Trust

Trust

Makilien Trilogy - Book 3

Molly Evangeline

Living Sword Publishing

www.livingswordpublishing.com

Trust
Makilien Trilogy – Book 3
Copyright © 2012 by Molly Evangeline

Published by Living Sword Publishing

www.makilien.com
www.mollyevangeline.com

Cover Design and Map
© Molly Evangeline

Cover Images
© Molly Evangeline
© Diego Elorza | Dreamstime.com

All Scriptures are taken from the New American Standard Bible, Copyright © 1960, 1962, 1963, 1968, 1971, 1972, 1973, 1975, 1977, 1995 by The Lockman Foundation. Used by permission. www.Lockman.org

ISBN 13: 978-0983774037
ISBN 10: 098377403X

Contents

DOLENNAR MAP
PRONUNCIATION GUIDE
CHARACTER GUIDE
BOOKS BY MOLLY EVANGELINE
ILYON CHRONICLES

To the One in whom I can place all my trust without any fear of betrayal, abandonment, or judgment. You are always right here to guide me, even when the path seems to end, and all I can do is be still, wait, and trust.

TRUST in the Lord with
all your heart and do not lean
on your own understanding.
- Proverbs 3:5

:Chapter One:

Orders

A cool breeze swept across Makilien's skin. She shivered, arms tingling, though not in reaction to the damp weather. Her eyes darted amidst the undergrowth of the forest, dark with moisture, and her brows dipped low in a frown when she found nothing to blame for her growing apprehension. All was quiet, peaceful even, despite the gray sky, but she couldn't shake the feeling. Glancing at her companion, she found Vonawyn kneeling in the dirt, studying one of the tracks they'd been following since just after dawn.

Casting another wary look into the forest, Makilien knelt beside her and whispered, "Something doesn't feel right."

"These are stag's tracks all right, and I think we're catching up to him." Vonawyn's voice rang out light and unconcerned, but a little louder than necessary. She caught her friend's eyes, giving a clear message. Makilien was not imagining things.

"How long ago do you think he passed this way?" Makilien asked, playing along.

Vonawyn shrugged. "An hour, maybe. Let's keep moving."

She rose and took the lead. Though Makilien kept a close watch, she said nothing, leaving it to her friend to determine their course of action. At over seventy years old, the Elf had much more experience in the forest than she did, not to mention superior sight and hearing.

They traveled another half mile before Makilien noticed the ground rising to their right. It had just occurred to her that this put them in a dangerous position when Vonawyn halted. Makilien stood stock-still and watched her, trying to keep up the pretense of unconcern, though her body didn't cooperate. Goose bumps rose along her arms, and her heart rate quickened.

"Get down!" Vonawyn gasped.

She caught Makilien's arm and dragged her to the ground. That very instant, something hissed through the air right above Makilien's head and slammed into a nearby tree. Sprawled in the grass, her eyes locked on the dark, quivering arrow—an arrow intended for her back.

Vonawyn grabbed her arm again, and they scrambled for cover behind two trees just wide enough to offer protection. Heart racing and gasping for breath, Makilien pressed her back against the trunk and looked over at her friend.

"How many are there?"

Vonawyn shook her head. "I only heard the one bow."

And thank Elohim she had. Makilien shuddered, almost able to feel the breath-snatching pain radiate from where the arrow would have struck.

Gripping her own bow, Vonawyn peeked around her tree. An arrow skipped off the trunk, inches from her face. She jerked back and blew out her breath.

"There are at least two of them, and they have good cover," she reported, voice taut with frustration. "No doubt they'll just wait for one of us to show ourselves. I don't think I could get a shot off and have time to hide again."

Makilien sighed and leaned her head back against the tree. If the Elf couldn't do it, she didn't have a chance either. She scanned their surroundings. Cover was too sparse for them to run. Vonawyn made the same observation. She put her fingers to her lips and imitated the loud, high-pitched call of a sparrow.

"Do you think they will hear it?" Makilien asked.

Vonawyn shook her head, grimacing. "I don't know. They can cover a lot of ground. They're probably more than a mile away from us by now."

She peeked around the tree again, this time on the other side. Another arrow came a second after she hid, this one sticking in the trunk. "They haven't moved. I'm pretty sure there are only two of them."

"Do you think they will move?"

"I wouldn't. We can't go anywhere, and they have a perfect position. Their best bet is to wait us out, it just depends on how patient they are."

Makilien took a deep breath, heart rate still elevated. "I didn't think we had to worry about this so close to home."

Vonawyn's brows furrowed. "Neither did I."

They fell quiet for a long time as the waiting game commenced. Occasionally, Vonawyn checked the position of their attackers. Arrows met her a couple of times, but the men soon decided to conserve them. It was getting close to midday now. Sweat trickled down Makilien's neck. Even though the breeze was cool, the air was muggy. She wanted to take off her cloak, but her tree wasn't wide enough to afford her any room to move. With utmost care, she shifted her weight. Her legs were beginning to cramp. She glanced up at the slow patter of raindrops on the leaves, and then looked at Vonawyn.

"Any plans?"

Vonawyn tipped her head a little. "Not yet. I'm hoping they get bored and try something daring. It's our only chance right now. If they don't move, we won't be able to try anything until dark."

Makilien frowned at the thought of being trapped here all afternoon, especially if rain fell heavier. *Elohim, I don't know who these men are or why they want to kill us, but please provide us with an opportunity for escape.* She had come on this hunting trip to have some fun and get her mind off more sobering things, but instead found her life threatened. *Please protect us.* She glanced at her friend again. "Apparently, they didn't hear your call."

Vonawyn just made a face as she fingered the sky-blue fletching on the arrow she had fitted to her bowstring, and silence came again. A squirrel scurried along the branches above Makilien and chattered down at her. She looked up.

"What do you have to complain about?"

Vonawyn raised an eyebrow and smiled wryly as some of the tension was relieved.

"Drop your weapons!"

Both women stood up straight at the shout that echoed from behind them. Someone scrambled in the brush, and two short cries of pain followed. Moving cautiously, Vonawyn peered around the tree.

"You can come out. It's safe."

Each of them released a great sigh and left the shelter of their trees. Up on the hill stood Elandir and Elmorhirian.

"Well, you two took long enough to show up," Vonawyn said, eyeing her brothers as they climbed the hill to join them, though she had a relieved smile on her face.

Elmorhirian feigned a hurt look. "Is that all the thanks we get for saving your life?"

But the friendly bickering ended as all four of them peered down at the two men lying motionless, each pierced by a well-placed arrow.

"You couldn't keep either of them alive to question?" Vonawyn asked.

Elandir shook his head. "We warned them and they turned on us. We didn't have a very good vantage point and weren't about to take chances. One of their arrows only just missed Elmorhirian."

He and his brother approached them and pulled up the men's sleeves, exposing their forearms.

"Just what we suspected," Elandir said.

Each man had a black snake tattoo.

"Zirtan's former men," Elmorhirian murmured. "I guess this confirms they are the ones attacking travelers through Eldinorieth."

"They're getting pretty bold to work their way this far south," his brother replied.

"Well, they wouldn't have made it much farther before meeting the sentries Father has posted."

Elandir gazed around the forest, eyes narrowed in suspicion. "We should see if they have horses nearby and make sure they are alone. We picked up their trail a ways back and realized they were headed this way."

"Good thing you did," Vonawyn told him.

He turned back to her and Makilien. "You aren't hurt, are you?"

His sister shook her head. "No, thank Elohim."

With this assurance, the Elf brothers took the lead and descended the backside of the hill. Makilien eyed the two men once more before following. Would those left of Zirtan's army always find ways to torment Eldor, she wondered? Hadn't they inflicted enough pain? *At least they aren't threatening all-out war again.* She had to be grateful for this. A few attacks along the forest road, while disturbing, wouldn't threaten their existence or freedom.

For over an hour, they wound their way deep into the forest. Most of the time, Makilien couldn't see the signs they followed, but Elandir and Elmorhirian were expert trackers and moved fast, knowing exactly where they were going. Makilien started to wonder if the men even had any horses, but then Elandir motioned for them to halt.

"There, just ahead in those pines."

Peering into the trees, Makilien caught the swish of a horse's tail. They moved on slowly now, approaching with caution until they were certain only two horses stood in the underbrush. The two brothers reached them first. Makilien and Vonawyn came up behind as Elandir dug through one of the horse's saddlebags.

"Doesn't look like much more than clothes and food."

Elmorhirian checked the other. Near the bottom, he stopped and pulled something out. "What's this?"

They crowded around him as he held up a tattered piece of stained parchment. Most of the dark wax seal that once held it closed was still intact.

"Looks like a V," Elandir pointed out.

The others agreed. Amidst a winding snake design, the letter V was evident.

"I wonder who that could be?" Elmorhirian murmured and opened the parchment, revealing a brief note. "'*Patrol the road just north of Elimar, but be wary of the Elves. Kill any travelers.*'" His brows rose. "Well, that makes it pretty clear. There is a mastermind behind this. Those men were under orders."

"Whose orders?" Vonawyn wondered aloud.

"If it were a Z, that'd be obvious, but it isn't."

Elandir took the note from his brother and tucked it into his jerkin. "We should get this information back home to Father."

The deep shadows of evening drew in when the four of them arrived at their destination. Crossing the shallow river, they entered Elimar. The glow of light from the houses dispelled some of the gloom of the rainy day. Near the center of the small city, they came to the Elves' home and reined their horses to a halt.

"That doesn't look like game you've brought back."

From just up the path, Torick strode toward them, eyeing the bodies secured to the two extra horses.

"Turns out attackers are more plentiful than game," Elandir replied, sliding down from his horse. "We suspected we were being followed, and then these two ambushed Vonawyn and Makilien this morning."

Torick looked to the two women. "Are you all right?"

They nodded, and Makilien answered with a smile, "We're fine."

"Zirtan's men?" Torick asked, glancing at the bodies again.

Elandir gave him a nod. "Both have a tattoo."

Torick scowled. "They just don't give up, do they?"

"They're not acting on their own. We found written orders in one of their saddlebags."

"Orders from who?"

Elandir shrugged. "Unfortunately, it doesn't say."

Torick following, the group entered Lord Elnauhir's house. Comfortable warmth enveloped them, and Makilien looked forward to changing into a dry pair of clothes. After a bit of searching, they found the Elf lord and Halandor in one of the studies. He greeted his children and Makilien and inquired about their trip. Elandir stepped up to explain the encounter with the two men and share their findings.

"I'm sure this will soon end trade with Aldûlir," the Elf lord said, expression weary. "Not that we rely on it, but the forest road is heavily traveled. There's no telling how many may be killed by making the journey." He shook his head. "But without knowing who or where the orders are coming from, all we can do is protect that part of the forest which lies closest to Elimar and pray the attacks will eventually come to an end."

"The men are so scattered we wouldn't know where to look if we did want to stop them," Halandor said in agreement. "The orders could be coming from anywhere."

"And any one of Zirtan's former captains could be issuing them," Torick put in.

Elnauhir nodded, resting against one of the chairs as he thought. "We will continue to monitor the situation. It appears to be nothing more than an attempt to make life difficult for us. If that changes, we'll speak to Lord Darian and figure something out."

Silence settled between them for a moment, and Makilien took the chance to exchange goodbyes with her friends before heading home. When she left the room, Vonawyn followed to see her out. They walked in silence most of the way, but Makilien noticed her friend's normally bright mood seemed to have sobered.

"Is something wrong?"

Vonawyn glanced at her and shook her head. "Not really . . . I guess I was just thinking about Aedan. When he comes home, he will have to travel through Eldinorieth." She gave a little shrug. "I worry about him."

"Me too," Makilien admitted, but a quick smile came to her lips. "Don't forget though, he has Tanzim with him. I bet anyone would think twice before attacking."

Vonawyn chuckled lightly before her tone became more serious again. "He's been gone a while. It's been two months since he left."

Makilien remembered watching him ride out that gray, misty day. There had even been a little snow still on the ground. It had been a difficult time for both her and Vonawyn. "I wonder if he is any closer to finding his father."

"I hope so. Every day I pray it will be the day he returns. I miss the times we spent together over the winter." Vonawyn's tone was wistful, but she was quick to apologize. "I'm sorry. I shouldn't talk about that."

A wave of emotion flooded up inside Makilien, something she'd spent the last year learning how to deal with, but she shook her head. "No, it's all right." She gave Vonawyn the best smile she could muster. "You're my best friends. I'm happy to see how things have grown between you. The last thing I want is for you to feel you can't share things with me."

Vonawyn smiled, though her eyes still clouded with sadness over the whole painful situation.

"Say hello to Leiya and your parents for me," she told Makilien at the door.

"I will."

Makilien stepped outside and found that one of the stable hands had taken care of Antiro, so she went on her way. Surrounded by the peacefulness of the Elven city, she followed one of the paths lined with an abundance of spring flowers, colors bright even in the dim light of dusk. But the beauty did not fully capture her attention as it usually did. Her thoughts lingered on the conversation with Vonawyn. The pain she still held in her heart made her chest ache. Aedan's absence had made it even more difficult to cope. Like Vonawyn, she prayed daily for his safe return. Losing him would be too much for her still broken heart. She took a deep breath. *Help me trust and not worry.*

Coming around a bend, the sight of a little house surrounded by maple trees, windows glowing, brought a soothing comfort to Makilien, and she hurried her pace. She ascended the porch steps and entered through the front door.

"I'm home," she called out as she set her pack down in the entry and shrugged off her moisture-heavy cloak.

From somewhere deeper in the house came a joyful exclamation of her name. In a moment, her little sister bounded into the room.

"Leiya," Makilien said with a grin and gave her a big hug.

The little girl peered up at her, eyes wide with excitement. "Did you get anything?"

"No, not this time. We saw a few deer, but not the big one we were after."

"Ah," Leiya said in disappointment.

Their parents had joined them by now, and Makilien greeted them each with a hug before continuing. "I think the game was scared off. Two men ambushed us this morning, but Elandir and Elmorhirian stopped them before anything happened."

Néthyn shared a look of concern with his wife. "Who were they?"

"Zirtan's men. Both had a snake tattoo."

"How many attacks is this now?" Hanna murmured, her face troubled.

"This is the fifth that we know of," Makilien replied. "We talked to Lord Elnauhir, but like he said, there's not much we can do. Hopefully, these men will grow tired of this and things will return to normal."

Her parents agreed. No one liked having this worry at the back of their minds. Steering the conversation toward less troublesome topics, Néthyn said, "You arrived just in time for supper. I believe your mother just about has it all on the table."

Makilien gave Hanna a warm smile. "Wonderful, I'm starving."

After washing up and changing, she joined her family in the dining room. Her father offered a prayer just before they dished up. As Makilien filled her plate, Leiya looked across the table at her and said, "A man from Minarald came to see you."

Makilien stopped, eyes jumping from the food to her sister, and then to her father. He too had paused, glancing at Hanna before focusing on his daughter. "Lord Elnauhir didn't mention anything to you?"

"No." Makilien let out a long sigh, trying not to let all her emotions take over at once. "Let me guess, another suitor?"

Her father gave a slow nod. "Yes. A young army captain. His name is Tylor."

Makilien's appetite deserted her, stomach reacting. She set the dish she held aside. "I wish they wouldn't keep coming all the way out here to Elimar just to be told no. Did you talk to him?"

"I did. We had a good talk." Néthyn passed a bowl to Leiya, but did not begin eating.

"And does he know not to expect anything from me?"

"I made it clear you would likely have no interest, and that, whatever your decision, he was to accept it. He was very good about it."

"But he's still going to be sent home disappointed." Makilien rubbed her forehead. It all gave her such a headache. She breathed out hard in frustration. "Maybe I should just go stay at the palace for a while. Then everyone can come ask to court me and get it over with without having to ride all the way out here."

Her father gave her a sympathetic look, but said, "It's their choice. Makilien, if this is really bothering you, you know I can send these men away without you ever having to talk to any of them."

Makilien considered this for a long moment. Finally, she replied, voice low with emotion, "When this first started, I thought I would be all right, but now I think it might be best if you did."

"Then I will do that," Néthyn told her. "I can go see Tylor in the morning to tell him."

"No," Makilien said resignedly. "He's already expecting to talk to me. I can handle it once more."

"Are you sure?"

She gave a quick nod.

Curled up on her window seat, Makilien stared out into the darkness, catching the glimmer of torches and lamps throughout the city. She tipped her head to hear the peeping of frogs from the streams, a sound she always loved. Taking in a deep breath, she looked down into her lap at her thick, leather-bound sketchbook. She had yet to open it, and hesitated. She knew she shouldn't do this to herself, not before bed, but, fingers trembling, she opened the cover and flipped through the pages. Halfway through the book, she stopped.

A painful weight settled on her chest, and each breath became labored. She closed her eyes against the burning of tears, and then opened them again to one of the first sketches she'd ever drawn of Sirion. The page was a bit crinkled in areas and some of the charcoal smudged from past tears. Fresh ones slid down her cheeks. She pressed her palms to her eyes, trying to hold them back.

Biting down hard, she breathed out deeply and leaned her head back against the window frame, staring out into the night again. This time, however, she didn't see the beauty of it, her thoughts caught in the past. After a long time, she blinked, falling back into the present. She glanced down at her sketch and closed the book, holding it against her chest. Another few tears dribbled down her cheeks.

"Elohim," she whispered, throat hurting. "I'm struggling so much lately. Please, strengthen me and help me focus on You and what is right now, not the past or what could have been. I know I can't live that way. I also ask for Your guidance tomorrow. I . . ." She shook her head, but forced herself to go on. "I ask that You would help me be open to Your will, even if it isn't what I want."

:Chapter Two:

Uncertainty

M akilien sat straight up in bed. Her heart thudded against her ribs, pounding blood through her body. Drawing in a deep breath, she put her head in her hands. No dream had caused this rude awakening. Just a strange sense of foreboding she couldn't understand that clung to her, even now. She slipped out of bed and went to her knees.

For a long time, she prayed what was on her heart. So much confusion tangled her thoughts, no matter how hard she tried to make sense of it. When she did rise, her knees ached, but she barely noticed. Reality and hope collided inside her. She shook her head. She could not let hope win. It would only cause her pain later. But . . . what if it was true?

"Ugh," Makilien murmured in frustration. "Impossible."

Blowing out a heavy sigh, she walked over to her wardrobe and stared inside for much longer than necessary before choosing an outfit. Mumbling to herself, she changed out of her nightgown and into the pale blue dress. Birds sang joyfully in the bright morning sun right outside her window, oblivious to the struggle in her mind. She stepped to the door and paused, closing her eyes.

"I just can't understand this, Elohim. When is any of it going to make sense?" She drew in another deep breath. "I really need You to guide me. I've never been so confused before."

She stepped out of her room. The sound of dishes came from downstairs. She hurried down and into the dining room where she found Leiya setting the table for breakfast.

"Good morning," the little girl said cheerfully.

Makilien couldn't help but smile as she responded.

Her mother came from the kitchen with breakfast in hand. "You girls can sit down. Your father will be here in a minute."

Makilien took a seat across from her sister as Leiya chattered about a fawn she had found the other day. Attempting to overcome her distraction, Makilien smiled and asked questions Leiya was quick to answer. Soon their parents joined them. After taking her first bite of eggs, Leiya asked, "What are you going to do today, Makilien?"

"I'll probably go over to Lord Elnauhir's house as soon as I'm finished at the stable and talk to Tylor." She glanced at her mother. "No use putting it off."

Leiya tilted her head as she too looked at Hanna. "Why are men coming from Minarald to see Makilien?"

Hanna gave her a smile. "Well, because they admire Makilien's accomplishments and what she has done for Eldor, and they believe she would make a good wife. They are hoping to win her affection."

Leiya stuck out her bottom lip. "I don't want Makilien to marry someone from Minarald."

"Now, Leiya," Hanna said gently. "That is Makilien's decision."

Makilien settled her eyes on her sister. "Don't worry. That isn't going to happen."

Leiya stared down into her lap. A sorrowful look came to her face as she murmured to herself. Though she didn't mean for anyone to hear, Makilien caught the whispered words. "I wanted Makilien to marry Sirion."

Makilien's throat squeezed, and she swallowed her breakfast with difficulty. It hurt to see how Sirion's death had affected not just her, but her family as well. They had come to love him so dearly in the short time they had been together.

She cleared her throat and took a drink of fresh milk to wash down the food. Whether her mother had heard Leiya's comment or only sensed the mood, she changed the subject.

"When are you going to begin your new dress, Makilien?"

"Um, soon." Makilien took a breath. "Maybe Vonawyn and I will go look for material today if there is time."

"I can't wait to see it when it's finished."

Makilien managed a smile. "Neither can I. Vonawyn told me what she has in mind, but I'm anxious to see it come together."

"I'm sure it will be just lovely," Hanna said, "and perfect for the celebration."

Talk of the celebration helped lighten the mood. The whole family looked forward to participating in all the upcoming spring activities in their new home. Such things had never been common in Reylaun.

As soon as breakfast was finished, Makilien and her father prepared to leave. Néthyn had work, and Makilien was anxious to get this talk with Tylor over and done with. Leiya followed the two of them to the entryway.

"Makilien, when you see Elmorhirian, will you ask him if he forgot his promise?"

"What promise is that?"

Leiya's face and tone turned very serious. "He promised he'd take me to catch tadpoles."

Makilien chuckled at her expression. "I'm sure he would never forget such a promise, but I will ask him."

Now Leiya smiled. "Thank you."

Reaching out to tickle her as she passed by, Makilien stepped outside after her father. Side by side, they walked toward the stable. It turned out they shared a deep love for horses, and since making their home in Elimar, Néthyn had secured a job working at the stable.

For a couple of minutes, they walked in silence, but Néthyn looked at his daughter keenly. "Are you all right?"

Makilien glanced at him. "Yes, I am," but she realized it didn't sound convincing. She shrugged. "I just have a lot on my mind."

Néthyn put his arm around her shoulders. He said nothing, but the comfort was enough.

At the stable, they parted after her father gave her a few encouraging words, and Makilien felt her spirits further lifted to find Antiro waiting for her at the entrance of his pasture. He nickered a greeting, and she hugged his neck.

"Good morning, boy."

He turned his head to nuzzle her face, his warm breath blowing softly across her cheeks. He could always sense her moods.

"Yeah, today isn't the greatest day," she admitted. She rubbed the velvety soft part of his nose. "I have another suitor to turn down."

Antiro stomped his hoof into the ground, and Makilien gave him a wry smile. "I agree . . . but this one will be the last."

She turned toward the stable and said over her shoulder, "I'll be right back."

When she returned, she brought a small bucket of Antiro's favorite grain and a brush. While he eagerly munched away, she brushed his black coat until it shone in the morning sunlight and took a step back to admire it. "Looks like that's it for your winter coat."

Finishing the grain, he nosed her for more.

"Nope. I don't want you getting fat."

Antiro shook his mane.

Makilien raised an eyebrow. "I'm serious. Besides, I have to go take care of Falene now."

With Antiro staring after her, she left the pasture, walking back to the stable. She stopped at one of the stalls inside, leaning against the door.

"Morning, Falene."

Responding to her voice, the gray and white paint mare turned and stuck her head over the stall door. Makilien ran her hand down the horse's face and smoothed her forelock. The horse sighed in contentment.

Opening the door, she led Falene outside, mindful of the mare's limping gate. In an area of the pasture fenced in just for her, Makilien let the horse go. She watched her take a few slow steps and stop to graze.

Makilien exhaled heavily, eyes a little misty. Most people had thought Falene should be put down after suffering such a severe injury to her hind leg, but after discovering she was still alive, Makilien just couldn't bear to let such a thing happen. She'd spent hours in the stable at Minarald caring for the horse, unwilling to listen to anyone who said she'd never be able to walk again. Her friends supported her though. Elmorhirian and one of the leatherworkers in the city had even helped her rig a special harness and hood so Carmine could carry Falene to Elimar. It was a lot to go through just for a horse, but Falene was one link she still had to Sirion, and she made it her personal goal to see his horse was well looked after for all the remaining years of her life.

Makilien lingered at the stable far longer than usual. It was a peaceful place for her, and she didn't want to leave it. But, at last, she resigned herself once again to the inevitable and trudged toward Lord Elnauhir's house. Her stomach gave a nervous flutter as she let herself in, but the first thing to greet her was Elmorhirian's distinct outburst of laughter. This could not help but bring a smile to her face, if only for a moment.

She followed the sound into the living room. Just as she came to the doorway, Elmorhirian said, "You're getting old, Torick."

"So you keep reminding me every chance you get," the man responded in an irritable tone.

Shaking her head, Makilien stepped inside. Halandor and Torick sat in two chairs while Elandir was on the sofa and Elmorhirian stood behind him. The two Elves were grinning at Torick, Elmorhirian still giggling.

With a look of disgust, Torick muttered, "You two are the bane of my existence."

Elmorhirian snorted again with laughter.

"You just wait until I'm gone, then you'll be sorry," Torick warned him.

"Oh, don't say that, Torick."

At the sound of her voice, everyone turned to Makilien.

"Good morning," Elmorhirian said brightly.

"Morning," she replied, just holding back a grin. The Elf brothers' humor was always contagious.

Elmorhirian's eyes jumped back to Torick. "You know, she's right. You still have plenty of good years left to enjoy our company."

Torick rolled his eyes, and now Makilien did smile as she walked in to stand near Elmorhirian. A moment of silence followed. The men exchanged glances, no doubt wondering if she would bring up Tylor, not wanting to themselves. Makilien tipped her head a little. "So, where is he?"

"Uh, I think he's with Father," Elmorhirian answered. "He wanted to see the library after breakfast."

"Do you want me to get him?" Elandir asked.

Makilien hesitated for only a moment. "Yes, please."

As the Elf rose, Makilien was aware of how closely Halandor watched her. Finally, he asked, "You're sure you are up for this?"

"I'm sure," she answered, with a nod to reinforce it. She wasn't really, and she doubted Halandor believed it, but she was determined to be strong and go through with this.

Elmorhirian turned to her.

"Just so you know," he said in a conspiratorial whisper, "last night Elandir and I made sure he was a decent guy, with some help from Torick."

"I do hope you were polite."

Elmorhirian snorted. "Polite? We're always polite."

Makilien raised her eyebrows, but couldn't suppress a smile, especially when he gave her that mischievous grin of his. "So what was your discovery?"

"We like him," Elmorhirian said with a nod. He paused. "But that doesn't mean you have to."

Makilien shrugged. "We'll see."

And so she waited, stomach squeezing and churning. For some reason, this time seemed harder than usual. Perhaps nearing the one-year mark of losing Sirion made everything more difficult. No one said much in the next couple of minutes, though Elmorhirian continued to make humorous remarks in an attempt to make her laugh and relieve the tension. She didn't laugh, but he could always draw a smile from her.

When the sound of footsteps approached the living room, Makilien pulled in a deep breath, reminding herself of all the far more threatening situations she'd faced in the past. This should be simple. Elandir entered first, followed by his father. And directly behind him came Tylor. He stepped into the room and his gaze found her immediately.

Though not in uniform, he held himself like a soldier, tall, disciplined, but the smile he offered was kind and genuine.

He was certainly one of the more attractive men to come calling—dark haired with brown eyes that reminded Makilien a little too much of Sirion. She swallowed hard, attempting to will away the stab of pain in her chest. This had suddenly become even more difficult. She was glad when Elnauhir stepped in to introduce them. She didn't know if she could have found her voice at that moment.

"Tylor, this is Makilien." The Elf lord turned to her. "Makilien, Captain Tylor."

The young captain stepped forward. "Makilien, it is an honor to meet you."

Giving him her best smile, she replied, "It is good to meet you, Captain."

"Tylor, please."

Makilien gave a quick nod, but her brain wouldn't supply her with a suitable reply. Neither one said anything for a moment. Glancing around the room, Makilien realized all eyes watched them, and this further scrambled her thoughts. Tylor must have noticed it too.

"Would you care to go for a walk?" he asked. "This is actually my first visit to Elimar. I'd love to see as much of it as I can."

"I'd like that," Makilien said graciously, praying for clear thoughts.

Tylor turned, allowing her to precede him on the way to the door. Just before leaving the room, Makilien turned back for a moment.

"Oh, Elmorhirian, my sister is expecting you to keep your promise to her."

"Already planning it," the Elf replied.

Makilien smiled. "I told her you wouldn't forget."

Out in the hall, Makilien and Tylor walked quietly side by side. Just before they were out of earshot, Makilien caught Torick say something about a walk.

"Goodness, Torick," Elandir exclaimed, "you're as protective as an old mother hen."

"What?" Torick growled. "I need to exercise this leg of mine."

"Sure."

Makilien chuckled softly and glanced at Tylor to find him smiling. She almost felt sorry for him. He had to feel anxious under the scrutiny of so many, and she couldn't imagine the number of questions the poor man had been subjected to. Not many young women were as blessed as she to have such a large group of protective friends.

At the door, Tylor opened it for her, and they stepped outside.

"It's been a beautiful spring, hasn't it?" he asked as they descended the stairs and turned right along the main path through Elimar.

"It has," Makilien agreed. "It's the first time I've witnessed it fully outside of Reylaun."

"What was it like there?"

Makilien took in the surroundings, mentally comparing it to her memories. "A lot less beautiful. There weren't many flowers, and everything was always so muddy. Between the mud and the dreary buildings, spring didn't hold the excitement and newness it does here."

For a time, the two of them continued to talk of things such as this—her past life and her adventures, avoiding the real reason behind their walk. With some relief, Makilien found Tylor easy to talk to, at least about day-to-day topics. Her first impression that he was a kind young man proved true. He smiled often and shared her love for things of natural beauty. He also had a good sense of humor, chuckling with her when they caught sight of Torick on his "walk" close by.

It was as they drew near to Lord Elnauhir's house once again, that the conversation reached its crucial point. They both stopped, and Tylor faced Makilien.

"I know I don't have to tell you why it is I've come here. I think just about the whole city is aware of my intentions," he said with a chuckle.

She gave him a quick smile though her stomach churned again. "Word gets around fast in a close community like this."

"I also know I am not the first to have called on you. I spoke with your father for a long time yesterday." He was serious now, voice gentle. "I want you to know, I am fully aware of what you are going through, and I don't think I can even begin to imagine it. The war caused incredible pain for so many people."

Emotion rose up inside Makilien faster than she could contain it, and she looked down at her hands, blinking as her eyes filled with tears. She didn't want to cry in front of him, knowing he would blame himself for it.

"Considering this, I think I already know your answer," he went on, "but I must ask, otherwise I'll regret it if I don't. You are an amazing woman, Makilien, one I would love to become better acquainted with and even court if you would allow it."

Makilien struggled to take a deep breath as her throat squeezed shut. Though she kept them from falling, tears glittered in her eyes. Seeing this, Tylor's expression fell.

"I'm sorry," he said. "I didn't mean to cause you more pain."

She shook her head, fighting to compose herself. All she could think of were Torick's words from a year ago, telling her not to give up on love. She wanted it, deeply, and she couldn't deny Tylor was the first one who had caused her thoughts to return to that conversation. But she could not let go. She just couldn't. Not yet.

Clearing her throat, she spoke quietly. "You are very kind, Tylor, and one of the most understanding men I've met in the last couple of months, but the truth is, even though he's gone . . . I still love Sirion just as much now as I did a year ago. I can't say whether I'll ever be able to love anyone else. Maybe, someday, but I just don't know. Because of that, I have to say no."

Tylor nodded without the slightest hint of persistence or frustration in his expression. "I understand. Thank you for allowing me the opportunity to speak with you. I know it wasn't easy. If you'd like, I'll escort you back to the house."

Makilien gave him a grateful smile. "Thank you, I appreciate your understanding."

They walked the remaining distance in silence. At the door, she stopped.

"I think I am going to the garden for a while." She looked up into his eyes. "Again, thank you for understanding."

He nodded and she turned away, but when he said her name, she looked back to meet his earnest gaze.

"I am deeply sorry for your loss. I hope, someday, if it is meant to be, you find someone worthy of your love."

Makilien's breath released in a painful sigh. "You too, Tylor."

She walked on, trying to sort through her emotions, coming to the fountain in the center of the garden. She visited this peaceful area often to think and pray, especially in the last few weeks. Taking a seat on the edge, she bowed her head and closed her eyes, thinking things over, exhausted by it all. The last time she remembered experiencing such turmoil was back in Reylaun before meeting Torick, and she didn't want it to be this way. She yearned for direction and peace.

Though she never heard any footsteps, Vonawyn came to sit beside her several minutes later. She looked at the Elf maiden, expression weary.

Vonawyn gave her a sympathetic look. "It didn't go well?"

"No, it was all right," Makilien answered. "He was very understanding. He's a good man."

Vonawyn agreed.

"And that's just the problem." Makilien exhaled slowly. "I almost wish he'd been one of the undesirable ones."

The Elf gave her a knowing look. "Are you feeling something for him?"

But Makilien shook her head. "No, not really. I mean, maybe I could, possibly, if I didn't still love Sirion." She met her friend's gaze, eyes filling again, and her voice came out thick. "This is *so* hard. I don't want to be alone all my life. I really don't, but I just don't think I can let him go."

Vonawyn took Makilien's hands in her own and squeezed them tight. "That may be true, but don't discount time. Time changes many things. It is still so recent, and the pain of it still so strong. I know it's difficult, but give yourself the time to discover what Elohim has in store for you."

Makilien closed her eyes, breathing heavily. Her friend was right, and she wanted it to comfort her, but the turmoil in her mind still weighed her down. All the conflict and confusion she'd experienced that morning when she woke hung over her, making everything harder to cope with.

"There's more, Vonawyn."

The Elf squeezed her hands again, worry shadowing her usual sparkling eyes. "What is it? What's wrong?"

Makilien hesitated. She didn't know how Vonawyn would respond to what she had to say when she didn't even know how to respond to it herself. "I haven't told anyone about this yet because, at first, I thought it was just because I missed him so much, but it's happening more often lately . . ."

She paused wondering if she was just crazy, if she was letting her grief affect her more than she realized, but she had to continue. Had to get it out in the open. She'd dealt with it on her own for too long. "I have times where I feel an overwhelming need to pray for Sirion. Like he's in danger or something."

Swallowing nervously, Makilien watched her friend, saw the surprise in her expression. She shook her head, feeling foolish. "I know it sounds crazy because why would that be if he's . . . gone? But that's the problem. I find these urges to pray for him putting hope in my heart that maybe . . . by some incredible miracle, he is still alive, somewhere."

She groaned. "But how could he be? I realize how this all sounds, but I just don't know what to do anymore. I don't know whether to let myself have hope or if I just need to let this go. I know I am torturing myself, but I can't help thinking of what my life might have been like these last months if he was here, where we might be now. What if it's the longing for what could have been that is making me feel this way? Do I just have to let it go and force it all from my mind?"

Vonawyn said nothing at first, taking in the implications of what Makilien had told her and considering her friend's emotions. Makilien stared at her, desperate eyes searching her face for answers.

At last, the Elf spoke carefully, "I'm not sure what to tell you." She paused in hesitation. "I do know Elohim can put it in our hearts to pray for those in need . . . but I can't tell you whether or not it could mean Sirion is alive or if it is just your longing for him. I won't tell you to ignore it if you do feel you should pray. I think it would be a good idea to talk to my father or Halandor . . . especially Halandor. He knows what you're going through."

Makilien nodded, both exhausted and relieved over finally sharing with someone.

"Why don't you have lunch with us?" Vonawyn suggested. "I know Tylor will be there, so maybe you don't want to, but then you could talk to my father or Halandor afterward."

Makilien didn't give an immediate answer. It would be difficult to see Tylor again, but easier now than before. "I think I will."

With a comforting smile, Vonawyn rose. "Good. Come on."

Despite the uncertainty surrounding her, Makilien quite enjoyed the meal. It was good to be with her friends, and Tylor still proved to be good company. But as soon as lunch ended, she focused once more on the reason she'd accepted the invitation. Stepping away from the table, she came to Halandor.

"I'd like to speak with you, if I could," she said.

"Of course."

They left the dining room and walked out to the terrace overlooking the garden. Taking seats across from each other, Halandor asked, "Is this about Tylor?"

Makilien shook her head. "No, actually, it's something else. I spoke to Vonawyn earlier, and she suggested I speak to you or her father. I chose you because you understand what I've had to endure these months."

Halandor gave an understanding nod, and she went on to tell him everything she had shared with Vonawyn.

"Did you ever experience anything like that? How am I supposed to react to it?"

She watched him hopefully, praying she would now receive guidance. He did not often look surprised, yet it was clear he had not expected what she told him.

"I can't say I ever did," he said slowly, thinking as he did so. "You're sure it's Sirion you feel this need for?"

"Yes, I'm positive," Makilien assured him. "I don't really know how to explain it, but the sense that he could be in trouble was strong enough to wake me up just this morning."

Rubbing his chin thoughtfully, Halandor stared off into the garden.

"Halandor."

His eyes returned to Makilien.

She swallowed, heart thumping. "Do you think it would be foolish of me to have a little hope?"

He stared at her for a long moment, noting how her eyes starved for an answer. The last thing he wanted was to raise her hopes unnecessarily, only to see them crushed, but he shook his head. "No, I don't."

A spark of light entered her eyes, a sight he had not seen in a long time, but he was quick to caution her, "Just be careful until there is something stronger to base your hope on. I don't have to tell you how unlikely it is that Sirion somehow survived somewhere, but I can't give you an answer as to why you feel the way you do. I think you should pray when you feel you should, but also pray Elohim will show you the truth in all this. I am certain He will at the appropriate time. I too will pray about it, and I'll talk to Elnauhir. Perhaps he will know more."

:Chapter Three:

Captives

Dawn broke over the open grassland. For the next half hour, the world would be gray, colorless—a fitting way for the day to begin. A new day of pain. A new day to find the strength to struggle on.

The last of night's chill breeze rustled the tall grass and swept over the prisoners. Sirion shivered, his body numb with the cold. He stared blankly at the shackles around his scarred wrists, the metal stained with blood long since dried. He tried to remember when he had been without them, but the days had all blurred into one never-ending nightmare. He hardly knew where or how it had begun. He remembered collapsing on the battlefield and believing he was dying. After that, only dim snatches of images, hollow voices, weakness, and pain. Though he had somehow recovered from his wounds, what followed were long weeks of sitting in dark, cramped cells, his only companions those bent on causing him misery. Grueling treks from one cruel place to another interrupted these times, and he had no knowledge of where he was now. Aldûlir, he guessed, but he could be anywhere. Wherever it was, he had never felt farther from home.

The harsh crack of a whip split the silence of early morning. Sirion flinched. An all too familiar pain radiated across his shoulders at the mere sound.

"Wake up, you worthless filth!"

Sirion squeezed his eyes shut, desperate to wish that awful voice away.

"I want to see everyone up now!"

With a heavy sigh, Sirion pushed himself to his knees. He swayed a little, stricken with a weakness he'd never known before this. Groans of misery rose up around him amid the clanking of chains. His tired eyes ranged over his fellow prisoners—thirty men and women of varying ages—ragged, filthy clothes hanging from their battered bodies.

A hulking tower of a man moved through the group, keen sight searching, almost hoping, for anyone who had failed to obey his commands. The long, coiled whip hung from his fist. Prisoners cowered around him, knowing even a wrong look could earn them a taste of its sting.

Halen—a name Sirion would forever attribute to suffering and the most abominable cruelty—moved in his direction, but he did not cower. One of the only things he had left was his dignity, and he held tight to the scrap of it that remained. He caught Halen's cold eyes and held them just long enough to prove that, even after all this long time, the man had not broken him as he had the others.

Once satisfied all his captives were awake, Halen ordered the guards to feed the prisoners. The men picked up three burlap sacks and tossed bits of food into the group. Sirion caught his portion before it hit the ground. He stared down at the meager breakfast ration, a hard, dry chunk of bread the size of his palm. Prisoners scrambled around him, fighting for every crumb.

"No! Please! I need food!"

Sirion's gaze jerked to the young woman chained nearest him. She reached out toward a skinny young man, but her chains held her back. The man clutched two bits of bread to his chest and turned his back on her. Eyes void of any hope, the young woman huddled into a little ball, hugging her knees up to her chest. Rocking back and forth, mournful tears trailed down her smudged cheeks.

Sirion stared at her, noting how tiny she was. His eyes fell to his piece of bread. It made him acutely aware of the deep, empty ache of his stomach and his hunger-weakened body. He needed food as much as anyone did. But, ignoring his own desires, he turned toward the young woman and extended the bread.

"Have mine."

One of the other captive men lunged for it, but Sirion held it out of reach, making sure it made it into the woman's hands. She guarded it like a precious treasure and stared at him with wide blue eyes.

"Thank you," she murmured.

Sirion nodded, but his attempt at a smile failed.

The young woman tore into the bread, gulping it down in seconds. Sirion watched and tried to ignore how he craved nourishment. His eyes dropped wearily to his chains. *I need strength, Elohim.* Heaviness descended on his heart. Elohim had seemed so distant and silent these past months of daily torture and misery. Sirion had waited every moment of every day for rescue from this nightmare. Now he despaired of it ever coming. But his faith had been tested in the past, and he knew above all he had to cling to it. Without it, what hope did he have? He had to trust that Elohim had a reason for keeping him alive on the battlefield and in the time since.

The guards moved through the group again, this time with waterskins. When they offered one to Sirion, he swallowed down as much as possible before they yanked it away. These few gulps of water would need to sustain him until midday.

"Everyone on your feet!" Halen bellowed as soon as they'd all had their water.

Sirion rose, stretching his sore muscles. His fellow captives rose around him, many struggling. This would be day six of their march to some unknown location, and Sirion wondered if all would make it.

Halen and his men mounted their horses.

"Move out!"

Slowly at first, the captives set out on their day's trek. The people walked in silence, faces bleak and resigned. On horseback, the men surrounded the group, watching. A couple rode behind, prodding them to move faster. It would get worse later in the day. Halen's whip was sure to be unleashed at some point.

The sun climbed up behind the captives, growing hotter with every hour. Sirion shrugged his shoulders as sweat trickled down his back and his hair stuck to his neck. Flies buzzed around him and the others like they were a herd of cattle. He gritted his teeth, allowing outrage at this treatment to keep him going.

Midmorning, the young woman he'd given the bread to stumbled. Glassy-eyed, she swayed. Sirion reached for her, but wasn't fast enough. She went down, crumpling into a pitiful heap and forcing the entire group to stop.

"Get up and get moving!" one of the guards shouted.

Sirion knelt next to the young woman and put his hands on her shoulders. "You must get up," he urged.

"I can't," she whimpered. "I can't go on."

Sirion gave one of the guards a pleading look. "She needs water."

Hoof beats pounded behind him, and he glanced over his shoulder. Halen yanked his horse to a halt and leapt out of the saddle, fury in his dark eyes.

"She can't go on without water," Sirion said, trying to make him understand.

But Halen ignored his words. He jerked his whip from his belt and let it uncoil.

Sirion's heart beat hard. "Please," he tried once more.

Halen strode toward them without pity, raising his whip as he advanced. Leaning to shield the woman, Sirion covered his head just as the whip snapped, hot pain streaking across the middle of his back. He bit down hard and swallowed his reaction to the pain. He held up his hands. "Stop. I can help her. Just let me help her walk."

In two strides, Halen was beside him. The man bent down and grabbed Sirion's hair, jerking his head so they were looking eye to eye.

"Then do it," the man growled. His voice lowered in hatred, and he spat through clenched teeth. "And don't you dare defy me again."

He released Sirion with a shove and stormed back to his horse. Sirion focused again on the young woman who lay there weeping.

"It's all right. You can make it," he encouraged her gently. "I will help you."

He took her by the arm and pulled her to her feet.

"Now get moving!" Halen shouted.

The group moved forward, and Sirion helped the woman take her steps, supporting most of her slight weight at first until she found her strength. He wondered how she had ever made it this far. Though not as skinny as some, there wasn't much to her. A small girl, the top of her head barely reached his shoulder. Her mournful sobbing cut into his heart, and he searched for a way to distract her from their circumstances.

"What is your name?"

The young woman sniffed and brushed the back of her hand across her face. "Irynna."

"I'm Sirion." He then repeated her name. "That means 'hope'."

She gave a joyless laugh. "It shouldn't. The last thing I have is hope."

Sirion looked at her, eyes full of sympathy. At times, he too felt he had no hope. "There is hope in Elohim," he murmured as much to himself as to her.

Irynna shook her head in defeat. "I don't think I can find hope in anyone. I don't even know how I will keep on."

Gathering strength and determination, Sirion gazed out across the grassland. "You see that lone tree ahead?"

Irynna squinted. "Yes."

"Right now, just focus on making it to that tree, all right? You can make it. We'll worry about the next distance when we get there."

Irynna drew in a deep breath, expression setting with her own determination. "All right."

They walked in silence for a time. Sirion winced, his damp shirt sticking to the welt across his back. The whiplash had not broken flesh this time, something Halen could have done effortlessly. Sirion didn't understand this. Halen had been more careful with him in the last few weeks. He couldn't imagine why since the man had never held back in the past. It certainly wasn't out of mercy.

"Thank you for helping me," Irynna broke his thoughts.

He looked down at her. "You're welcome."

Irynna stared ahead to the tree that was their goal and then back up at Sirion. "Why are you helping me?"

"Because it's right, and I hate cruelty," he told her, the spark of anger over their treatment returning to burn in his heart and fuel his perseverance.

"You're stronger than the rest of us," Irynna murmured and swallowed hard. "I don't think right and wrong matters to us anymore, only survival."

Sirion knew this was true. He had seen proof of it in the young man who'd stolen Irynna's bread, but he could hardly condemn them after all he'd endured himself. He knew just how difficult it was to fight the despair and the instinct to do whatever was necessary to survive. "How long have you been a captive?"

Irynna hung her head. "A year, almost."

"What happened?"

Acute pain crossed her face. Sirion quickly apologized. "You don't have to talk about it."

"No," she replied, voice sad. "Keeping it to myself won't make it not be." She grimaced, tears sparkling in her eyes. "Slavers raided my village. They killed my father and brothers when they tried to stop them from taking me. I'm not sure what happened to my mother."

"I'm sorry," Sirion said, burdened by what she and the others around him had witnessed. His voice lowered. "My family was killed by Shaikes when I was a boy."

"Is that how you got here?"

Sirion shook his head and shared what little he knew about his captivity. Once he'd finished, one question burned in his mind, one that had plagued him for so long.

"Irynna, have you heard of Makilien?"

She glanced up at him with a quick nod. "Yes."

He hesitated, suddenly afraid. Could he live with the answer to his next question if it wasn't the news he prayed for every single day? Could he bear that on top of all this? Words catching in his throat, he asked, "Do you know if she survived the battle in Minarald?"

Irynna peered up at him, and Sirion held his breath.

"I'm sorry, I don't know."

He exhaled, both disappointed and relieved, and once again, he prayed.

After another short time of silence, they continued talking quietly. They talked of both their lives prior to captivity, sharing their dreams and regrets. Soon they reached the tree Sirion had set as a goal, but because of their conversation, barely noticed. After all the months of only enemies for company,

Sirion found great relief in having someone understanding to talk to.

Evening descended with the sun sinking into a shimmering haze on the horizon ahead of them. Sirion breathed heavily, muscles cramping and weak, and head pounding with dehydration. Beside him, Irynna was close to collapsing again. Sirion forced himself to keep on, for her sake. Praying they would soon make camp for the night, he looked up, eyes landing on a city wall in the distance. The first sign of population in almost a week.

"I think we've reached our destination," he murmured to Irynna.

She glanced up, though she had to put effort into raising her head. "Just so long as we stop soon."

They came to a well-worn road making travel a little easier on the prisoners. In another half hour, they arrived at the city gate. Sirion took in the surroundings, trying to discover clues to their location. A rough stone wall rose up twenty-five feet and circled around as far as he could see.

Through the gate, they entered a sprawling city. The streets teemed with people. Sirion studied those they passed. A few were dressed richly and looked down upon the prisoners with disdain. But most, he noticed, appeared nearly as bad off as they were—grimy, underfed men, women, and children with grim expressions. When they passed an intersection crowded with people, full understanding hit him. At the front of the crowd sat an auctioning block, and behind, rows of slaves waiting to be bid on. The city was a slave trade center, and the majority of the inhabitants were themselves slaves.

Travel was slow for the group. They wound their way down the crooked streets lined by dirty plaster buildings squeezed together to take advantage of all available space. People bumped and scowled at them, shoving them out of the way if they were especially ill tempered.

In the end, their journey brought them to a massive warehouse. Halen and a few of the guards led the prisoners inside. Only four windows high above allowed in any light. Sirion choked on the heavy air as soon as they entered. It reeked of sweat and waste, stinging his nose and throat. As his watery eyes adjusted to the low light, he saw the building was divided into cells. Many already contained large groups of captives. A man met them in the wide aisle leading across the building. Older and hunched, he peered up at Halen through strands of wild gray hair.

"I've got new merchandise," Halen told him.

The man studied the prisoners, the last bit of sunlight glinting in his cold, void eyes. He grunted and shuffled to the nearest empty cell, unlocking the door. It swung open with a loud shriek that sent a shiver down Sirion's spine.

The guards moved the prisoners along, herding them into the cell. As most collapsed inside, the door slammed shut behind them. Sirion watched Halen stride off and sank to his knees. For a long time, silence hung around them except for the heavy breathing of the prisoners. No one said anything until Sirion heard Irynna sniff.

"Are you all right?" he asked.

"They're just going to sell us off like livestock," she cried, voice trembling and so quiet he almost couldn't hear her.

Sirion put his hand on her shoulder, wishing he had words to encourage her. In a way, the prospect of being sold gave him a spark of hope. His new master might not watch him as closely as Halen, providing opportunity for escape. And if he did, he already determined to find Irynna and take her with him. He could never live with leaving her behind, but to tell her where the others might overhear would be unwise. He couldn't save them all.

The inside of the warehouse darkened. Feeling around for space, they settled in as comfortably as they could. Just when they expected to be left in peace for the night, the warehouse door creaked open. In came Halen, the man with the keys, and a handful of new men, clothed in black. A couple held torches aloft, the flickering orange glow surrounding them as they marched down the aisle.

Sirion watched them come right to the cell containing him and his fellow captives. As soon as the door was unlocked, a fearsome man with a harsh expression walked in with Halen who glared down at Sirion. "Get up."

Sirion glanced once at the other man and rose to his feet. Halen promptly detached his shackles from the main chain and shoved him toward the door.

"Keep him secured," Halen ordered the other men.

Two of them grasped Sirion's arms. Even if he'd wanted to pull away, he wouldn't have had the strength.

Halen turned back to the man still inside the cell. "Which ones?"

The man eyed the prisoners.

"Those three and the girl."

Halen unchained the three strongest young men in the group and Irynna. Her eyes, wide and fearful, jumped to Sirion as they led her out. With their prisoners between them, the men proceeded out of the warehouse. Outside, the area glowed eerily with lanterns and a nearby pit fire. Someone shoved Sirion from behind. They moved on, heading in the direction away from where they'd entered the city. Sirion scanned the streets. Where would they be taken this time?

:Chapter Four:

The Fortress

Shadowy figures slunk away from them, disappearing in narrow alleys as they marched down the darkened streets. Bursts of harsh laughter floated through the city, and a faint scream echoed from a distance. Apprehension churned Sirion's stomach, and the overwhelming sense of evil and suffering in the air chilled his blood. *Why do You want me here, Elohim?* he wondered. *Please show me what purpose there is in this.*

In a few minutes, they arrived at the city's farthest gate. Guards stood at a fire alongside the arched opening, but let them pass without questioning. Once outside, moonlight reflected on a wide river flowing ahead of them. Sirion's gaze was drawn to the looming, black silhouette on the other side—a great stone fortress. Jagged against the night sky, it appeared to be broken down, but as they drew closer to the bridge spanning the river, he realized the structure was still under construction.

They crossed the long, plank bridge and approached the wall of the fortress. Torches at either side of the gate glinted on the black armor of two guards. These men opened the door, and they entered the silent, shadowed courtyard. Sirion glanced at the others. Irynna walked with her head down, but fear filled the eyes of the other three young men, their gazes darting all over the compound. Their heavy breathing competed with the sound of their reluctant footsteps.

Across the courtyard, one of their captors grasped the iron ring of the fortress door and pulled. The door groaned open to reveal a long, torch-lit hall, which eventually disappeared into darkness. As they passed through the doorway, Sirion leaned close to Irynna and whispered, "I will try to find a way to escape, and I'll find you."

The men yanked him away, but Irynna sent him a grateful look.

Once all were inside, the door closed with an ominous rumble. Sirion looked over his shoulder. Would he ever pass back through that door, out of this dark place? The group marched down the hall, finally coming to a halt at an intersection. Here, Halen turned to the men.

"Take care of the others," he ordered.

Sirion could only watch as they led Irynna and the other young men down the dark hall to the right. Soon, they disappeared, and Sirion feared where they might be taken. Halen faced the two men still guarding Sirion and jerked his head. They continued on. Aside from their footsteps echoing in the hollow hallway, the fortress was deathly quiet. The cold, damp air and eerie surroundings made Sirion's skin prickle. And why had he been singled out of the captives?

At last, they arrived at a tall double door. Halen pushed it open, leading the way into a cavernous room. The tall, arched ceiling was shrouded in shadows. Only two torches burned at one end where a raised platform stood. The stone seat on the platform confirmed Sirion's suspicions. This was a throne room.

The men shoved Sirion forward to stand before the throne. Halen stepped in front of him, giving him an ugly sneer. Sirion held his poisonous gaze, struggling to tamp down his hatred for the man.

"His lordship will be here shortly."

Turning on his heel, Halen left Sirion in the hands of his guards. Once his footsteps died away, silence settled. The two men stood like statues on either side of Sirion. He could hear his heart beating, and one of the torches sparked and sizzled. He glanced to the side door where Halen had left and waited for several long minutes. He shifted his arms and his shackles jingled. His eyes roamed the room. Whoever it was for must like it empty and foreboding. The throne was the only furnishing.

After a time, footsteps broke the dead silence. Sirion looked again to the door as they drew closer. From the distinct sounds, he guessed at least four people approached. Halen entered first, but Sirion's eyes focused on the next three people, each one familiar, yet only one surprised him. The first was the Dark Elf, though, as usual, he had his face obscured by a hood and a black cloth covering all but his eyes. He stopped at the side of the throne and stared. Sirion held his gaze for a moment, but found something unnerving about his intense eyes. The next man stopped beside the Elf. Sirion's eyes narrowed as he glared at Derrin. Clad in deep red and black, he fit right in, but his face was drawn and shadowed. He glanced at Sirion, but immediately dropped his gaze to the floor. His expression hinted that he had seen many things he'd never expected or wanted to see. Perhaps, after a year, he had realized just what a grave decision he had made.

But Sirion's attention did not linger long on the two. His gaze settled on the third man, jaw clenching. Though shorter than those around him, the man walked with his chin held high. His black cloak billowing behind him, he stepped up to the throne and faced Sirion.

"You," Sirion said in disgust.

"Yes, me," Vayzar replied with a scornful smile. He sat down and leaned casually on the armrest, altogether pleased with himself.

"You're the one behind my captivity," Sirion said through gritted teeth.

"In a way, yes," Vayzar acknowledged, his grin widening. "I was the deciding factor, you might say. The voice of reason that stopped Derrin from uselessly killing you."

Sirion shot a glance at the young man, but he would not look up.

"So yes, I am responsible. Welcome to my humble abode." Vayzar waved his hand around the room and gave a low chuckle. "I am the self-appointed lord of Carel."

Hope flamed to life inside of Sirion. Eldinorieth was only a day to the southeast. If he could get free of the fortress and reach the forest, they would never be able to find him. Already his mind jumped to work on a plan.

Silence filled the room, and Vayzar stared at him expectantly. When he did nothing, Halen shoved him forward.

"Kneel," he ordered.

Sirion nearly scoffed. They were crazy to believe he would willingly bend a knee to the evil man. Vayzar's eyes narrowed, and he looked past Sirion, giving a subtle nod. A whip crack echoed in the room. Pain seared across Sirion's legs, forcing him to his knees. He bit down hard and suppressed a groan.

"Better," Vayzar said with satisfaction. "Now," he went on, sitting up straighter and leaning forward a little, "how have you fared the last several months?"

Sirion ground his teeth together, chest rising and falling heavily as he gave Vayzar a cold, hard stare. How could he ever recount the suffering he'd endured?

But this was all Vayzar needed. "Exactly what I thought. Therefore, I have a proposition for you. Work for me and your days as a miserable captive will be over."

Sirion gave a forceful shake of his head. "I would *never* work for you."

Vayzar glanced past him again, and Sirion tensed. The whip cracked, and this time tore into his right shoulder, opening a new wound. A cry caught in his throat, but he swallowed it down. He breathed hard, fighting the pain.

"You will learn to call me lord," Vayzar told him, voice low and certain. "That is why I've kept you alive all these months. You see, I saw the value in your life. The value in having you on my side." He left the throne and stepped down. Bending close, he whispered, "And I always find a way to get what I want."

Sirion looked right into his cold eyes. "This time you are going to be disappointed."

He anticipated another biting lash from Halen's whip, but Vayzar just cocked an eyebrow. "We shall see."

Vayzar straightened and commanded, "Take him to a cell where he can sit and consider the generosity of my offer."

Looking down at Sirion again, he added darkly, "And the consequences of refusing."

The guards grabbed Sirion's arms and jerked him to his feet. His eyes locked with Vayzar's in a battle of wills until the men shoved him toward the door. He glanced at the Dark Elf who watched him all the way out.

Exhausted and distracted by the throbbing pain of his shoulder, Sirion lost his sense of direction and how many halls they traveled. Winding around in the massive fortress, they came to a short corridor with a handful of small cells. The guards opened one door and shoved him inside. As they walked away, he dropped to the stone floor. He wanted nothing more than to sleep and escape the nightmare of reality.

One hand propped on his knee and the other holding a net made from a piece of an old bed sheet, Elmorhirian bent down close to Leiya and spoke in a low voice. "Now, move very slowly so you don't scare them. Tadpoles are very, very sneaky."

Eyes large with seriousness, Leiya nodded. "Okay."

Watching from the bank of the pond, Makilien giggled at their expressions. With cautious steps, they waded through the water until Elmorhirian reached out to stop Leiya.

"Ah! Right there. See them swimming?"

Leiya bent over to peer into the water. "Yes! I see them!"

"All right, I'll show you what to do. For this part you're going to have to be quick."

Elmorhirian's net hovered over the surface for a moment, and then he plunged it into the water. When he pulled it back up, water gushed over the sides. Leiya watched with delighted expectation as the net drained.

"You got some!"

Elmorhirian grinned. "I told you I was the best tadpole catcher in Elimar. Here, you can put these in the bucket."

He handed her the net and she trudged to the bank where they had set a bucket of water.

"Look, we've got five already," she said excitedly as Makilien helped her transfer the wiggling baby frogs. "Now, I'm gonna try."

She splashed back into the pond to rejoin Elmorhirian. Brows sunk low in concentration, she tried several times to fill her own net with tadpoles. At first, she could not catch anything, but after a little help from the Elf, she returned to the bank with a couple of the tiny creatures.

"This is fun," she said with a giggle. "Come in and try it, Makilien. You can borrow my net."

Makilien cocked her head as her sister stared up at her persuasively. The distractions she'd faced lately made it difficult to join in with things, but a grin broke out.

"All right."

Leiya jumped up and down in excitement. Chuckling at her, Makilien pulled off her boots, rolled up her pant legs, and tucked her skirt up into her belt. Following her little sister, she stepped into the cool water, mud oozing around her feet. It reminded her of her time as a child when she used to play with Aedan in the stream running through Reylaun.

They'd had such grand imaginary adventures back then, never knowing the real ones they would one day face.

For the next while, the three of them waded around the pond, laughing and adding many more tadpoles to their bucket. Poised to catch a few more, Makilien heard a loud splash behind her. Leiya shrieked, and Elmorhirian gave a mischievous chuckle. She turned to them. Water dripped from Leiya's hair and the front of her dress.

"Oh yeah?" she exclaimed with a giggle.

She dropped her net and used both hands to scoop up water to splash Elmorhirian.

"Now this is war!" the Elf declared.

Leiya shrieked again when he came after her. Makilien folded her arms and watched them wryly. But this didn't fit Elmorhirian's plans. As he passed her, he splashed a handful of water up in her face. Makilien sputtered and stood stunned for a moment as Elmorhirian flashed a wicked grin.

"Oh, now you're going to get it. Let's get him, Leiya!"

Leiya laughed in delight, and they both charged the Elf. A full-scale water fight ensued, filled with shrieking and laughter. By the time they sloshed to the bank, they were dripping wet and tired. Leiya dropped down next to the tadpole bucket with a happy sigh.

"That was fun."

Flopping down on his back, Elmorhirian agreed. Makilien smiled with the contentment they each felt and would have spoken, but Elmorhirian suddenly looked up.

"Do you hear that?"

"Hear what?" Leiya asked.

He gave her a grin. "Dragon wings."

"Really?"

He nodded. "Probably someone from Minarald. Come on. Let's take care of the tadpoles and see who it is."

The three of them hurried to Makilien and Leiya's house where Elmorhirian carefully poured the tadpoles into a large basin where Leiya could watch them grow. Still wet, they went on to Elnauhir's house. When they arrived, the sight of a majestic emerald green dragon greeted them. Beside him stood a much smaller dragon, about the size of medium-sized dog, with even darker green scales.

"Emaril and Jade!" Leiya exclaimed.

She rushed on ahead. When the little dragon spotted her, she let out a shriek of excitement and bounded forward to meet her, half running, half flying.

A wide grin spread across Makilien's face. She couldn't believe how much Jade had grown in the couple of months since she'd visited Minarald, but she supposed it was only natural for young dragons.

Happy voices and giggling filled the air. Makilien loved how her sister and the dragon were such good friends. Makilien's family had been in Minarald shortly after Jade's birth, and she and Leiya had bonded immediately even though Jade couldn't speak yet at the time.

As she and Elmorhirian passed the two of them, Makilien said, "Hello, Jade."

The dragon gave her a toothy grin. "Hello, Makilien. Hello, Elmorhirian," she replied, a giggle in her young voice.

She was a beautiful little creature, and would become a stunning mature dragon, but she had some growing to do. Her horns and spikes were just little dark knobs, and her spring green eyes were a bit large for her head. However, it made her all the more endearing.

As Leiya and Jade chattered on, Makilien and Elmorhirian greeted Emaril, but before they could move on to conversation with him and the others present, Jade came bounding back.

"Father, can I go play with Leiya?"

"Of course," Emaril replied. "Go on."

The two of them dashed away, and Leiya exclaimed, "Let's play hide and seek!"

Chuckles were shared over their enthusiasm.

"Jade sure is growing," Makilien said.

"She is indeed, and abounding with energy," Emaril replied. "She begged and begged to come with me. Insisted she was strong enough to fly all the way, so I relented. She gave it her best effort, but spent half the journey riding on my back. We stopped to rest last night or I would have made it sooner. But it's good for her to be out and about . . . and for Indiya to have a little time of peace and quiet."

"I bet she's exhausted," Lorelyn said, a wry smile crossing her lips.

Emaril chuckled. "At times, yes, but we couldn't be happier."

Lorelyn's smile grew. "I'm glad."

"So what brings you to Elimar?" Elnauhir asked.

"Just to bring word of Lord Darian's plans for the celebration," Emaril answered. "Lord Gébrale will be returning to Tûrenth shortly and then Lord Darian will set out for here. You can expect him in perhaps eight or nine days."

"Excellent. That will give us time to visit before the celebration," the Elf lord said.

"Lord Darian also requested I bring back any new information on the situation in Eldinorieth."

Elnauhir nodded. "I'm glad you mentioned that. I do have information for him. Makilien and Vonawyn were actually ambushed by two men while they and the boys were out hunting a couple of days ago."

The dragon glanced at Makilien. "That is disturbing news. How close to the city did this happen?"

"Only about fifteen miles from here," Elandir joined in.

The dragon frowned at this.

"Come," Elnauhir invited him. "Let's all go to the garden. We can discuss this further and you can rest from your flight."

:Chapter Five:

Mysterious Meeting

Darkness so thick he could not see his own hands engulfed Sirion. He had spent more time in darkness during his months of captivity than he had in the light, a trial for someone with Elven blood. In this deep darkness, time did not exist. But the longer he sat, the more he craved food and water. He leaned one shoulder against the cold wall, mindful of his wound, and blew out his breath. How long would he be locked away this time?

He prayed, begging for something to take his mind from the situation. He tried to think of better days—days of freedom and time spent with his loved ones. He thought of Makilien and smiled faintly, but then wondered again if she was even alive.

Sirion hung his head. Despair gnawed at his heart and mind. He dragged the edge of one of his shackles across the floor. It grated against the stones, and then silence. Utter silence. He had not heard a single thing for however long he'd been here. It was as if the earth had swallowed him up to be forgotten forever.

But the ever-fighting spark of determination flared to life inside him, and he rose to his feet. Hand to the wall, he took weak steps along the perimeter of the cell and found the door. Searchingly, he ran his fingers over every inch of it, pushing and prying at every crack and crevice. He worked at it until sweat beaded on his forehead and his breath came in frustrated puffs. With a defeated sigh, he sank back to the floor and wiped his tattered sleeve across his forehead. The door was solid.

He could grope around in the dark to try to find something useful inside his cell, but for now, his strength was spent. Leaning back again, his eyes slid closed. He tried to imagine his home in Silnar, but the image was vague. This nightmare he was living had caused his previous memories to dim, becoming more like dreams he couldn't quite grasp.

He did not know for sure if he had drifted off, but he sat up straight and listened. Yes, he did hear footsteps. They had not been imagined. He put his ear to the door. At least two people approached the cell. He pushed to his feet as dim torchlight filtered through the tiny barred window of the door and peered out through the bars. Two guards appeared. With grim, silent expressions, they unlocked the door. It swung open with a mournful shriek, and the men glared into the cell.

"Lord Vayzar wants to see you," one of the guards said and jerked his head.

Sirion gladly stepped out of the cell though he wasn't as mentally prepared for another confrontation as he would have liked. The men marched him down the dim, winding halls lit intermittently by torches. This time Sirion tried to keep a clear sense of direction. After multiple turns, they stopped at a door in an empty hall. The guards opened it and pushed him inside. His eyes searched the small room, taking in every detail. It was almost bare except for a table in the center and a chair beside it. A three-candled holder sat on the table with a large basin and pitcher and a pile of clothing.

One of the guards walked around in front of Sirion and took his wrist. He looked down as the man unlocked one side of the shackles and then the other. Sirion rubbed his raw wrists, breathing deep in relief to, at last, be rid of the things.

"Wash up and change," the guard snapped. "And be quick. His lordship is waiting."

The guards stepped out and closed the door. Sirion glanced over his shoulder. It was tempting to try something now that he was unshackled and left unattended. But with the guards armed and right outside the door, he resisted the temptation. Breathing out, he walked to the table and surveyed the items. Clear water filled the pitcher. His parched throat ached in reaction. Whether it was for washing or not, he didn't care. He picked up the pitcher and drank. When he set it down with a sigh, half the water remained.

With time ticking, he poured it into the basin and found a clean cloth on the other side. Dunking it into the water, he washed away all the months of dirt and grime revealing the signs of old and newer wounds. But he'd become numb to them.

After washing, he changed into the new clothes. They were very plain—a simple, off-white shirt and dark linen pants—but they could have been a prince's attire compared to the tattered rags he had been wearing. The shirt hung a bit on his thin, hunger-weakened frame, but the clean material felt good.

He had just finished when the door swung open, and one of the guards stepped in. The man said nothing, but motioned for Sirion to follow. He was relieved when they did not replace the shackles.

They continued through the fortress. Sirion's confidence had returned now that the water had revived him. In just a few moments, they arrived at yet another door. Beyond this one was a much larger room. Two round, iron chandeliers with dozens of lit candles hovered over a long table lined with high-back chairs. The dining room, apparently. But the inspection of the room ended when Sirion's eyes settled on Vayzar.

"Ah, there he is." The man grinned. "Welcome." He waved his hand at the guards. "You can leave us."

Sirion's gaze followed them out of the room before returning to Vayzar.

"You look a sight better," the man said. He motioned to the table. "Come, come. Have a seat." He pulled out a chair near the head.

But Sirion just stared for a long moment at the odd little man.

"Well, don't just stand there," Vayzar said, voice a bit clipped.

Sirion took slow steps toward the table, suspicious gaze never leaving him. Despite the man's strange show of friendliness, Sirion could see the blackness of his heart reflected in the devious glint of his eyes.

He sat in the offered chair, and Vayzar promptly took the seat at the table's head.

"Very good," he said as he settled in.

He motioned across the room, and Sirion now realized servants stood at a second entrance. They hurried forward bearing two trays. A large plate was set before Sirion, and his eyes beheld a feast. His mouth watered and his stomach squeezed in reaction. Only sheer willpower kept him from devouring the food. Why would Vayzar offer him such a feast? It did not make sense, therefore he did not eat.

Trying desperately not to notice the tempting aroma wafting up from the plate, he leaned back and glanced at Vayzar. The man, his own plate before him, watched Sirion with a look of expectation.

"Well? Don't tell me you're not hungry." He eyed Sirion. "You can't be that picky. What did the Elves feed you?"

Sirion broke his silence. "Is it poisoned?"

He looked hard at Vayzar, but the man just laughed.

"Poisoned," he chuckled. "Of course not. Trust me, if I wanted to kill you, I could think of a much more creative and entertaining way to do so than poisoning your food."

He and Sirion stared at each other for a long moment. Then Vayzar reached out for Sirion's plate and swapped it with his own.

"There. Feel better? Now eat up. We have to build up your strength."

Sirion tensed. "For what?"

Ignoring him, Vayzar dug into his plate, smacking loudly. "Delicious."

Sirion sighed, eyes landing on his plate, and could stand it no longer. He gave in to the desperate craving of his stomach. Whether it fit Vayzar's plans or not, he did need to regain his strength. He brought a forkful of succulent meat to his mouth and closed his eyes for a moment. Never had food tasted so good. For several minutes, he just ate hungrily, forcing himself to forget Vayzar's pleased expression.

"There, see? I told you it was good."

At last, Sirion's plate lay empty and his stomach more content than it had been in ages. Energy and strength warmed his muscles and gave him a fresh sense of determination. His gaze settled on Vayzar, and he sized him up. He was confident he could take him if he wanted, but what then?

Vayzar smirked, reading his eyes. "I wouldn't try anything." He brushed back the edge of his jerkin revealing a long dagger.

Knowing he had to bide his time, Sirion leaned back in his chair. "Why would you want to build up my strength?"

"Well, you're no use to me half-starved," Vayzar stated, completely matter-of-fact.

Defiance sparked in Sirion's eyes, but Vayzar saw that too.

"And don't give me any of that 'I won't help you' talk," he warned. "You've actually been quite helpful already."

Sirion's brows crunched down. "How have I helped you?"

"Patience," Vayzar replied, sounding ever more like he was addressing a child.

Sirion gritted his teeth, wanting more than anything to force some answers out of the man. "What are you up to here?"

Vayzar grinned, only too pleased to say, "What do you think? I'm after Eldor, of course, but unlike others before me, I'm actually using my brain and not recklessly attacking straight-out."

Sirion gave a humorless laugh. "When will you people ever quit? How many failures will it take?"

"Ah, but you see, I'm not your average, rash conqueror. As I said, I'm using my brain . . . and his."

Vayzar's gaze shifted.

Sirion frowned and looked off to his right. He jerked back when he saw a man standing right beside him. It was as if he had just appeared there, for Sirion had not heard his approach. Sirion's eyes climbed upward. His heart skipped a beat. The man's face was thin and bony, his coloring a sickly gray. The skin on the left side of his face and neck was horrifically scarred, seeming to ooze down into his collar, and his eye on that side was clouded. His good eye, however, was dark and piercing. Sirion's stomach lurched. The sickening stench of death and decay exuded from the man. Sirion swallowed involuntarily, frozen under his cruel gaze.

"I'd like you to meet Wormaw." Vayzar's voice broke in, low with sordid amusement. "He's an alchemist, among other things."

Sirion tore his eyes away from the frightful man and back to Vayzar.

"He is my guarantee of success in Eldor. You see, Eldor won't be able to stop us because no one will anticipate my attack. I will weaken the country slowly from the inside first. And then, when I'm ready, I'll deliver the killing blow. Thanks to Wormaw here, I possess a wonderfully despicable concoction that, when released on Minarald, will wipe out more than half the city. The people won't know what hit them. I'll be able to march right in, unhindered, and crown myself king. Ingenious, isn't it?"

Vayzar grinned maliciously, revealing his stained teeth. Sirion tried not to let him see how the news disturbed him. Speaking with more confidence than he truly felt, he said, "What none of you seem to realize is that Minarald has more than walls and an army for protection."

"We shall see about that. Very soon, in fact." Vayzar rose from the table. "It is time to strike the first major blow . . . and it involves you."

Sirion paced the room, the same he had dressed in before the meal, and kicked at a pebble on the floor, sending it skittering into the far wall. He glanced in frustration at the closed door. No matter how he tried to discover what Vayzar's final comment had meant, the man had refused to answer, simply grinning again and telling him he had someone he needed to meet. Sirion had been promptly escorted back to this room after that. Nearly half an hour had passed now, and he was growing impatient and increasingly apprehensive.

He ran a restless hand through his hair and murmured, "What does he have planned?" But his resolve was steadfast. He would do anything in his power to keep from being used by Vayzar.

Footsteps came at last. Sirion stopped pacing and faced the door. When the knob turned and the door swung open, the Dark Elf slipped into the room. He closed the door silently and turned to Sirion.

They eyed each other. Sirion could only see a small portion of the Elf's face between his hood and face covering. He did notice now that they were both the same height, and the Dark Elf's penetrating eyes were the same shade of brown as his own.

Sirion's fists clenched as indignation rose inside him. "How can you betray your people?" he questioned, frustration thrumming in his voice. "How could you shame them like this?"

The Dark Elf did not reply. He took his eyes from Sirion and advanced farther into the room. When he stopped, Sirion stared at his back.

"Why are you here? What do you want with me?"

Still, the Dark Elf gave him no acknowledgement, but he reached up and pushed back his hood, his dark hair falling to the middle of his back. Moving slowly, he turned around and pulled down his face covering.

The blood drained from Sirion's face. He stumbled backward, grabbing the edge of the table to steady himself. His heart nearly stopped in his chest.

:Chapter Six:

Reunion

A steady rain soaked the city, and low thunder rumbled overhead. Makilien pulled on her boots and reached for her cloak hanging on a peg near the door. As she put it over her shoulders, Leiya came tromping into the entry from outside. Rainwater trickled from the ends of her hair.

"Makilien, can you help me? The tadpoles' basin is overflowing. I need to put it on the porch or they'll get washed out," the little girl said in distress.

Makilien smiled. "Of course."

She clasped her cloak and pulled up the hood, reaching out to lift Leiya's as well.

"You should keep your hood up."

"I know, but it gets in the way," Leiya pouted.

Makilien chuckled and followed her outside and around to the back of the house where Leiya spent hours watching the tadpoles swim around and eat. They had grown in the last few days. Some even had two tiny legs.

She helped her little sister carry the basin up to the porch, and Leiya looked up at her happily. "Thank you."

"You're welcome," Makilien replied, smiling down at her. "I'm going over to Lord Elnauhir's house now to work on my dress with Vonawyn."

"Okay."

Makilien stepped down from the porch and followed the path away from the house. Raindrops pattered on her hood, and she pulled her cloak closer. It was an ideal day for her and Vonawyn to work on their celebration dresses. After almost a week of work, they only had the trim left to finish.

As she neared Lord Elnauhir's house, a commotion caught her attention. Several of her friends were gathered around two wet and muddied horses. An unfamiliar, petite young woman held the reins of one, but Makilien's eyes went straight to her friends who lifted someone off the other horse. Ignoring her own advice, she shoved her hood back to see better. Her breath came in a gasp, heart pounding into her ribs. She tried to keep her mind from racing ahead of itself, but it was too late for that.

Her feet seemed to move of their own accord, slowly at first, but breaking into a run. She had almost reached the group when Vonawyn turned to her, eyes wide and expression blank with shock. Her words came out breathlessly. "It's Sirion."

Makilien let go a small cry, hands covering her mouth. Her legs nearly gave out, and she stumbled, but Vonawyn grabbed her by the shoulders and steadied her.

"He's alive," the Elf said, adding gently, "but he's injured."

"H-how badly?" Makilien's heart hammered away in her chest, and she felt dizzy with a spinning mix of shock, fear, and joy.

"I'm not sure yet. Come on."

They turned and ran after the others. Makilien moved as close as she could to Sirion, straining to see his face. Halandor and Elandir carried him between them. She caught a glimpse of blood staining his shirt. At last, she saw what she wanted. His eyes were closed and his skin pale, but it was his face. Emotion rose up in a flood, choking her throat and sending tears to her eyes. *Please let him be all right,* she pleaded.

In a spare bedroom, they laid Sirion on the bed. Makilien could see now that the blood came from an unseen wound to his right side. They carefully pulled off his shirt, and Lorelyn took over. She peeled back the bandages around his chest to reveal a long cut across his ribs. Though it did not bleed freshly, the edges were inflamed.

Lorelyn turned to Vonawyn, voice sure and calm. "Take Elmorhirian and get the supplies I will need."

Vonawyn gave a quick nod, and she and her brother rushed from the room. Those who remained stood around the bed, looking on as if not one of them could truly believe the sight. No one spoke at first. Makilien clutched the post at the end of the bed as she tore her eyes from Sirion to Lorelyn. Her voice barely made it through her throat.

"Will he live?"

She gave Makilien a quick, reassuring smile. "Yes, I believe he will. The wound is not too serious."

Makilien released a great sigh, and right there it sank in that Sirion was alive—truly alive—and had returned. Tears spilled over her eyelids. What a glorious day it was! Halandor came up behind her and put his arm around her trembling shoulders. She glanced up to give him a teary smile.

69

When Vonawyn and Elmorhirian returned, Lorelyn and her daughter skillfully tended Sirion's wound. Before long, they had him bandaged and resting comfortably though he remained unconscious. Now curious eyes turned to the quiet young woman who had ridden into Elimar with him.

"I think perhaps we should let Sirion rest and have a talk with our guest." Lord Elnauhir smiled kindly at the girl and motioned for everyone to follow.

They filed out of the bedroom to gather in the living room. Lorelyn handed the young woman a blanket to wrap around her wet shoulders as Lord Elnauhir turned to her and asked, "What is your name?"

"Irynna," she answered softly.

"Irynna, may I ask how you came to be here? I'm sure you can see how shocked we are. For months we have believed Sirion to be dead."

The woman nodded in understanding. "Yes, he said you would believe that. We were slaves, the two of us. We met a couple of weeks ago. He promised me if he could escape, he would find me and take me with him."

"And he did escape?"

Irynna tugged the blanket closer, fists balled in the material, and nodded again. "Yes. We barely made it, but he was so determined. I was on the verge of giving up completely." She stared across the room with misty eyes. But then she focused on Elnauhir again to say, "He gave me hope."

A feeling of warmth and love surged inside Makilien as she thought of how Sirion had helped the young woman. She wanted nothing more than to go back and find him awake, but she forced herself to stay.

"Where were you being held captive?" Elnauhir asked.

"Carel."

The Elf lord nodded slowly. The infamous reputation of the city was known even this far south. "Did Sirion say how he came to be a slave?"

"Yes, but I don't think I can give you all the details he can." Irynna dipped her head apologetically.

"That's all right. We can wait. I'm sure it won't be long before he wakes," Elnauhir replied. "And I hope you will excuse the bombardment of questions, but you said outside that you were attacked by two men in Eldinorieth?"

Irynna nodded, eyes large.

"That does not come as a surprise," Elnauhir sighed. "There have been frequent attacks lately. When did the attack occur?"

"Yesterday morning," Irynna answered. She looked at the floor and shook her head in regret. "Sirion was hurt protecting me. We didn't have any weapons, but he fought them off as well as he could. I think eventually they realized we weren't worth the trouble and ran off. I did what I could for Sirion without any supplies. I was afraid I wouldn't even be able to get him here once he fell unconscious. Luckily, he was awake long enough this morning to get on his horse."

"You did well," Lorelyn assured her. "The temporary bandage stopped the bleeding and kept the wound clean."

Irynna smiled shyly, not fully meeting her eyes. Suddenly, her stomach growled, and she put her hand over it.

"Sorry," she said, blushing.

"No, let me apologize," Elnauhir replied quickly. "You must be starving. I'll have a meal prepared." He turned to his wife. "Will you see that the cooks prepare something?"

Lorelyn nodded.

"Vonawyn," Elnauhir went on. "Why don't you show Irynna a room and find her dry clothing. After that, show her to the dining room. The food should be ready by then."

"Yes, Father." Vonawyn turned to Irynna with a warm smile. "Come with me."

Once the two of them had gone, those remaining stood silent for a moment so surreal it could have been imagined. Makilien shook her head.

"I can't believe it," she murmured in a daze.

Halandor smiled at her. "You were right."

Makilien nodded with a smile still mingled with tears. "Can someone let my family know about this? I would like to go sit by Sirion, if that is all right."

"Of course," Elnauhir assured her. "I will send someone."

With a murmur of thanks, Makilien returned to Sirion's bedroom. He still lay unconscious, but did not appear as pale as when they had first brought him in.

Taking a chair from the table nearby, she set it next to the bed and sat down. She just stared at him at first. It seemed like a dream that, if she wasn't careful, she could wake up from. Finally, she reached out and gently clasped her fingers around Sirion's hand. She smiled, tears coming fresh.

"You're really here," she whispered. "You're back."

She took in every detail of his face, hardly able to wait to see his warm eyes and kind smile. Her heart had ached so deeply for it.

Makilien's mind was hazy as she drifted on the edge of sleep, but her first conscious thought was of Sirion. She sat up, wide awake. It was still a little dim outside, but the sun had risen. She scooted out of bed, dressing with great haste. Stopping at the mirror, she smoothed the front of her dress and fixed her hair. She realized she looked a bit tired. After all, she hadn't taken Vonawyn's advice to get some sleep until sometime after midnight, hating to leave Sirion's side. But, regardless of looks, she didn't feel at all sleepy this morning. Just anxious.

With a deep breath, she left the bedroom. Sirion's room was just down the hall. At the door, she gave a light knock. Vonawyn opened it, a sparkling grin stretching across her face. Makilien gave her a questioning look, but when Vonawyn's gaze shifted to the bed, her heart leapt with joy. Those brown eyes she had longed to see for so long met her own. Her throat tightened, and tears blurred her vision.

"You're awake," she gasped, and rushed to the side of the bed, unable to keep the tears from falling. She took his hand, treasuring the feeling of his fingers closing around hers.

"It's so good to see you," Sirion said, smiling up at her. "I didn't know if you were still alive."

"Yes, I'm alive," Makilien half laughed, half choked. She brushed her free hand across her face and attempted to control her tears. "I'm sorry, it's just so wonderful to see you awake and have you back. I don't even know what to say."

Sirion's smile gentled, and he squeezed her hand.

Vonawyn came up behind Makilien and touched her shoulder. "He just woke up a couple of minutes ago. I was just coming to get you."

When Halandor spoke, Makilien realized most of her friends were present.

"Sirion was telling us how he was injured during the battle. Zirtan's men took him while he was unconscious. That is why we could not find him."

"And they've had you all this time?" Makilien's heart ached to think of it.

Sirion grimaced. "Yes."

"Why did they take you? Were any others taken from the battlefield?"

"I don't know about others, but they intended to use me for some plan of theirs."

"And they were keeping you in Carel?" Halandor asked.

"For a couple of days, yes. They moved me a lot, but Carel was the last place. I kept waiting for the right opportunity, and then one day when they brought me food, I was able to break free of the guards. It was the first chance I had to get away."

"Thank Elohim," Makilien breathed.

Her friends murmured their agreement.

"Are you hungry, Sirion?" Elnauhir asked.

"I am," he answered eagerly.

"Good. I'll have food brought to you right away."

"No, that is all right," Sirion stopped him. "I would like to get up and join you. I just needed some rest. I feel fine."

"Are you sure?"

Sirion nodded.

"All right. We will let you get dressed and see you in the dining room. Elmorhirian can stay in case you need any assistance."

Everyone but Elmorhirian filed out of the room. Giving Sirion another quick smile, Makilien reluctantly let him go and followed.

The dining room filled with joyful chatter as they all gathered around the table. Sirion's miraculous return added a new height of excitement to the household. A couple of minutes later, Irynna joined them, all cleaned up and wearing a lovely lavender and green dress. Makilien hadn't noticed the day before how pretty the young woman was.

Irynna paused and looked around, her expression shy and a little uncertain. Unendingly grateful to her for helping Sirion make it to Elimar, Makilien met her at the door.

"Good morning, Irynna. Come sit down."

The young woman smiled and followed her to the table. "Is Sirion awake?" she asked as she sat.

"Yes, and he's going to join us. He's looking very well this morning," Makilien answered with pleasure.

"Good," Irynna said, relief in her voice. "After everything he has done, I couldn't stand the thought of something happening to him on account of me."

In a short time, Sirion and Elmorhirian joined them. Everyone had questions for Sirion over the meal, but mostly they talked of what had taken place in Eldor after the battle. Sirion had missed so much. It was as if a whole year of his life had been stolen from him.

"You're just in time for the Alliance celebration," Elmorhirian piped up near the end of the meal. "It's in four days. Darian will be here too. He'll be overjoyed to see you."

"Perfect timing," Sirion replied with a smile.

"Speaking of Darian," Elnauhir said. "I've sent a message to Minarald with our fastest rider to let him know of your return. I'm sure one of the griffons or dragons will bring the news to your uncle. No doubt he'll set out for Elimar as soon as he receives word."

"I hope he does." Sirion looked across the table and caught Makilien's eye.

She smiled at him, her mind abuzz with excitement and joy, thinking of all the summer would now hold, and how much more the coming celebration would mean.

:Chapter Seven:

Questions

"Good morning, Makilien."

"Good morning, Leiya." Makilien flashed her sister a smile as she walked into the kitchen and asked their mother, "Can I help with anything?"

"Will you please take the milk into the dining room for me?" Hanna requested.

Makilien did this, and in a couple of minutes, her family gathered at the table for breakfast.

"What are you going to do today, Makilien?" Leiya asked her usual question as they dished up a hearty meal of fresh eggs and potatoes.

"I was thinking of asking Sirion if he wants to go for a walk." She paused to take a bowl from her mother. "We really haven't spent much time together these last two days. Elandir and Elmorhirian seem to have kept him busy and worn out."

"They certainly enjoy having him back," Néthyn said, eyes twinkling with amusement.

Makilien had to chuckle. "Yes."

She didn't mention her disappointment that Sirion had not sought to spend more time with her, aware it was her own selfishness that wanted it. After all Sirion had been through, he needed time to recover. She turned her eyes to her father. "I will probably have supper at Lord Elnauhir's house tonight if that is all right since Darian is supposed to arrive this afternoon."

"Sure," Néthyn replied. "We'll probably be over there as well."

This led to talk of the celebration, which took up most of the meal. Once they had finished, Makilien helped her mother and Leiya clear the table and then followed her father to the stable. It was a lovely spring day, the fresh leaves on the trees lit up brilliantly by the sunlight. A perfect day for a walk if Sirion agreed to it.

When they arrived, Makilien found both Sirion and Elmorhirian inside at Falene's stall. She smiled to see Sirion reunited with his horse, something she had only ever dreamed of seeing.

Elmorhirian spotted her first. "Morning, Makilien."

She gave him a quick smile as she joined them, but her eyes focused on Sirion as he gently rubbed Falene's forehead.

"Good morning. I wasn't expecting to see you two here."

"I was telling Sirion about what happened to Falene, and I thought he'd like to see her," Elmorhirian explained.

"Well, I don't want to interrupt you, but I thought I'd ask if Sirion felt like taking a walk with me as soon as I'm done taking care of Antiro."

Elmorhirian gave her a knowing grin. "Of course. We were just wasting time anyway."

Makilien chuckled. "Why don't you show him Falene's paddock while I feed Antiro?"

"Will do."

Gathering a bucket of grain and the grooming supplies, Makilien met Antiro in his paddock.

"Good morning," she greeted, spirits bright.

He responded with a whinny, making her grin. As he crunched his grain, she groomed his coat and told him briefly of her planned walk and hopes to spend more time with Sirion today. The horse paused halfway through and tossed his head in agreement.

As soon as she'd finished, she met Sirion and Elmorhirian at the fence of Falene's pasture. Taking this as his cue to leave, Elmorhirian said, "There are a few things Father wants me to see to this morning before Darian arrives." He stepped away from the fence. "I'll see you two later."

"We'll be around," Makilien told him. "I don't want to miss Darian's arrival."

As the Elf walked away, Makilien stood beside Sirion at the fence, and they both watched Falene for a moment. Makilien waited for him to speak, but when he remained silent she said, "She really missed you. I could tell."

"And I missed her," Sirion said with a faint smile. He glanced at Makilien. "Thank you for taking care of her. Elmorhirian told me how much you've done."

"I just couldn't let her die. Not after losing you." She breathed out a sigh, thinking back to the intense pain of that time. It still made her chest ache. Shaking it off, she looked from the horse to Sirion. "So, do you feel up to a walk? We don't have to go far."

Sirion nodded slowly. "Sure."

He pushed away from the fence, and Makilien fell into step beside him. She was quiet at first, uncertainty pricking at her. There had seemed to be a slight hesitation before Sirion's answer. She told herself it was nothing, that she was just overly sensitive, but it lingered at the back of her mind nonetheless.

Fighting the discomfort of her thoughts, she looked up at him. "I'm so glad you're here. Everything finally seems right again."

Sirion smiled at her, but said nothing.

Makilien looked away, letting out a quiet sigh. Oh, how she wished he would talk to her, the way he used to. They had so much they could talk about, but he said very little about the last several months. She realized he might not want to relive it by discussing it, but still, she would have expected him to share more with her.

Reluctant to bring it up, she asked in a low voice, "Was it terrible, your captivity?"

Sirion's expression sobered, jaw clenching and brows sinking low. "Yes," he murmured, staring ahead, memories playing through his mind.

Makilien swallowed hard, emotion and sympathy welling up inside. "I'm sorry."

He looked at her now, his expression still troubled. She continued, "I know how difficult it must be, but if you ever need to talk about it, I'm always here. You know that, right?"

His face relaxed a little. "Yes, I do."

A smile resurfaced on Makilien's lips, and she changed the subject as they wound their way through the city. She did most of the talking, but she enjoyed Sirion's presence despite the earlier uncertainty.

Sometime later, they ended up at the fountain in Lord Elnauhir's garden. They walked up to it, and Makilien stared down at the brightly colored fish swimming there. Memories flashed in her mind, remembering the time she and Sirion had sat here before she left to return to Reylaun. She'd been so comforted by his words and his confidence in her return. She wondered if he remembered it. She watched him, waiting to see if he would speak. He didn't, but noticed her hopeful gaze. He turned his head to look at her.

Emotion again built inside Makilien, and tears moistened her eyes. "I missed you so much."

"I missed you too," he replied quietly.

Makilien's heart sank. There it was again, the hesitation. She couldn't have just imagined it. A lump rose in her throat, but she tried to conceal her distress by looking into the water of the fountain. Was she being silly? Why would Sirion ever hesitate to tell her he had missed her?

Trying to shake the assailing questions, she said, "You don't have to stay here with me. I'm sure Elandir and Elmorhirian would love to have your company again."

She looked back up at him, forcing a smile. He smiled in return, but she now noticed something different about it. It didn't hold the same affection that it used to, and that put a painful ache in her heart.

"Thanks for the walk," Sirion told her, sounding almost normal.

Makilien tried to take comfort in that. "You're welcome."

With that, he walked away, leaving her standing alone at the fountain. She watched him leave the garden, and then sank down on the fountain's rim. She pulled her knees up and rested her arms on them as she stared off at nothing. A cold emptiness had settled inside her, leaving so many unanswered questions.

It just didn't make sense. They had been so close before the battle. She still remembered with almost painful clarity the feel of him holding her when she had so desperately needed it and the kiss he'd placed on her forehead after their declaration of love for each other. Her love was just as strong today as it was then, but what about his? *What has happened, Elohim?* Tears clogged her throat, but she would not let them rise any further.

Was she overreacting? Confusion joined the chaos of her thoughts. Had Sirion changed, or was it her somehow? She stared down at her reflection in the water. *I'm not different, am I?* She skimmed her fingers along the water's surface, distorting the image.

"Makilien?"

Her gaze jumped up as Vonawyn joined her at the fountain. She tried to erase her sadness, but her friend read the pain in her eyes.

"What's wrong?"

Makilien had difficulty speaking at first, but at last, she confessed, "It's Sirion. I don't know if he loves me anymore."

She had not let the thought fully develop until now. Speaking it aloud made tears sting her eyes and nose.

Vonawyn reached for her friend's hand. "Oh, Makilien, I'm sure he does."

Makilien wasn't so sure. Her lip quivered, and her voice broke. "But I don't see or feel it. He's different, Vonawyn."

Her friend looked at her in sympathy and rubbed her shoulder. "Maybe he just needs more time. We don't know everything he went through. I think it was probably much worse than he will tell us. Maybe he needs time to deal with it before he can show his other feelings."

Makilien nodded, clearing her throat. Vonawyn's words helped more than she could say. "You're right. He's barely been back for two days. I can't expect things to be normal. I am being selfish."

"No," Vonawyn replied, shaking her head. "You've just craved his love for so long."

Makilien smiled. "Thank you, Vonawyn."

They stood, and Vonawyn gave her a tight hug. "I'm sure everything will turn out fine."

At the sound of hoof beats, everyone rushed outside as a large company of uniformed horsemen bearing the blue banners of Eldor trotted up to the front of the house. The man at their head gave the welcoming group a sparkling grin.

Dismounting, King Darian handed the reins of his horse to one of his men and met those from the house at the base of the steps.

"Welcome, my lord," Elnauhir greeted.

"It is good to be back," Darian replied with much enthusiasm. "Especially now." His eyes searched the faces, and when he found Sirion, his smile broadened. He went to him and put his hand on his shoulder. "Sirion, thank Elohim you are alive. There was much rejoicing in Minarald when we received the news. I sent Tôr to Silnar straight away. I'm sure your uncle has heard by now."

"I can only imagine his joy," Sirion responded.

"Indeed, it is a miracle to have you returned to us."

Following their greetings, Lord Elnauhir ushered everyone inside to the sitting room where servants brought refreshments. Taking a glass of punch, Elmorhirian gave Darian a teasing look.

"And where is the lovely Lady Demera? I half expected you to bring her with you."

Darian glanced down, cheeks flushing slightly. A bashful little smile grew on his face. "I would have liked that if she could have remained in Eldor longer. Gébrale had to return to Tûrenth, and I didn't want Demera to be forced to travel without him."

Elmorhirian didn't think this was a good enough answer. "Well, you could have sent her home with one of the dragons."

"Oh stop, Elmorhirian," Lorelyn scolded her son. "Quit pestering poor Darian."

Elmorhirian's mischievous expression remained, and he shared a chuckle with Elandir, but Darian didn't appear bothered. Instead, he gave the Elf a wry look.

"Just wait," he warned. "Someday it will be you."

"Yeah," Elandir chimed in, giving his brother a devilish grin. "Just wait."

All mischief left Elmorhirian's eyes as he narrowed them at Elandir. Lorelyn chuckled at them before telling the king, "Despite my son's teasing, we're all very pleased for you."

Smiling warmly, Darian replied, "Thank you. I admit, it was unexpected, though not unwelcome."

Catching the light rekindling in his youngest son's eyes, Elnauhir spoke before Elmorhirian could jump in again. "So how are things with Gébrale in Tûrenth?"

"Very well. The city is growing. They have many of their buildings and houses completed, and many more nearly finished. He said the city is beginning to look as it did when his father reigned. They are very pleased with the progress."

"How wonderful for them to rebuild," Lorelyn said.

Darian agreed, and they all settled in for the afternoon to discuss the happenings in Minarald. With Darian added to the group, it seemed like old times. Makilien treasured every moment of it, praying this was the beginning of life returning to normal.

:Chapter Eight:

Shattered

"Leiya, you must sit still or I'll never get your hair right," Hanna told her daughter, laughter in her voice.

Makilien chuckled at them, watching her sister wiggle around in the chair in front of the mirror.

"I'm just so excited," Leiya replied. "I love celebrations!" She tried to look at Makilien.

"Leiya."

"Oh, sorry, Mama," she apologized, and stared ahead, trying mightily not to move.

Makilien walked behind her so she could see her sister's face in the mirror.

"Do you think I'll get to dance?" Leiya asked hopefully, adding with a little pout, "I didn't get to dance at Darian's coronation."

"I would certainly think so. Why, I bet Elmorhirian and Elandir both ask you to dance," Makilien replied.

Leiya's smile beamed. "Really?"

Makilien chuckled again. "Absolutely."

"There we go," Hanna said when she finished Leiya's hair, an adorable arrangement of long ringlets. She smiled at Leiya's reflection. "All done."

Leiya hopped off the chair and admired the hairstyle and the sunny yellow celebration dress Hanna and Makilien had sewn for her. She twirled, grinning.

"You look beautiful, Leiya," Makilien told her.

"Yes, you do," Hanna agreed.

Leiya hugged her arms around her mother's waist. "Thank you."

Makilien stared at them with a deep feeling of contentment. Her mother was lovely too, dressed in her new green celebration gown, her dark hair hanging long. She loved the two of them so much.

Breaking from her thoughts, she said, "I better get over to Lord Elnauhir's house to change. Vonawyn is probably waiting for me."

"We'll see you there," her mother replied.

Over at her friend's house, a buzz of voices met Makilien as she stepped inside. Many from around the city had already arrived for the celebration. The festive atmosphere made her stomach flutter with excitement, and she paused a moment to take in the sight of the decorations. Bright flowers and ribbons had been hung everywhere.

"There you are."

Makilien turned to Vonawyn's smiling face. "Sorry. I should have been here sooner, but I was helping Mother and Leiya."

"Don't worry. You're just in time."

The two of them hurried upstairs to Vonawyn's bedroom where the Elf pulled open her wardrobe doors. Inside, both their dresses hung, pressed and ready. She brought Makilien's out first. Makilien grinned as she held it up to admire. Made of lavender gossamer fabric, it had a beaded bodice that added a little sparkle and short, flowing sleeves. It was a perfect springtime celebration gown, and she had the added satisfaction of knowing she'd made most of it. Just seeing it made her as excited for the celebration as her sister. She laid the dress on the bed to change and noticed a smaller, pink satin gown.

"Who is this for?"

"Irynna. She'll be up in a few minutes to change," Vonawyn answered. "I borrowed it from Anlia. They are about the same size, don't you think?"

Makilien agreed and changed into her gown. Once Vonawyn had also dressed, she sat Makilien down in a chair to fix her hair, braiding it back into one elegant braid into which she wove tiny purple and white flowers that matched her dress.

While she worked, Vonawyn said with a smile in her voice, "I bet you have been especially looking forward to today since Sirion arrived."

A grin jumped to Makilien's lips. His arrival had indeed changed everything. "Yes. The time I spent with him at the celebration in Minarald is one of my most cherished memories. I'm hoping we can relive a little of it today."

Vonawyn gave a light sigh. "The only thing that would make today even better would be to have Aedan here too."

"I wish he was," Makilien said with feeling, "but, I was thinking, when he does get back, we should have a celebration in honor of Sirion's return."

"That is a wonderful idea," Vonawyn replied enthusiastically. "I'll mention it to Father."

In a moment, she had finished with Makilien who rose to look in the mirror.

"You did a beautiful job, as always," she told her friend.

A short time later, a light knock came from the door. Makilien answered it.

"Come in, Irynna," she invited.

The young woman stepped shyly into the room. Over near the bed, Vonawyn held up the extra dress and asked, "What do you think of this one?"

A smile started on Irynna's face and grew to be the widest Makilien had seen her wear as her large eyes took in the sight of the gown.

"It's beautiful," she murmured. "Are you sure I can wear it?"

"Of course." Vonawyn placed it in her hands.

Irynna ran her fingers over the soft fabric. She gave a little laugh of pure joy. "I've never worn such a dress. We were just poor farmers."

Makilien smiled, sharing her joy. "I know what you mean. My family lived on a little village farm too. I never saw anything like these dresses until I came here."

Eagerly, Irynna changed into the gown, and Vonawyn went to work on her hair, braiding it in a fashion similar to Makilien's. When she finished, she guided Irynna in front of the mirror. The young woman's dark blue eyes grew and sparkled in delight.

"I look . . ." her voice trailed off in wonder.

"Like a princess," Makilien finished for her. "That's what my sister would say."

Irynna's cheeks flushed, and she flashed a grin.

Vonawyn looked between the two of them. "Are you ladies ready for a celebration?"

"Definitely," Makilien responded.

With Vonawyn in the lead, they left the bedroom. Downstairs, they came into the ballroom where all the guests gathered. Since only a few from Minarald had come, most of the guests were Elves, and Makilien took a moment to admire their unique and elegant beauty. Searching the crowd, she found her family and walked over to them. They smiled at the sight of her.

"Oh, Makilien, you look so beautiful," Hanna breathed. "Your dress is so pretty."

"Thank you, Mother."

She looked up at her father whose eyes were beaming.

"How did I get so blessed with two such lovely daughters?" her asked.

With a warm smile, Makilien gave him a quick hug. "Because we have a very loving Lord."

"Indeed," Néthyn replied.

In just a short time, Elnauhir invited all the guests into the dining room for the celebration feast. Many long tables filled the room, decorated with white tablecloths and a variety of flowers. Amid much happy conversation, they took their seats. Makilien, her family, and friends had the honor of sharing a table with Lord Elnauhir and Lord Darian.

Before the meal began, the Elf lord came to his chair and the entire room quieted.

"Thank you all for gathering here to celebrate such an important event in our history." His strong voice carried through the room. "Today we look back and remember the beginning of our close and unbroken friendship with the people of Eldor. Since the start of our alliance, we have faced times of both prosperity and great adversity together. And we here know of this even better than most generations before us. Through it all, Elohim has kept us strong and preserved the alliance. Let us now give thanks for our friends and this opportunity to gather together."

All heads bowed, and Elnauhir thanked Elohim for bringing the Humans and Elves together, and for their prosperity, which allowed for such a celebration. After the heartfelt prayer, the feasting began in earnest. Between conversation and eating, stories were shared about the Humans and Elves that had been passed down for generations. Makilien enjoyed tales she'd never heard before of Baltar and the founders of Eldor. It gave her great joy to be a part of a country with such a rich history.

Halfway through the delicious meal, Darian stood and, once again, everyone's attention turned to the head table as conversation died away. He smiled, eyes sweeping across each table.

"I want to take a moment to thank those here in Elimar for your unwavering friendship throughout the years. Without the aid of the Elves, Baltar and those with him may never have gone on to found Minarald. And now today, there are many times in the recent past where we would have faltered without you." The king raised his glass. "To the alliance between the Eldorians and the Elves. By Elohim's will, may it always remain strong."

Exclamations of "Hear, hear!" echoed through the room, and all drank with Darian.

With feelings of great joy, they finished the remainder of their meal before returning to the ballroom. As night fell, the musicians set up to play for an evening of dancing. This was Makilien's favorite part of the celebration. Just as she had told her sister, Elmorhirian asked Leiya to dance right away. Makilien grinned at her little sister's delighted giggles as the Elf took her out onto the dance floor. Néthyn and Hanna soon joined in, and Makilien found herself standing alone.

She searched the faces around her, eyes finally landing on the person she sought. She'd had little chance to speak with Sirion since the start of the celebration, but she hoped now would provide a better opportunity. Sirion had seemed a little more himself since Darian's arrival, and it encouraged her.

She shared a smile with him as she approached.

"You look beautiful tonight," Sirion told her.

"Thank you," she replied, a little color rising in her cheeks. She paused, waiting a moment to see if he would speak. When the silence grew awkward, she asked, "Do you think you'll be able to dance tonight?"

Sirion touched his side. "I'd like to. I don't know how well I'll manage. It has been a while."

"Well, I certainly wouldn't mind if you need to go slowly, but you don't have to if you'd rather not," Makilien told him, though she would be disappointed, deep down.

Sirion glanced at the dancers. "I think I'll be all right."

Together, they walked onto the dance floor. Sirion took her hand and slipped his other around her waist. They did not speak at first, but then Makilien said, "It's a beautiful celebration, isn't it?"

"Yes," Sirion agreed. "And such an important time in Eldor's history."

"It is amazing to think of all that has taken place since the alliance was formed." She paused, trying hard to think of more to say. For some reason, she still felt awkward, nothing like she had during her first celebration. She just didn't understand it. What had changed so much?

She glanced up to Sirion's eyes, but they were on something behind her. Feeling her mouth go dry, Makilien swallowed nervously. She wanted to ask him what had happened to them, but she didn't know how, and it didn't seem to be the appropriate time or place. She tried to keep in mind everything Vonawyn had been telling her, but uncertainties and questions overran her mind.

When the dance ended, she couldn't help feeling relieved. All her dreams of reliving the past had ended with it, at least for tonight. She worked hard not to show how much the awkwardness between them affected her. If something was bothering him, the last thing she wanted was to add to his burden.

"Thank you for dancing with me," she said, forcing a smile, something she found herself doing far too often these days.

"It was my pleasure," Sirion replied.

Makilien lingered for a heartbeat or two, even now hoping for more. In that moment, it hit her what was so different. Ever since returning, Sirion had been kind to her, yet distant. She couldn't recall anything he'd said to her, since his arrival, that had been of a personal nature.

When he did not speak further, she moved on, aching in her heart to know why. She paused in the middle of the crowd and looked around forlornly. What now? She wasn't in much of a celebratory mood anymore, but she couldn't just leave so she made up her mind to make the best of it. She didn't lack for dance partners. She'd barely moved before Elmorhirian came to claim her for a dance.

For the next couple of hours, she kept busy dancing with her friends. She even enjoyed it despite the nagging questions in her mind. When the night grew late, her parents took their leave to get Leiya to bed, despite the little girl's reluctance to do so. With plans to spend the night here, Makilien hugged them goodnight.

Sometime after they had gone, she took a break from dancing and walked to the refreshment table. Pouring herself a glass of punch, she stepped back to watch those on the dance floor while she sipped the sweet liquid. The dance and the air of celebration still ran strong and made her smile. Her eyes shifted from one couple to another until they landed on Sirion. She watched as he glanced around the room and then stepped out to the garden.

Makilien stared at the empty doors, wondering why he had left. She hoped he didn't feel poorly. After all, it was a lot of excitement for someone recently injured. She bit her lip. All her questions came fresh. She wanted so badly to know what was wrong between them and if they could fix it. Wondering tore her up inside.

Taking a resolute breath, she made up her mind. She would never know anything if she didn't come out and ask him. Even if his answers might be hard to hear, she needed them, and this was as good a time as any. Her wondering had already robbed most of the celebration's joy.

Setting her cup down, Makilien made her way to the door where Sirion had left. Glancing over her shoulder, she stepped outside. The air was cool, but refreshing. She walked into the garden, leaving the glow from the house, but the moon offered plenty of light to see by. Her eyes searched for Sirion, but she didn't see him on any of the nearby benches. Quiet voices caught her attention. She walked around a tall rose bush and came to an abrupt halt.

Sirion stood a short distance away, but he wasn't alone. Irynna stood in front of him, her soft dress and fair skin bathed in moonlight. She smiled sweetly up at Sirion, eyes twinkling. Sirion smiled down at her and took her hands in his, moving close.

The reality of coming upon such an unexpected sight struck Makilien like ice water and drove a dagger deep into her heart. Her throat constricted, cutting off her air. As Sirion's head bent closer to Irynna's, the answer to all of her questions stood right in front of her. Sorrow flooding in, she turned and fled, tears burning her eyes.

She stumbled to a halt at the door, bracing herself against the wall as she dragged in a fortifying breath before entering the house. She could not allow herself to break down in front of everyone. Desperate to remain composed, she hurried around the perimeter of the room, keeping well away from the guests. But her eyes swam with moisture making it almost impossible to see. She blinked rapidly but was fast losing the battle.

At last, she reached the opposite door. Leaving the ballroom behind, she ran to the end of the darkened hall where the full weight of what she had seen crushed down upon her. With a gut-wrenching sob, she dropped to a bench and covered her face with shaking hands.

Sirion was in love with another. It shattered her heart into a thousand pieces. *How could this have happened?* It went against everything she'd believed about him. Shoulders heaving, she choked out sob after sob.

"Makilien?"

Her head reared up as she turned to find Halandor join her with a grave look of concern. She fell into his arms, weeping bitterly.

"What is it? What's happened?" he asked, feeling her trembling and heavy sobs.

Makilien squeezed her eyes shut tight and shook her head against his shoulder. The pain stole her voice. He let her have another moment, but then gently pulled her away so he could look into her eyes.

"What is wrong, Makilien?"

Her voice broke as she choked out, "Sirion is in love with Irynna."

A fresh burst of tears overtook her, and, for a moment, Halandor could only stare dumbly.

"I saw them," she cried, "out in the garden. He was about to kiss her!"

"Oh, Makilien." Halandor pulled her close again and rubbed her back, letting her cry.

She shook her head, desperately wishing she could forget what she saw. "I don't understand. I knew something was different, but I never would have expected this. Not from him."

"Neither would I," Halandor murmured, almost as stunned as she was. The Sirion they remembered would at least have had the courtesy to tell Makilien that he no longer felt the same about her.

Makilien sniffed, swiping her hands across her cheeks, but tears still flowed. "It feels like he's dead all over again." Her voice didn't come as much more than a whisper.

Halandor put his arm around her shoulders, and she leaned against him.

Miserably, she asked, "Is there something wrong with me? Is that what made him change his mind?"

"No, no, not at all," Halandor soothed, rubbing her arm. "I don't know why Sirion made this choice. He was gone for a long time, and we don't know what happened during that time, but this has nothing to do with you, all right?"

Makilien's lip trembled. "I thought, when he came back, things would be as they were. I was so looking forward to it. Now I'll have to see Sirion with someone else. I want to be happy for him, but . . . it's so painful."

Halandor sighed. "I know. It will be painful for a long time, but your life will go on. All you can do is cling to Elohim."

She gave a weak nod, but could hardly imagine how she would cope with the next few days.

Makilien stared out the window, eyes unfocused and indifferent. The sun had already risen past the treetops, but she remained in bed. She didn't feel she had the strength to face the day. She had never experienced pain like this—pain of rejection, of betrayal.

A tear slid down her cheek. She brushed it away.

"I don't want to do this," she murmured, fighting a flood of tears.

A thought floated through her mind, one in which she wished Sirion hadn't come back, that she could be left with her memories of him, but she immediately hated herself for it. How could she not be glad Sirion was alive and had returned? She should be happy for him. He was clearly happy with Irynna. She was just being selfish. Didn't she love him enough to be pleased for him even if he had chosen someone else?

More tears leaked out, and she pushed herself up. Head hanging, she closed her eyes tight.

"Help me, Elohim," she whispered. "I don't know how to react to this."

As she sat and prayed, her thoughts grew clearer. Sirion was not, and never had been, the most important relationship in her life. Her relationship with Elohim was. She believed it was the only relationship truly necessary, and He would never betray her.

Still, to let go was painful, and it would take time for her wounded heart to heal fully. Drawing what strength she could, she slipped out of bed and dressed. Standing in front of the mirror, she lamented her appearance. She looked wretched, her face rather pale and her eyes red and a little puffy. She hoped no one would notice.

Makilien left her room with tentative steps, dreading what the day might bring. The thought of seeing Sirion and Irynna almost sent her back to her room. She pushed on, but felt sick to her stomach, and she prayed to find some reason to pass on breakfast. What she needed right now was to go home and talk to her mother.

As she passed the hall where Darian's bedroom was located, she heard a thud. Something tipped over and crashed to the floor. She frowned. Concerned, she hurried to the door and knocked.

"Darian?"

Shuffling came from inside.

"Makilien!"

Though muffled, the urgency in Darian's voice sent a chill down her spine. In a fraction of a second, the thought flashed through her mind that she had no weapon, but it did not stop her. She flung open the door and burst into the room. The sight that greeted her froze her in place.

Across the room, Darian struggled against an assailant with a dagger, and the attacker was Sirion. Makilien's knees almost gave out, and she grasped the doorknob. Sirion looked over his shoulder, his eyes meeting hers.

"Sirion!" she gasped.

In this moment of distraction, Darian managed to knock the dagger from Sirion's hand. At the same time, some protective instinct snapped Makilien out of her daze. Her eyes flew around the room, landing on Darian's sword. She lunged for it, but as her fingers found the hilt, Sirion bolted for the window and jumped out.

Makilien rushed to Darian's side as he groaned and sank into a chair. Blood soaked his right sleeve. He clasped his hand over a deep wound near his elbow, but the blood trickled through his fingers at an alarming rate. Fear seized Makilien's breath. The king was bleeding to death before her eyes.

She dropped the sword and spun around. *Elohim, help me!* Her mind scrambled, finally locking on a thought. She raced to the window, yanking the tieback from the drapes.

Rushing back to Darian, she tied it around his arm above the wound, pulling it as tight as she could.

"Someone help!" she screamed, finding her voice.

"What is going on?"

Makilien looked over her shoulder to find Irynna in the doorway, staring wide-eyed.

"Go get help! The king is wounded."

Irynna turned and ran for help. Makilien turned back to Darian, and their eyes met and held as the truth of what had just happened sank in for both of them. Makilien's blood turned to ice. Sirion had just tried to murder their king.

:Chapter Nine:

Misplaced Trust

T his has to be a nightmare, Makilien told herself over and over as she stared at the closed door. But it wasn't. It was real. She glanced at each of her friends. Deep confusion, disbelief, and horror haunted the eyes of their drawn faces. No one could understand what had taken place, but none were more affected than Makilien. She had witnessed it. Witnessed her truest friend, the man she loved, try to kill Darian. She shuddered, wishing she could erase the memory, but the images were stuck there and ran unchecked through her mind.

She ran her hands up and down her arms, chilled with overwhelming fear and sadness. *Please don't let Darian die,* she prayed with all her heart. Waiting for news was killing all of them. It felt like they'd been waiting in the hall for hours, and everyone was on edge. What would happen to them, to their country, if they lost their king?

At last, when they weren't sure how much longer they could stand the torturous wait, Vonawyn and her parents stepped out of the bedroom. Aided by one of his men, Darian came with them.

"He'll be all right," Lorelyn said, taking in the sight of those waiting so anxiously. "He's just a little weak."

They breathed a collective sigh, and tears burned Makilien's eyes. She drew in a shaky breath and thanked Elohim for sparing the king's life.

The men helped Darian to the sitting room where the household gathered. At first, silence hung over them, no one sure how to express their thoughts and emotions. Finally, Elandir broke it, eyes pained. "You're sure it was Sirion?"

Both Makilien and Darian gave a miserable nod. Makilien wished with all her heart and soul it was a mistake, but facts were facts. Wishing couldn't change reality. She knew that well by now.

"Can you tell us what happened?" Elnauhir asked.

They all turned to Darian. He glanced at each of them, eyes lacking their usual sparkle, and shook his head, still not sure how to believe it. "He came to my door and said he'd like to talk. Of course, I let him in, quite happy to speak with him. I turned my back for a moment as I asked what was on his mind, and in the next instant, he had a dagger to my throat. I tried to ask him what he was doing and he put more pressure on the blade, but he hesitated. All I knew was that I had to act or I'd be dead, so I grabbed the dagger and we fought for it. That's how my arm was cut. Thank Elohim that Makilien was near or . . . Sirion would have finished me off once I was too weak to fight him."

Silence settled again like a heavy blanket. With hard, painful heartbeats, Makilien asked, "How could he do this?"

"I don't know," Elnauhir murmured, his troubled expression putting deep lines in his forehead.

"This just isn't like Sirion at all," Halandor said, emotion thickening his voice.

Elnauhir let out a great, burdened sigh. "There can only be one reason. Whoever held him prisoner forced him to do this."

Halandor shook his head. "What must they have done to him?"

Large, hot tears spilled from Makilien's eyes, rolling down her cheeks. "But to actually try to kill Darian? How could he? He has always been so strong. How could he give in? He never gave in when he was tortured in Beldon. I would have believed he would die first."

Blank looks met her questions.

She rubbed her eyes with her palms, trying to rub away the tears. But the cold, hard facts were too much. The Sirion she'd known and loved was gone. Destroyed by the enemy, though she couldn't imagine how great the torture must have been to change him so completely. At the painful squeezing of her heart, she choked on a sob as she thought of what type of monstrous things had been done to him.

And then, in the midst of this pain and confusion, a thought flickered to life. A thought so profound her heart slammed hard against her ribs, making her gasp.

"What?" several of her friends asked.

She rose, trembling as she tried to make sense of a flood of thoughts and memories. Looking around at them, even she couldn't believe the words that came from her mouth.

"It's not Sirion."

They stared at her, uncomprehending.

"What do you mean?" Elmorhirian asked.

Makilien shook her head, her thoughts flying as her heart raced. "It's not Sirion who tried to kill Darian. It can't be."

Her friends exchanged glances, not sure how to respond to this.

"Makilien, I know this is difficult, but . . ." Halandor's voice trailed off with uncertainty.

"No, I'm not just saying it, I have a reason," she explained, voice rising in a whirlwind of emotion, desperation, and hope. "When Sirion was held prisoner in Beldon, he was beaten and has scars from it. I've seen them. But, when Lorelyn was tending his wounds when he arrived here, I saw his back. There were no scars! Not even faint ones. It didn't occur to me at the time, but whoever this is can't be Sirion."

Expressions changed, brows drawing together, as they considered her words, sifting through their own memories.

"But . . . how can that be?" Darian stammered. "How can it *not* be Sirion?"

Elnauhir looked at Makilien, eyes intense as he asked, "Are you absolutely certain about this?"

Makilien gave a firm nod, and Lorelyn added, "I don't remember seeing any either."

"But, they could have disappeared over time . . . couldn't they?" Elandir asked.

Lorelyn slowly shook her head. "I don't know. Scars like that . . ."

"Makilien is right."

The solemnity of Elnauhir's voice cut through their conversation. All eyes jumped to the Elf lord, searching for answers, including Makilien.

Elnauhir paused for a moment, letting the weight of the discovery sink in. Once he was sure, he glanced at each of them. "There is something few know because it was too painful for Sirion to ever talk about. You all know Shaikes murdered his family, but most of you have never heard that it wasn't only his parents who were killed. Sirion had a twin brother, Ryelan."

Eyes widened, realization hitting everyone.

"Everyone believed Ryelan was killed, though his body was never found in the remains of the house or when a party was sent after the Shaikes. If it wasn't Sirion who tried to kill Darian, there can be only one possibility. Somehow Ryelan survived all these years and came here pretending to be Sirion."

Feeling suddenly weak, Makilien sank down on the couch and covered her face. A wealth of emotion flooded her to know Sirion wasn't responsible for any of this. He didn't try to murder Darian, and he hadn't fallen in love with Irynna. She released a small sob of relief and felt Halandor's hand on her back as she worked to control herself. She looked up, hope filling her heart.

"We must find Ryelan. Sirion has to be alive, and Ryelan must know where he is. He knows too much about us not to have talked with Sirion."

Elnauhir agreed. "The guards have been searching for a half an hour now. Ryelan is likely hiding somewhere here in the city."

"Well, I'm going to join the search," Torick said, pushing up from his chair.

A fire had lit in everyone's hearts. They would not rest until they found Ryelan and learned Sirion's location.

"Make sure you are all armed," Elnauhir cautioned ominously. "I don't want to see Ryelan hurt, but we have no choice but to consider him extremely dangerous. If he is working for the enemy, who knows what else he is capable of."

They nodded, understanding the danger, and moved to retrieve their weapons.

"I need to run home to get my sword and tell my parents what has happened," Makilien said. "I will join you as soon as I can."

She left the house and jogged toward home. A thousand thoughts spun through her mind. She thought of Sirion, still a prisoner somewhere, and steely determination hardened inside her. Focused on this, she almost missed someone call her name. She skidded to a halt. Irynna hurried to catch up to her.

"What is it?" Makilien asked.

"You have to come with me," Irynna said, expression grim. "I know where Sirion is hiding."

Makilien's eyes grew large. "Where?"

"In the forest. I'll show you."

"Good, I'll get my sword and we'll tell the others."

Makilien turned away, but a razor sharp point dug into her back. She froze.

"If you don't come with me quietly, your sister will get hurt."

Makilien gasped and tried to face her again, but Irynna's dagger cut deep into her skin. She gritted her teeth. "What have you done with Leiya?"

"She's safe, for now. That is if you cooperate and don't alert anyone," Irynna's low voice came from just over her shoulder.

Makilien clenched her fists, but didn't fight. Irynna took the dagger away from her back.

"Good, now just walk to the stable, and remember, if anything goes wrong, you won't *ever* see your sister again."

Swallowing hard, Makilien walked on, this time toward the stable. She hardly noticed the stinging cut or the blood trickling down her back. Her thoughts focused on Leiya and how things had gone so wrong.

"So you have been in on this all along," she accused, voice taut. She glared over her shoulder at the young woman who wasn't nearly as harmless as she appeared.

"Just keep quiet and keep walking," Irynna snapped.

Makilien watched her just long enough to see her look around, eyes darting nervously.

At the stable, Irynna scanned the entire area before nodding ahead. "Into the forest."

Makilien obeyed, pleading with Elohim to keep Leiya safe and show her a way out of this mess. They trudged through the undergrowth, winding their way into the trees. Half a mile inside the forest, she spotted two horses, but her gaze jumped to something of far more importance. Leiya sat on a fallen log nearby. Makilien rushed forward, but Ryelan blocked her path, sword in hand.

"That's close enough."

Makilien glared at him, seeing him now with new eyes. Her breath came out heavily as the emotion built again. "Let my sister go."

Ryelan's gaze swung past her. "Irynna, get the shackles."

She left Makilien's side and hurried to the horses. Makilien's eyes remained locked on Ryelan.

"Where is Sirion?" she demanded.

A brief moment of surprise flickered in his eyes.

"Yes, I know who you are now, *Ryelan.*" She laughed a sad, humorless laugh. "I, of all people, should have known all along. Sirion would never break my heart the way you did. He is a good, kind, caring man. You may look the same, but that's as far as your similarities go."

Ryelan's jaw shifted, but he said nothing.

In a moment, Irynna returned with a pair of shackles. She reached for Makilien's wrist, but Makilien pulled away. Ryelan gave her a hard look.

"If you want your sister to remain unharmed, you won't resist us."

Makilien looked around in desperation, but Ryelan and Irynna had all the control. With a defeated sigh, she raised her hands. Irynna locked the shackles around her wrists and guided her forward to stand before Ryelan.

"You have what you want. Let Leiya go," she requested, a pleading tone mixing with the edge to her voice.

"She will remain here until we are well on our way." Ryelan turned to the little girl. She stared up at him, defiance in her eyes. "Remember what I told you. You will stay right here until someone finds you or it starts to get dark, do you understand? If not, I'll be forced to hurt your sister."

Leiya's gaze flicked from him to Makilien. She was being incredibly brave, but there was fear in her round eyes.

"Makilien?"

"It's all right, Leiya," she assured her. "Do what he says."

Tears welled up in Leiya's eyes as she looked back to Ryelan. "Please, don't take her."

Makilien thought she caught a flash of guilt cross Ryelan's face, but she had her doubts. If it had been there, a hard expression replaced it in an instant as he took her arm and guided her none too gently to the horses. At a tall bay gelding, he told her to mount. She hesitated, desperation willing her to fight.

But Ryelan squeezed her arm and leaned close. "*Now.*"

Looking back, she held his gaze. She swallowed at the dangerous look in his brown eyes, a look she would never have found in Sirion's.

Setting her jaw, she grasped the saddle and pulled herself up.

Irynna mounted the other horse, and Ryelan settled behind Makilien. From the saddle, Makilien stared down at Leiya. Tears rolled down her sister's cheeks.

"It will be all right, Leiya," Makilien said to comfort her. "Elohim sees what is happening." She looked over her shoulder, catching Ryelan's eyes again. "He sees everything."

Jerking the reins, Ryelan kicked his horse and it took off at a lope. Makilien strained to look back again, catching one last glimpse of Leiya before the forest swallowed them up.

:Chapter Ten:

Jered

Sirion lay on his back and stared up at the ceiling, which was lit dimly by one lantern hanging outside the cell. He had nothing to occupy his mind but the memories and questions that replayed thousands of times. The moment Ryelan had revealed himself haunted him often. He blew out a long breath. How could his own brother, his twin, betray him like this?

And Irynna. He bit down hard. She'd played him. All those personal things they'd discussed on the walk to Carel, all the information he'd freely shared out of the relief to have someone to talk to, Ryelan now used against everyone he cared about.

He groaned. "Elohim, please protect them from Ryelan."

How many times in the last days had he prayed this prayer? He rubbed his hands over his face. Though he'd grown used to the idea of Ryelan being alive after all these years, the reality of it hit him hard sometimes. Under any other circumstances, he would have rejoiced over the miracle, but this was a nightmare.

Overwhelmed, he pushed himself up and paced the cell. Restlessness ate at him. After regular meals for days, he had almost fully regained his strength. Every day he waited for an explanation as to why Vayzar was doing this, but no one came with answers, only to bring his food.

Just as he hit his fist against the wall and hung his head, a door opened from farther down the hall. He lifted his eyes to watch the cell door. No doubt it was time for his next meal. However, when two guards appeared, they brought no food this time. One unlocked the door.

"Lord Vayzar wishes to see you."

Sirion had to be thankful for this chance to leave his cell, but apprehension mingled in. Perhaps now he would gain answers to his persistent questions, but he was sure he wouldn't like them. Keeping his breaths slow and even, he prayed along the way over what was to come. The guards guided him through the winding passages to Vayzar's throne room where the despicable man stood waiting for him.

He looked Sirion over, nodding in satisfaction. "Ah, you've filled out nicely. Very good."

Sirion ground his teeth together, hating for the man to be so pleased. Working to maintain a good handle on his emotions, he asked, "What do you want from me?"

"Well," Vayzar clasped his hands behind his back, "since I can't trust you to be on my side, which would have earned you a much more comfortable position, you will be doing hard manual labor, building my fortress. I'm always in need of strong young men, and you will do nicely until I have future plans for you."

He walked up to one of Sirion's guards. "Take him outside and put him to work. Pair him up with that what's-his-name who lost his partner. Can't have him lazing around all day."

The guard jerked his head in a nod, and they took Sirion's arms to lead him away. Giving Vayzar one final glare, Sirion moved with them. This time, they took him through a part of the fortress he had not seen before. When they reached a door and swung it open, bright sunlight blinded him, but it felt wonderful on his skin. He closed his eyes, savoring it for a moment.

Once he could see again, his eyes took in all the sights. The door they'd exited led out into the back courtyard surrounded by the half-finished wall, which bustled with activity. Hammering, chiseling, and grunts of exertion drew Sirion's gaze to dozens of young men working to complete the wall. Bent over their grueling work, their exposed skin glistened in the heat of the sun. Almost as many guards stood at the base of the wall, watching them closely.

One of Sirion's guards jerked him to the right and his focus shifted. Just ahead rose a large wooden stockade, and beyond that, two more buildings, which appeared to be warehouses. As they drew near, he peered through the narrow gaps between the stakes of the palisade, but could see nothing.

At the structure, the guards unlocked the chain holding the door closed. Inside the stockade was a semi-circle attached to a large lean-to. The area was quiet and empty, except for one young man sitting against one of the lean-to's support beams. He had one knee bent up and his arms folded across his broad chest. Black hair framed a strong face, and his dark blue eyes followed their approach.

When they neared him, one of the guards snapped, "On your feet, Jered! It's time for you to get back to work."

At first, the young man did not move, but then he rose slowly, taking his time. He was well built and perhaps taller than Sirion. He eyed the guards, a noticeable smirk lifting one corner of his mouth.

"What? Vayzar can't bear to let me have a day off?"

The guards scowled, and one of them backhanded him solidly across the chin. "That's *Lord* Vayzar. And keep your mouth shut or you'll be headed to the grinding house next."

The man shifted his jaw and scoffed but said no more. His gaze turned to Sirion, though Sirion couldn't tell behind those steely eyes if it was out of ill-will or not.

One of the guards produced a long chain and clamped one end around Sirion's ankle and the other around Jered's.

"You'll show him what's expected of him," he instructed Jered.

The young man, arms crossed again, just stared at him, his expression bored.

"Let's go," the guard ordered.

They prodded Sirion and Jered out of the stockade. The chain was just long enough for them to walk, if they were careful not to get ahead of each other. No one said a word, though Sirion had many questions. They crossed the courtyard and exited through an uncompleted archway. Turning left, Sirion's eyes followed a well-trodden road, where about a mile in the distance, lay a quarry. Many pairs of young men worked there as well, carving huge blocks out of the dark gray stone.

When they had traveled the distance and arrived at the quarry, a man handed Sirion and Jered each a large hammer and chisel from a supply wagon.

"Get to work over in that section," he ordered with a jerk of his head.

Still silent, Jered led the way. They left the guards behind, but when Sirion looked around, he counted many overseers, just as there had been at the wall. His focus returned to Jered when they stopped at a large slab of rock that had already been started. Here, Sirion's companion turned to him.

"I'm Jered," he said, introducing himself, and Sirion detected no animosity in his voice.

"Sirion."

"You an Elf or something?"

"Half-Elf," Sirion answered.

"Ah."

From somewhere above, one of the overseers shouted at them to get working.

"Welcome to paradise," Jered muttered, his voice edged with sarcasm. He turned to the rock. "We've got to get this piece chiseled out."

The two of them got down by the rock and started chiseling.

"So how did you get here?" Jered asked, delivering powerful, ringing hammer strokes to his chisel.

Sirion hesitated. The last time he'd shared this kind of information, it only helped Vayzar, but he realized the man already had all the information he needed. With a sigh, Sirion explained in brief about his captivity. Jered didn't speak, but nodded every so often.

"What about you?" Sirion asked when he'd finished. "How did you get here?"

"Out of my own stupidity and arrogance," Jered answered in a biting tone of disgust. He glanced at Sirion, his expression wry. "I wanted to get out and see the world so I left home. A couple months ago, I ignored the warnings about Carel and came in for supplies. I was pretty much grabbed right off the streets. Within a day they had me working out here."

Sirion shook his head and looked around them. So many young men forced into service.

"Do they make everyone work in pairs?"

Jered nodded. "Makes it nearly impossible for one of us to try to escape."

Sirion glanced at the chain between them. Two men would have to work in perfect unison to get very far with any speed. He looked at Jered again, hesitating a moment before asking, "What happened to your old partner?"

He caught a glimpse of the young man's blue eyes as he glanced at him, an expression of deep regret flashing across his face. "He didn't work fast enough and complained one too many times in front of the overseers. They took him to the grinding house yesterday."

Sirion frowned. "What's that?"

Jered wiped his sleeve across his already sweaty forehead and lowered his voice. "I'm not sure exactly what's going on here, but Vayzar has two operations going. One is to complete his fortress. Now the other I don't know much about, but he's growing fields of Shadelin. You know what that is?"

"It's a poisonous flower, isn't it?"

"Yeah. Well, he's got women and the weaker men bringing in bushels of it. They dry it out, and then bring it to the grinding house where it's ground into powder. After that it's given to that alchemist Vayzar has working with him."

Sirion listened with keen interest as all this information flowed into his mind. Whatever they were doing with the Shadelin powder was certain to pertain to Vayzar's plans for Eldor. He looked toward the fortress, now seeing the fields of pale, dusty orange Shadelin flowers beyond it. Though the plant wasn't common in the south, he remembered hearing that a meal or drink laced with Shadelin would kill a grown man. Dread clutched his stomach.

"You don't know what he's doing with the powder?"

Jered shook his head. "No, but I do know they're mixing it with something. I heard they did an experiment on some of the weakest slaves. They burned the mix and the plume of smoke it caused killed everyone in minutes."

Realization struck Sirion like a physical blow. "If Vayzar were to bring barrels of this powder into Minarald, he could kill thousands without there ever being a struggle."

Jered gave him a grave look.

"Get back to work!"

Sirion glanced up at the overseer, realizing he'd stopped working. Though his hands shook with the horror of what he'd just discovered, he hammered again on his chisel, mind racing with a thousand different thoughts. Forcing himself to calm down, he asked, "Is there much of this powder?"

"I don't think so. Not yet, anyway," Jered answered. "Fortunately, I've heard it takes a whole lot of Shadelin flowers to get a decent amount. The thing about it is, they're shorthanded and lose workers almost daily. The powder not only affects their skin, but breathing in the dust every day eventually kills them. You get sent to the grinding house, and you're as good as dead."

Sirion paused for just a moment to give Jered a sympathetic look. "I'm sorry about your partner."

Jered sighed, shaking his head again. "Should have been me. I'm more outspoken than he ever was, but they won't send me. I'm about the strongest one here and they want to keep me working, at least until the fortress is complete." He gave Sirion a pointed look. "I don't know what will become of us after that."

Thunder rumbled low and ominous in the distance. Already, clouds had gathered overhead, and the forest grew dim as evening approached. After a long afternoon, Ryelan reined his horse to a stop and looked over his shoulder at Irynna.

"We'll set up shelter here tonight."

Dismounting, he took Makilien by the arm and helped her down from the horse. On the ground, her shoulders slumped. The emotional toll and non-stop riding had been exhausting. Her weary eyes took in the surroundings. All around stood only trees and deep shadows. She shivered. Eldinorieth didn't seem friendly in this gloomy twilight, and the present company didn't help.

Releasing his grip for a moment, Ryelan reached into one of the saddlebags and pulled out a chain. He turned back to her.

"Over to that tree." He gestured to a small maple nearby.

Makilien obeyed with silent resignation. She'd been in this position before and hadn't once escaped without outside help. At the tree, Ryelan locked the longer chain around it and secured the other end to Makilien's shackles, allowing her to move around a little. She had to be grateful for this luxury, though it confused her why Ryelan would bother. He said nothing more to her before turning back to unsaddle his horse.

Once he and Irynna had finished, they set up a small camp, stretching a canvas tarp between the trees to keep all three of them dry once it began to rain. During this time, Makilien watched Ryelan's every move. She found it deeply unnerving how identical his appearance was to Sirion. It was like watching Sirion work, and it put a deep, longing ache in her heart.

Finally, she spoke, the longing she had to learn about Sirion coming out in her voice. "Please, tell me, is Sirion alive?"

Ryelan glanced at her, but would not answer.

"Is he?"

She received the same response. Her brows dropped low, and indignation rose up inside her. She wouldn't take this abduction quietly, not without some answers. "I will not stop asking until you've answered me."

Ryelan blew out an exasperated breath. He looked at her, eyes flashing in annoyance, but she met it with her own stubborn look.

"All right, *yes*, he's alive," Ryelan conceded.

Makilien's heart leapt inside her. "Thank You, Elohim," she whispered, eyes sliding closed in relief. But they snapped back open, focusing again on her captor. "Are you taking me to where he is?"

Only silence. Makilien stared hard at him. Her tone changed, lowering accusingly.

"Why are you doing this? How can you?" She shook her head. "How can you be so different from Sirion?"

"*Enough*," Ryelan snapped. His fists squeezed. He looked to her again, and his voice lost a bit of its edge. "No more questions."

Makilien held his gaze for a long moment before he turned away, busying himself with the shelter. She waited for a few minutes, but too many questions tumbled through her mind to heed his command. Again, she would not make this easy for him.

"So, the injury, that was self-inflicted, wasn't it?" she asked as he passed her. "You weren't really attacked. You just did that so we'd be concerned about you, so we wouldn't ask too many questions."

She might as well have been talking to the tree, but she pressed on. "That's what gave you away, you know."

Ryelan paused, but did not face her.

"It's true. Had we never needed to tend your injury, I never would have seen that you don't have Sirion's scars." She added in a murmur, "And we would all still believe Sirion was responsible for this."

Whether Ryelan reacted or not, she couldn't tell, but when he did turn, he had no hint of emotion in his expression and would not look at Makilien. Instead, he walked over to Irynna.

"I'm going to backtrack and cover our trail. The rain should take care of anything I miss." Now he did glance at Makilien and lowered his voice. "Just watch her carefully."

Irynna gave a solemn nod. "I will."

And with that, Ryelan disappeared into the forest. Irynna busied herself with a cold supper. She gave a little to Makilien, but neither one said a word. About an hour later, the rain began and both huddled beneath their shelter, staring out into the wet, growing darkness.

"So what is in this for you?"

Irynna's eyes jumped to Makilien. "What?"

Makilien tipped her head. She figured the more she would learn from her two captors, the better. "What do you gain from all this? Power? Money? What?"

Irynna shrugged. "I just do as I'm told."

"Why?"

The other woman shifted, swallowing, and her gaze swung back out to the forest, voice dropping. "Because if I don't, I'll end up back where I was."

Makilien read the fear in her expression. Irynna pulled her knees up to her chest and sat silent for a long moment. At last, she spoke again, though the rain almost drowned out her quiet voice.

"I was a slave. I watched slavers murder my father and my brothers, and then they dragged me off to Carel. Ryelan found me on the auction block and rescued me. There's no telling where I'd be if he hadn't come along."

"How long ago was this?"

"Not quite a year."

Makilien gave a slow nod of understanding. "So if you don't do as you're told, you'll be sold as a slave again?"

Irynna's silence was answer enough.

"By who?" Makilien asked. "Ryelan?"

"No." Irynna's gaze snapped back to her. "No, not Ryelan."

"Who then?"

Irynna shook her head, toying with the cuff of her sleeve. "I can't say."

Makilien rubbed the metal around her own wrists, thinking a moment before asking, "Why can't you just run away and be free of whoever is behind this? You could easily escape now."

Irynna released a sad sigh. "I won't leave Ryelan."

Makilien said nothing to this. Enemies or not, she could understand that. Leaning back against her tree, she too sighed. She closed her eyes, her mind full of a million things to pray about.

Sirion's muscles cramped and painful spasms shot up his arm and through his shoulders so he could barely lift his hammer. He drew in a deep breath, but his lungs burned. His body could only endure so much more of the strain.

The sun had already sunk halfway below the horizon, giving the workers relief from its heat, but Sirion wondered how long they would work on and if his strength might fail before then. He hated to think of the consequences of that and was relieved when, a short time after this thought, a voice bellowed, "Everyone gather up."

In one action, everyone ceased hammering and the quarry grew unnaturally quiet. Letting his arms fall limp to his sides, Sirion pulled in one heavy breath after another.

"You all right?" Jered asked.

Sirion gave nothing more than a nod.

"Give it a few days. You'll get used to it," Jered said, resting a sympathetic hand on his shoulder.

Now, the two of them trudged down to where the men gathered to return their tools, and the entire group marched toward the fortress. From horseback, the overseers followed, eyes alert for any who might try to bolt. But after a full day, that wasn't likely. Sirion wasn't the only one ready to collapse. At the fortress, the men filed into the stockade where they were unchained.

Jered motioned for Sirion to follow him. They walked beneath the shelter where Sirion noticed straw pallets laid out. In the farthest corner, Jered pointed to an empty pallet. "This can be yours."

Sirion dropped down, ready to go right to sleep. Jered knelt on the pallet beside him.

"They'll have supper for us in a few minutes."

In his weariness, eating hadn't even occurred to Sirion, but his stomach was empty. They waited without speaking until a guard called out for the men to come for their meal. Sirion pushed himself up with a groan, body screaming in protest at the orders from his brain, but Jered stopped him.

"You just stay put. I'll bring your food."

"Thanks," Sirion replied, more than grateful to his new friend.

Jered left the shelter and joined the group waiting at one end of the enclosure. Sirion rested back against the wall, his weary eyes sliding closed as fragments of the information he'd learned from Jered tumbled around in his mind. Now that work was finished for the day, determination to get warning to Eldor consumed him. He must find a way, and meeting Jered could be the key. The man had been here for long enough to be familiar with the routine and this area of the fortress. Perhaps together they could find a weakness in Vayzar's grip over them.

In a moment, Jered returned with two large wooden bowls. He sat down and handed one to Sirion who eyed the contents. He was surprised to find it filled with a hearty soup.

"They always feed us well," Jered explained, "to keep us working hard."

As the two of them ate, three young men came and sat down with them. Jered nodded to each of them and glanced at Sirion.

"This is Ren, Tavin, and Jon," he said, introducing them. To the three, he said, "This is Sirion, my new partner."

Ren, a red-haired kid in his late teens studied Sirion with a look of puzzlement. "I've seen you before. Don't you work for Vayzar?"

All eyes landed on Sirion. He shook his head. "It's not me. It's my twin brother, Ryelan."

Jered's brows shot up. "Your brother? What went wrong there?"

"I don't know," Sirion answered, voice tired. "Until now, I've believed him to be dead."

"So he's working for Vayzar and you're Vayzar's slave. Does he know?"

"Yes. He's partly responsible for why I'm here."

Jered just shook his head. "If only you could convince him to change sides. He might be able to get us all out of here."

"If only," Sirion agreed. *If only he were here and not destroying things in Eldor under my name.* He grimaced at the thought.

:Chapter Eleven:

A New Ally

Makilien stretched her tight muscles and rolled her shoulders with a labored sigh. Four full days on the trail was tiresome in any circumstance, let alone as a prisoner. She had no idea where they were, only that the surrounding forest had all looked the same for days.

Her eyes focused on Ryelan. He dug through his pack, pulling out a large chuck of dried meat and a jent from the trees they'd passed the day before, and offered Makilien the food. She took it, but her eyes remained on his face.

"You don't owe them anything, you know. They only want to use you."

He met her gaze, his expression unreadable, but kept silent, as usual, and walked away. Frustrated, Makilien sat back to eat her breakfast. She bit into the jent, contemplating a conversation the night before.

She had finally talked him into telling her how he'd been captured by the same Shaikes who had killed his parents, and then had been rescued, as he told it, by Zirtan's men. Since they raised him, he somehow felt indebted to them, though Makilien pointed out the men were on the same side as the Shaikes, a fact he must be aware of. She'd tried to convince him to walk away from it all, but the conversation ended there.

It wasn't the first time she'd tried. She had made countless attempts to get through to him during their journey. She sensed conflict at times, but he refused to let it take hold. Now, she wasn't sure what more she could say.

She pulled off a strip of meat and nibbled on it. "Are we almost to Carel?"

Their destination was another bit of information she'd been able to pry out of him, though she'd already guessed as much.

Ryelan glanced at her. "We'll make it by evening."

When he spoke without a hard or annoyed edge to his voice, he sounded just like Sirion.

Before long, they had the horses saddled and left camp. Ryelan had kept a fast pace on this journey. He knew as well as Makilien did that her friends trailed them. Unfortunately, Ryelan was an expert in the forest and covered their trail whenever possible. Still, Makilien didn't doubt Halandor's tracking abilities. He would find them, even if it took time.

The sand-colored walls of Carel rose up before them, casting long shadows as the sun neared the horizon. Makilien tipped her head back to look up, but it wasn't much of a sight. The walls were dull and in poor repair, full of cracks and crumbling away at the top. Her eyes dropped when they stopped at the main gate. She peered through the large archway. Even from here, she could see the narrow streets crowded with people streaming in one direction or another.

"Should we go around?" Irynna asked.

Ryelan shook his head. "It will be faster to go straight through."

"The horses won't like it."

But Ryelan was already dismounting. "You lead them, and I'll watch her."

He helped Makilien out of the saddle and locked his hand around her arm. Irynna took up the reins of the horses, and they entered into the city. The pushy crowd quickly swallowed them up. Makilien could understand now why Irynna was concerned about the horses. Each of them were constantly bumped or jostled by passersby. She cringed every time since most were big, filthy men who almost made Ryelan seem safe. She stayed close to him, avoiding everyone she could.

It became worse farther into the city. The horses snorted and stepped skittishly behind her, nervous by the close quarters and confusing buzz of conversation everywhere. But, inside Makilien, a spark of hope burned to life as she realized this was the perfect opportunity to attempt an escape. Distracted by the people, Ryelan's grip had loosened, and the crowd provided the perfect cover. No doubt she could move through them faster than Ryelan could. Yet, what if someone else caught her? Someone worse?

A shiver crawled along her arms, but she made up her mind. It was now or never. What was the alternative? Saying a silent prayer, she glanced at Ryelan and took a deep breath. Once sure his focus was elsewhere, she looked over her shoulder, determining her escape route. She would run back the way they had come and find somewhere to hide until she could get out of the city. Irynna stood in her way, but was too concerned with the horses to react fast enough to catch her. And she'd never overpower Makilien anyway.

Mouth dry and heart thumping, Makilien licked her lips and breathed another desperate prayer. *Here it goes.* With a strong jerk, her arm came free of Ryelan's grasp. Before he even had time to realize what had happened, she spun around and bolted.

"Hey!"

Racing past Irynna, Makilien kept her gaze straight ahead. But Ryelan's pursuing footsteps echoed just behind her, and she could feel his presence. Adrenaline spiking, she ran almost blindly, squeezing between person after person. Her nerves tingled at the anticipation of Ryelan grabbing her from behind. She puffed out short breaths and made herself run faster. Her heart pounded as fast as her feet, and blood rushed in her ears. She bumped shoulders with a stranger who growled a complaint, but she did not slow. She would not let Ryelan deliver her to certain death.

Realizing she no longer heard his footsteps, she risked a glance back. She caught a glimpse of him still in pursuit, but it was just as she'd hoped. A little more distance and he would lose sight of her in the crowd. Hope surged hot through her veins, and she found another burst of speed, charging ahead. Just a little farther and she could find a place to hide. She could almost feel freedom again.

Suddenly, a tall man crossed in front of her. She gasped, but without room to slow her momentum, she crashed into him. He hardly moved, but Makilien tumbled backward, slamming to the ground. Sprawled out in the dusty street, she lay in a daze, her ears ringing from the impact. She slowly pushed herself into a sitting position, coughing and gasping to regain her breath. That's when she heard Ryelan shouting for people to move just a little ways up the street. He was gaining on her. Desperation ignited again, and she scrambled up. But she'd barely reached her feet when she froze, her eyes locking on the face of the man she had run into. Icy cold fingered her spine at those familiar dark eyes and black hair. Jorin.

Caught between two dangerous enemies, Makilien didn't know where to turn. The indecision cost her. Before she could run, Jorin grabbed her by the arm. She struggled against his hold, but could not escape his strong grip. *It's over*, she realized, heart plummeting.

The man dragged her along with him, hurrying her off the street and around the corner of a building where he released her with a push. Makilien stumbled, and her eyes darted around, frantically searching for an escape. Dread knotted her stomach. It was a dead end alley. Her heart pummeled her ribcage. *He's going to kill me!* She spun around to face him, backing away. However, he had his back to her now, peering around the corner into the street. Makilien eyed the gap between him and the other building. She wanted to make a run for it, but she'd never make it past him.

From right outside the alleyway came Ryelan's voice. She shrank farther into the shadows, pressing her back up against the wall. She held her breath. Did he know she was here?

A long, slow minute passed, and with it, Makilien's fear of Ryelan finding her. Yet, a new, heightened fear of Jorin took its place. At least Ryelan had no intention of killing her, but not so with the other man. After two failed attempts on her life, how much more determined would he be now to finish the job?

Drawing in a deep but shaky breath, she watched Jorin turn to her, his towering height especially evident. He looked the same, though his black hair was a bit longer and he had a haggard, less kempt appearance than she remembered. She took an involuntary step back as he came toward her.

"He's gone," Jorin said, his voice low and emotionless. "If you stay out of sight, he won't find you."

Makilien swallowed, eyes jumping from him to the entrance of the alley. Something changed in Jorin's expression, softening just slightly. "Go, if you wish, but I wouldn't advise it."

Her survival instinct urged her to run, but she resisted. She worked to slow her breathing, and her brows dipped low. "You won't kill me?"

"No."

Makilien's mouth opened in astonishment, remembrances of his hatred for her flashing through her mind. "Why not?"

Jorin shifted and just watched her for a moment, crossing his arms. "I'm repaying the favor."

"What favor?" she asked, frown deepening.

"You saved my life when you should have let me die."

The memory of intervening when one of Gébrale's men had been about to kill Jorin halted all others. She'd thought for sure he'd been unconscious, yet somehow he knew she'd saved him.

Watching her understanding dawn, Jorin's already deep voice lowered even more, to the point Makilien almost had a hard time hearing him. "It has haunted me every day since then. Why did you do it? Why would you?"

The tension slowly eased from Makilien's body. She shrugged one shoulder. "I didn't think it would be right to let them kill you while you were defenseless. I don't believe Elohim would have wanted that."

Jorin stared at her, his face unchanging, but thoughts and emotions flickered in his eyes. Finally, he said, "Come with me."

Makilien blinked in surprise. "Where?"

"I know someone who will keep you safe. He can help you get out of the city. I can't go past the wall."

When he turned, she hesitated for a moment more, but then hurried to follow him to the entrance of the alley. Once he'd checked for any sign of Ryelan or Irynna, they continued on.

"Why can't you leave?" she asked, coming up beside him.

He glanced at her, and appeared to be debating before he brushed back his hair. "Because of this." A circular shaped brand scarred the exposed side of his neck. "I'm a slave."

Makilien's eyes grew bigger. Jorin, a slave?

"After I lost you the second time, Zirtan had no more use for me," he explained, voice resigned.

She said nothing to this, more surprised than ever that he did not wish to kill her right here, right now.

In silence, the two of them wound their way deeper into the city. Makilien's eyes scanned each person they passed, afraid they would come upon Ryelan. Neither she nor Jorin possessed any type of weapon should he find them. Still, she felt a strange sense of security with Jorin. She had an idea, odd as it was, he wouldn't just hand her over willingly.

At last, they came to what appeared to be a stable, but when they walked into the shadowy building and Makilien's eyes adjusted, she saw a glowing forge. The beating of metal upon metal rang ahead of them. A broad-shouldered man with short dark hair stood at an anvil, striking his hammer against a red-hot horseshoe. After two more beats, he looked up. A kind smile creased his face.

"Jorin." He had a deep voice like the man he addressed, but a warmer tone. Dousing the horseshoe in a bucket of water, he asked, "What brings you here today?"

"I need you to look after someone and see she gets out of the city safely," Jorin said. He motioned back at Makilien who stepped forward. "This is Makilien."

She caught the reaction in the blacksmith's eyes, but he smiled at her. "Makilien. What a surprise. I am Beregon."

Makilien smiled in return, and Jorin said, "She ran into me on the streets with one of Vayzar's men after her."

"Vayzar!" Makilien nearly choked on the name. She looked up at Jorin, wide eyes filling with questions.

He nodded. "I assume that's who Ryelan wanted to take you to."

"So Vayzar is the one behind all this?"

Again Jorin nodded. "He pretty much has the entire city under his control."

A burn of indignation and disgust rose up in Makilien's chest, and her fists clenched thinking of the evil man. She wanted to know more, but didn't get a chance to voice any further questions.

"I need to get back," Jorin told Beregon. "Will you see to her?"

"Of course," the blacksmith answered without hesitation.

With a last glance at Makilien, Jorin left the shed. She watched him disappear and then focused her attention on Beregon. Before either could speak, a soft female voice came from behind Makilien.

"Beregon, is that Jorin?"

They turned to the open door at one side of the shed. In the doorway stood a woman, her dark hair in a single braid over her shoulder. She stared ahead, her sea-blue eyes unfocused. Beregon went to the woman's side. "He was here, but he had to leave. Come, I want you to meet someone."

He took her by the hand and led her toward Makilien. She was a lovely woman, but Makilien saw deep scars on her cheek, near her lip, and along her jaw line. Makilien's throat squeezed with emotion, wondering what had befallen the poor woman and if it had caused her blindness.

Smiling at Makilien, Beregon said, "This is Sophine, my wife." He placed Sophine's hands in hers. "Sophine, this is Makilien."

The woman's face lifted in surprise, but also delight. "Truly?"

"Yes."

A smile broke across Sophine's face. "How wonderful to meet you, my dear."

Makilien smiled in return, though Sophine could not see. Something about this kind, gentle woman pulled at her heart and almost made her cry. "It's wonderful to meet you too."

Then Sophine's slender fingers found the metal around Makilien's wrists. Her smile faded. "You were a prisoner."

"Yes," Makilien confirmed. "I was captured and taken from my home a few days ago. I managed to escape in the crowd when we arrived here."

"Jorin found her and brought her here so I can help her out of the city," Beregon explained.

"Praise Elohim," Sophine murmured. Still holding Makilien's hands, she asked, "Are you hungry? I was just about to start supper."

"Yes, I am."

"Good." Sophine turned her head in Beregon's direction. "Why don't you see to removing these chains and I'll put supper on. When you're finished, bring her inside."

"Yes, dear," Beregon replied lovingly, and he led her back to the door of the house.

Ryelan stalked down the torch-lit hall, brows crunched low. He was tired, sweaty, and hungry, yet before seeing to any of those needs, he had to face Vayzar's wrath. The man was sure to be livid. Ryelan could only imagine how he would react to not one, but two failures. He grimaced. While he didn't truly fear Vayzar, apprehension churned his gut. In a fury, the man might do anything.

Halfway to the throne room, footsteps hurried up behind him. He looked over his shoulder as Irynna caught up.

"Did you find her?" she asked, her eyes searching his.

Ryelan's face contorted in disgust over the turn of events. "No."

Irynna's mouth dropped open. "But surely—"

Ryelan held up his hand. "She just disappeared somewhere. I'm sorry, we can't speak of it now. I've got to see Vayzar, and I'd rather you stay far away from this exchange."

Silenced, Irynna fell back as he marched on. At the door of Vayzar's throne room, he put his hand to the knob and paused. Shaking his head, he pushed the door open. Inside, Vayzar was meeting with two of his advisors. They all looked to the door.

"Ah, Ryelan, you've returned," Vayzar said, voice rising in enthusiasm. To the advisors, he ordered impatiently, "Leave us."

They bowed and promptly exited the room. Vayzar rose from the throne and approached Ryelan with a wicked grin stretching his lips wide.

"Do tell me the king is dead. I want to know every gruesome detail."

Ryelan steeled himself, grimacing again. "There were complications."

The grin dropped from Vayzar's face. "Complications? The king is not dead?"

Ryelan shook his head. "Makilien heard the struggle and came in. I would have had to kill her in order to finish off the king. I figured you were more interested in having her alive."

"Well, that puts a damper on things," Vayzar pouted, "but very well." That malicious and unnerving smile of his returned. "So where is she then? You didn't tell her about me, did you? I can't wait to see the look on her face when ..."

Again, his smile faded at Ryelan's sour expression. "She is here, isn't she?"

Ryelan licked his lips and shifted his weight from one foot to the other. "There were ... other complications."

An icy glint flickered in Vayzar's eyes as they narrowed. "What *other* complications?"

Ryelan hesitated.

"What other complications!" Vayzar snapped.

"She got away."

Vayzar's face was first wiped of expression, but then flushed a deep shade of red. "She got away!" he exploded. "How in the name of Zirtan could she get away? You're supposed to have Elven reflexes and senses, aren't you?"

Ryelan scowled and retorted, "I'm only Half-Elf."

"Well, you're close enough! After all, you've been going around masquerading as one for years. The point is, how did you let her get away?"

"We were coming straight here through the city, but along the way, she pulled away from me and was able to disappear in the crowd."

Vayzar threw his hands in the air. "You were *that* close and you let her escape? She's just a girl. You're twice her age and twice as strong. How could you do something so stupid!"

Ryelan glared at Vayzar before speaking, his own anger about to snap. Through a clenched jaw, he said, "The good news is she's still somewhere in the city. I've checked with the guards, and they will not let any young women or wagons out of the city without coming to me."

Vayzar matched Ryelan's intense stare, his voice like the edge of a dagger. "You'd better find her." He stepped closer, eyes narrowing. "Because if you don't, your girlfriend may just end up back where you found her, as a slave. And trust me, she'd fetch a fine price."

Rage boiled up inside Ryelan. "Don't you dare lay a hand on her."

"That depends on you," Vayzar snapped. "And you better be *very* careful to remember who is in charge here."

With those words, he spun around and stormed out of the room. Scowling, Ryelan went in the opposite direction. He marched through the halls, muttering to himself while his eyes searched until they landed on just the person he sought.

"Derrin!"

The young man stopped and spun around. Ryelan strode past him, ordering, "Come."

Derrin hurried to catch up and kept stride. "Where are we going?"

"You are going to help me find Makilien."

"*Find* Makilien?"

Still fighting back a flood of anger, Ryelan said, "She managed to escape in the city. You and I are the only two besides Vayzar who would recognize her."

Silence.

If not for Derrin's footsteps, Ryelan would have thought he was talking to air. He looked at the other man, finding his expression unsure.

"That won't be a problem, will it?" Ryelan asked, the anger adding a dangerous tone to his voice. He was in no mood to deal with Derrin's growing uncertainties.

Derrin hesitated, but answered, "No."

"Good."

:Chapter Twelve:

Price of Information

Reaching down to pat his loyal buckskin's neck, Aedan took in all the familiar sights of Andin. Everything looked just as he remembered it—a wide assortment of shops, taverns, and housing lining the dirt streets. It wasn't the cleanest town, but neither was it the worst he'd seen. Nudging Lokye with his heels, they moved down the main street, careful of the bustling foot traffic.

"We'll see about supplies," Aedan said to his steed whose ears flicked back at the sound of his voice. "Then you and I both are going to have a nice rest before morning. Tanzim may be comfortable in the forest, but a bed sounds good to me."

He turned off the main road to a familiar street. When he reached his destination, he pulled Lokye to an abrupt stop. His heart thudded. Where Laena's store had been, there lay only a blackened heap of charred wood and ash. Tiny wisps of smoke still rose like miniature phantoms.

Aedan jumped down and approached the destroyed building. *What's happened here?* he wondered, his eyes searching the debris. He prayed Laena had not been inside when the store had gone up in flames. He took a step farther into the destruction.

"What do you want here?" a female voice asked with apprehension.

Aedan spun around. Laena stood near Lokye. Her tense face softened when she recognized him.

"Oh, you," she breathed, and she joined him at the edge of the burnt store. "Aedan, right?"

He nodded and cast his gaze once again to the destroyed building. "What happened?"

"Some men came for supplies—Zirtan's former men, I suspect. They started messing up the store and getting a little too friendly. I was able to get out and go for help, but this is what they did in the meantime." Laena shook her head in bewilderment.

"When did it happen?"

"Two days ago."

"I'm sorry," Aedan murmured, and a terrible thought occurred to him, making him sick to his stomach. "The men, did any of them look similar to me or were called Jaeson?"

Laena looked at him and gave a slow nod. "Actually, yes, on both accounts. Do you know him?"

Aedan breathed a deep sigh and rubbed the back of his neck, hesitant to speak. "He is my father. I've been tracking him for months, but he's always one step ahead of me." He shook his head. "I'm really sorry he was part of this."

"Well, I don't know that he was exactly," Laena said. "He didn't seem pleased with what the others were doing."

Aedan found some small comfort in that, and it restored a little of his hope, which had been waning in the last weeks.

"Do you know if they are still here in the village?" Perhaps he had finally caught up to his father and could confront him.

"I don't know," Laena answered. "It's possible. You can check the inn."

Aedan nodded, his concern for her and her situation returning. "Do you have a place to live?"

"I'm staying with friends." Her eyes roamed the area. Funny how small it looked when there was naught but rubble. "This store was my husband's livelihood and all I had when he died. Now that it's gone, I'm hoping to travel to Eldor, but with talk of attacks in Eldinorieth, I dare not go now."

Aedan considered his options. He felt he should help Laena, but if his father was so close, he couldn't wait. "I need to look for my father. I'm not sure if I'll find him here, or will have to move on, but as soon as I can, I'll return and take you to Eldor."

"Oh, no, you don't have to do that," Laena told him.

"I want to," Aedan assured her.

She smiled gratefully. "Thank you." Glancing back at Lokye, she asked, "Were you here for supplies?"

Aedan nodded.

"Well, I know one of the other shopkeepers. He's less than honest and charges too much, but if I'm there, he'll give you a fair deal."

Now it was Aedan's turn to thank Laena. Taking hold of Lokye's reins, he followed her through the village to the other shop.

Makilien rubbed her wrists, glad to be rid of the shackles. She'd felt the discomfort of restraints far too many times already in her young life and hoped this would be the last.

"So you don't know what Vayzar is up to?"

Beregon shook his head. "I'm afraid not. He arrived last fall. I don't know what he told the slave owners, but within weeks he had the city under his control and began his fortress. That has been his main operation until this spring when he planted fields full of Shadelin."

Makilien frowned. Every child in Reylaun had been strictly warned about the poisonous plant since it sometimes grew up along the palisade wall. If it was as dangerous as her parents said, then a man like Vayzar collecting such a vast amount of it was something of great concern.

"I wonder what he could be using it for?"

"Considering the amount and that it's lethal, who knows?"

Makilien thought on this while Beregon put away the tools he'd used to break the chains. Turning back to her, he said, "You should probably lie low for a day or two. Vayzar's men will be combing the city if they aren't already, and the gate guards will be watching for you. Once the initial search is over, I will find a way to sneak you out during the night."

"I can't leave," Makilien replied. At Beregon's look of surprise, she went on, "Not until I find someone."

"Who would that be?"

"His name is Sirion. I believe Vayzar is holding him prisoner." Makilien paused, emotion coming on strong at how near he might be. She swallowed and cleared her throat. "We're very close."

"I'm afraid finding him will not be easy," Beregon said gently. "The only way into Vayzar's fortress is if you bear Zirtan's mark, are one of his slaves, or you're invited in personally."

But Makilien was not in any way deterred. "I'll have to figure out something. I won't leave without him. I've had to live with believing him dead for too long."

Beregon considered her for a moment. "Very well. I'll see what I can do to help."

"Thank you," Makilien told him. "And I'm hoping more help will come soon. My friends from Elimar came after me when I was captured, I have no doubt of that. I don't know how far behind they are, but if I can somehow get word to them, they can help us."

"I think I know someone I can trust to send out with a message. How about I see him first thing in the morning?"

"I would be very grateful if you would."

"Tomorrow morning then." He motioned for Makilien to follow. "Come. I'll show you the house."

The two of them walked inside. "It's small, but you'll be safe here."

He led her down a narrow hall and gestured to a room on the left. "This is the living room. The bedroom is here on the right, and the kitchen is straight ahead."

In a moment, they entered the kitchen and dining area— the largest room of the modest dwelling. Pots clanked as Sophine prepared beef and a variety of vegetables for supper. Despite her lack of sight, she worked with comfortable ease in the familiar setting.

"Please, sit down," she invited. "Supper will be ready shortly."

Makilien sat at the small round table while Beregon went to the washstand. After washing up, he stepped behind his wife and put his hands on her shoulders. "Is there anything I can help you with?"

"You can bring the bread and dishes to the table."

When the two of them joined Makilien at the table, Beregon gave thanks, and they dished up their plates. Makilien took a bite of meat, savoring the taste of real food again. Being blind certainly did not affect Sophine's cooking skills.

"This is delicious, Sophine," she told her.

The woman smiled. "Thank you. I'm glad. It's taken me a while to become comfortable in the kitchen."

While they enjoyed the meal, Makilien shared with them everything pertaining to her capture, Ryelan, and Sirion. They listened and responded with a great deal of sympathy and encouragement. When she finished, Sophine said, "Vayzar must have Sirion locked up somewhere in his fortress."

"That's what I'm expecting, though, unfortunately, he could be anywhere," Makilien replied with a sigh. "I couldn't get Ryelan to tell me that."

At this, Sophine turned toward her husband, her voice lowering. "You could get in and find out."

Beregon stared at her for a moment. "I could." He paused. "It depends on whether or not you want me to give in."

"You wouldn't be giving in," Sophine replied. "Not now that you have a reason to go."

Beregon nodded quietly to himself. His eyes switched to Makilien who said nothing but took great interest in the exchange.

"Vayzar has been pressuring me to do the metalwork in his fortress for months. I always refused to give him any type of aid, but now, if it would help someone else . . ."

"So you could get into the fortress?" Makilien said, unable to hide the hope in her voice.

"Yes. I don't know where I would be allowed or how closely I'd be watched, but I would be inside." He glanced again at his wife, thinking it over. "I'll go see Vayzar tomorrow."

Sophine smiled, and Makilien said with the deepest sincerity, "Thank you so much."

Leading Lokye behind him, his saddlebags filled with fresh supplies, Aedan followed a narrow street toward the inn. His heart rate was a little higher than normal. This could be the day he would come face to face with his father again since their meeting on the battlefield, bringing an end to months of searching. Then he could go home. The thought set him to praying that all would be as he hoped. Every day his desire to return to Elimar grew stronger.

Near the end of the street, he spotted a lone man leaning against the side of a building. The man watched him approach out of the corner of his eye. Drawing closer, uneasiness prickled up Aedan's back. Something didn't feel right. But he walked on determinedly. Just before he passed, the man pushed away from the building and stepped in front of him. Aedan stopped, tensing, and held the man's sinister gaze.

"Excuse me," he said firmly.

The man crossed his arms, eyeing Aedan up and down. "Where are you off to in such a hurry?"

"None of your business."

The man smirked, and Aedan noticed too late when the man's eyes swung past him. Sharp steel pressed into his back, and his sword and dagger were pulled from their sheaths before he could react. With a strong shove, the man behind forced him into an alley where two more men waited.

Heart pounding, Aedan turned slowly in a circle, eyeing each of them. "What do you want? You want my money and supplies? Take them. It will hardly be worth the trouble once you split it up between you."

The man who had stopped him ambled forward, filthy teeth showing in an expression somewhere between a smirk and a scowl. "You're the one who's been trailin' us."

Aedan's heart beat a little harder at this. These men had been with his father. But he kept his expression controlled.

The man stepped closer, forcing him back. He could sense the other men closing in around him.

"What business do you have with us, boy?" the man sneered.

Aedan stood taller, unwilling to be intimidated. "I'm looking for Jaeson."

"What for?"

"It's personal."

"Well, we don't take kindly to pursuers."

The man balled his fists, and Aedan knew one way or another, he was going to take a beating. Before the men behind could secure him, he threw the first punch, sending the leader back a couple steps. A tiny window of opportunity opened for him to bolt, but it wasn't enough. The men caught him by the arms and spun him around to face another man who wound up for a strike. Yet, before he could take a swing, Aedan kicked him hard in the gut.

By this time, the leader of the group had recovered. Aedan barely saw the blow coming. Stars flashed as the man's fist drilled into his chin. A second blow came to his ribs. He gasped as the air rushed from his lungs, but adrenaline surged through him. He threw his weight into the man to his right, ramming him against the wall. When the man's grip loosened on impact, Aedan drove his elbow into his side and yanked himself away. He spun, his momentum delivering a powerful punch to the other man's stomach.

Though free of the two men, Aedan couldn't get away before the leader's fist again slammed into his face, shooting fiery pain through his jaw. He stumbled, almost losing his footing, but caught himself. If he went down, he wouldn't get back up.

All four men descended on him at once, pummeling him with their fists. Aedan tried to defend himself, but didn't have a chance of taking on so many. He could see it now—lying bloodied, battered, and half-dead in the alley for someone to stumble across. His instincts screamed to fight, but to try opened him to attack.

At the moment he lost hope, one of the men gave a surprised yelp and sailed through the air. He slammed into the wall where he crumpled in an unconscious heap. A second man was backhanded with such force that he landed a few feet away, out cold. The remaining two retreated in panic, but strong hands caught the leader by the jerkin, lifted him up into the air, and threw him into the last man as he tried to flee. Both slammed to the ground. The leader clutched his arm, writhing in pain while the other man lay motionless.

Aedan wrapped an arm around his throbbing ribs and braced his other hand on his knee, bent over in pain. He glanced up at the towering, dark-skinned, fierce-faced being standing over him. The creature's shoulder muscles and fore-arms bulged as he squeezed his fists, waiting for anyone who might challenge him.

Breathing heavily, Aedan spit out a mouthful of blood and a molar. He wiped his lips with the back of his hand and straightened with a wince.

"Tanzim," he gasped. "I thought you were staying in the forest."

"Forgot to tell you to get me some sweets," Tanzim replied, his voice edged in a deep growl as he glared at the other men.

A laugh broke from Aedan despite the pain it caused his bruised ribs. He shook his head. "Only you, Tan. Thank Elohim your sweet tooth saved me from losing more of mine."

A groan came from the only conscious man, attracting Aedan's attention. The man leaned back against the wall now, cradling his broken arm. Aedan's relief over rescue turned to steely determination. He strode over to the man, who tried to scoot away, and grabbed a fistful of his jerkin. Looking him in the eyes, Aedan demanded, "Where is Jaeson? Is he here in the village?"

The man scowled and set his jaw stubbornly.

Aedan pulled him closer, lowering his voice to a menacing tone. "Either tell me what I want to know, or I'll let him get the information for me."

He nodded to Tanzim. The Shaike growled deep in his throat and cracked his knuckles with loud crackling pops. The man swallowed, his eyes climbing the Shaike before switching back to Aedan.

"He's not here," he said at last. "He went on to Carel to join up with Vayzar."

Aedan's brows shot up. "Vayzar? What is Vayzar doing in Carel?"

The man shook his head. "I don't know. We told Jaeson we were done getting mixed up in these crazy schemes so he went on without us."

Aedan peered at him, his eyes narrowing. "You're telling me the truth?"

"Yes."

"How long ago did he leave?"

"Two days."

Aedan glanced at Tanzim and rose. "Let's get out of here."

Leaving the man and his unconscious friends, they exited the alley. Lokye stood faithfully in the street where Aedan had left him. Before he took the reins, Aedan dug through one of the saddlebags and pulled out a small sack.

"Tan."

He tossed the sack to his friend. When Tanzim opened it, he found it filled with hard maple candies.

A grin of pleasure broke across his otherwise scowling expression. "Mmm, my favorite."

He dropped a couple into his mouth as he and Aedan walked on, coming to the main street.

"Do you know where Carel is?" Aedan asked.

Tanzim gave a quick nod. "'S'bout a day and a half southeast of here. Ain't a friendly place neither."

"What do you mean?"

"It's a slave city. The slavers'll grab most anyone to sell if they can get a good price. A strong lad like you's worth his weight in gold."

"Well, it's a good thing I have you to watch my back then."

:Chapter Thirteen:

Punishment

On and on the hammers rang out through the day. Sweat dripped from Sirion's face. He paused, brushing his hand across his forehead. The sweat stung his cracked knuckles, dry from the scorching sun and demanding labor. His muscles ached and weariness was a constant companion, but Jered had been right. Even after just five days, he was growing used to the grueling routine.

One of the overseers came around with a waterskin as he did every so often. Sirion set aside his hammer and drank deeply. Determining when he'd had enough, the overseer yanked the skin away and gave it next to Jered. In this brief time, Sirion allowed his body to rest. He glanced at the sinking sun. In less than an hour, they would march back to the fortress.

As soon as the overseer took the waterskin from Jered, the two of them bent back to their work for the final push of the day. Sirion lost himself in the rhythm of his hammer until Jered's voice cut through the steady beating.

"I've noticed the two guards to my left get awfully bored this time a day. I don't think they've even looked this way the last half hour."

Sirion glanced at them and added a mental note of it to all the other information he'd been gathering. Jered was more than willing to join him in the search for an escape, and the last few days they'd spent studying their guards' positions and habits, looking for the perfect opportunity to slip away.

They worked on, saying no more. The sun sank lower, soon turning a blazing orange that spilled across the cloudless sky. Suddenly, above the beating of hammers, a shout echoed through the quarry. Sirion and Jered looked up. On the far side of the quarry, two men ran away as fast as they could. Not far behind, the overseers scrambled to their horses.

"No," Jered murmured under his breath. "They have nowhere to go."

Dread twisted Sirion's stomach. The only chance of escape was to sneak away undetected. To make a run for it was suicide. *Go!* he mentally urged the men on, but already the guards had mounted and raced after them. An uneasy hush settled over the quarry as all watched. The men gave it all they had, but would never outrun the horses.

It all came to an abrupt end when one of the men got too far ahead of the other and tripped when their chain went taut. The overseers were on them in an instant. At this distance, most could not see what happened, but Sirion saw everything—the way the overseers jumped off their horses and beat the men without mercy. He dropped his gaze, biting down hard. When he did look up again, the overseers led the men back toward the fortress.

"Let that be a lesson to the lot a ya!" another overseer shouted. "Now get back to work while there's still daylight left."

Sirion turned, meeting Jered's gaze, and saw fire in the man's eyes. Jaw clenched tight, Jered did not speak, but his expression said everything. In silence, the two of them worked on until the sun had disappeared.

When everyone returned to the fortress for the night, they found the two men who'd tried to escape tied up in the courtyard, their arms stretched out between tall posts. They stood defeated, heads bowed as torchlight flickered on their bruised and hopeless faces. All looked on them in pity. This pity turned to confusion when the overseers gathered them around the escapees. Sirion and Jered exchanged uncertain glances. Heart thumping with dread, Sirion began to pray.

A moment later, Vayzar strode out into the courtyard. With him came Halen and Sirion's detest for the heartless man.

"I hear we had an escape attempt today," Vayzar said as he stopped between the two guilty men, facing the group. "A very foolish action to be sure, and one I will not tolerate. It wastes time, energy, and gives others foolish notions as well. I suggest any of you with such notions get them right out of your head, because if you don't, you'll end up just like these two, severely punished and sent to the grinding house. And just so that it is very clear, you will all witness their punishment."

The guards tore off the men's shirts, and Halen uncoiled his whip. A deep shudder ran through Sirion's body. At each crack of the whip, he could feel their pain burning in his own nerves. He wanted to look away, but couldn't drop his eyes. He watched the men fight the pain at first, but eventually give in to agony. His throat constricted, emotion and haunting memories building up inside. Jered stood like a statue beside him, though his chest rose and fell heavily. Had they not been chained together, he may have acted despite the consequences.

After long, torturous minutes, the men had been beaten nearly unconscious, and the rest of the captives were led to the stockade, a heavy silence blanketing all. Once free of their chains and in their corner of the shelter, Jered slammed his fist against the wall with an angry cry.

"This is all so wrong!" He faced Sirion, eyes flashing. "Elohim never meant for men to treat each other in such a way. Vayzar and Halen are animals." He dragged in a deep breath and walked closer to Sirion, his voice lowering. "I can't do it. I can't plan an escape for myself and just leave all these men here. If I go, we all go."

Slowly, Sirion nodded in agreement. It had to be all or nothing.

Makilien insisted on helping Sophine with the supper dishes while Beregon went out to see how much of a stir her escape had caused. This menial task brought a welcome time of peace after the days on the trail as a captive. She quickly grew to love Sophine's companionship. The woman listened with honest interest as Makilien spoke of Sirion and the turmoil of the past year. Makilien had a feeling the woman knew better than most how she felt.

Little more than an hour later, Beregon returned, finding Makilien and Sophine enjoying a cup of tea at the table. Makilien set her cup down, focusing on him.

"Did you see anyone looking for me?"

"Quite a few guards," Beregon answered. "The city is buzzing with interest. Vayzar is clearly making a determined effort to find you. You will have to be very careful for the next few days."

"What if they come looking for her here?" Sophine asked in concern.

"I thought of that." Beregon turned and bent, pushing back a rug in the middle of the floor to reveal a trapdoor. He lifted it and motioned for Makilien. "If anyone comes by, you can hide down here. Hopefully, no one will know."

She looked down into a small, dark food cellar. It was a perfect place to hide as long as no one thought to look under the rug.

"I will put a sword down there for you, just in case," Beregon told her.

Makilien smiled her thanks, now knowing how she would ever be able to show her gratitude to him and his wife.

They joined Sophine at the table again, and Beregon poured himself a cup of tea, glancing at Makilien. "It's very fortunate Jorin found you today. In a city like this, anyone would have been happy to turn you in if they thought it could benefit them."

With a nod of agreement, Makilien said a silent prayer of thanks. Looking at Beregon curiously, she asked, "How do you know Jorin? As you probably know, the two of us have a bit of history."

"Yes, he told us about your encounters." Beregon looked over to Sophine. "We've known Jorin for a few months now. He came in periodically with work his master needed done. At first, we didn't speak, but I knew he had a lot of uncertainties. Finally, I started asking him questions and he slowly shared his story with me. As hesitant as he was at first, I think it gave him relief to discuss things. He's more open now, and he comes in more often, at times of his own accord."

Makilien rested back in her chair, rubbing the faint scars on her wrists from the last time she'd been Jorin's captive. "That is amazing. I can't believe how he has changed. I'm still reeling over the fact that he saved my life."

"Don't forget, you saved his first at a time when you were still bitter enemies. I don't believe he'll ever forget that. It has caused him to do a great deal of thinking. I think you'll be very pleased to know it has even made him open to the subject of Elohim."

Makilien's eyes grew a bit larger. "Really?"

"Yes," Beregon said with a nod of confirmation. "Sophine and I both have spoken to him regularly on matters of our faith. While I can't say he has responded to it, he listens and has never resisted us."

For a long moment, Makilien just sat and considered this, how her intervening had changed the course of Jorin's life, and may even, one day, result in him believing the truth. In any case, had she not intervened, she may have been sitting helpless in Vayzar's clutches right now.

Once the three of them finished their tea, Sophine rose and beckoned Makilien to follow. They stepped into the bedroom, and Sophine opened a wardrobe at one end. Feeling the dresses and shifts hanging inside, she pulled a couple out and turned to Makilien.

"I hope these will fit you."

Makilien took the clothing with a smile, noting how nice the clean material felt. "I'm sure they will. Thank you for your generosity."

Sophine's expression grew into a soft smile. "I am very pleased to help you. Both Beregon and I are."

"And I hope you know how grateful I am to both of you and Elohim for the shelter I have here. You must know the danger in what you are doing."

Sophine shrugged. "We're not worried." She reached out, touching Makilien's arm. "Come, I'll help you make a bed in the living room where you can sleep."

:Chapter Fourteen:

Offered Service

Letting out a soft groan, Aedan rolled over onto his back. He rubbed his eyes and gingerly touched his swollen jaw as he ran his tongue over the gap in his teeth. Pushing himself up with a wince, he put his arm around his chest and blew out a breath. Tanzim eyed him from across the fire.

"You all right?"

"I'll live." Aedan rubbed his sore ribs thinking he felt just about the same as the man Tanzim had thrown against the wall. He lifted a brow wryly. "A bed would have been nice."

"The forest is safer."

Aedan had to agree with him in this instance.

Tanzim handed him a plate of fried eggs. Aedan had no idea where they came from, and didn't ask. He'd learned to accept whatever the Shaike offered, though, at times, their opinions on what was edible differed.

Swallowing down a bite, Aedan said, "We should find my father, finally. If he's only a couple days ahead of us, I can't see him leaving Carel before we get there."

"We'll have to be wary of this Vayzar fellow."

Aedan agreed, memories of living under his rule in Reylaun still fresh. "And find out what he's up to. I don't like the sound of the attacks in Eldinorieth, and I'm willing to bet he has something to do with it."

Tanzim grunted. "What'll you do if your father won't listen to reason?"

Aedan chewed his food, not answering. He would only ever be able to answer that question when the time came.

Makilien rose from her knees and smoothed her dress. She was in a difficult situation. Her deepest desire was to do something, anything, to get to Sirion, yet she realized she was stuck here, helpless, and had to leave everything in Elohim's hands. A long time of prayer had helped bring peace and patience into her heart. Even so, she was anxious to see what the new day would bring. Stepping out of the living room and down the hall, she found Sophine and her husband already preparing breakfast.

"Good morning, Makilien," Sophine said in a cheery voice as soon as she'd entered the kitchen.

Makilien marveled over how good her hearing must be. "Good morning. Can I help with anything?"

"Thank you, but I think we're about finished. Please, have a seat."

Makilien took her place at the table, and it wasn't long before the couple joined her. During Beregon's prayer, he made particular mention of Sirion, and Makilien felt a deep gratitude for the care and understanding of others. Beregon and Sophine had already proved to be a wonderful blessing to her in light of the absence of her family and friends, and she added her own silent prayer of thanks.

As they began their meal, Beregon said, "When we're finished, I'll go see the young man I mentioned yesterday. He is a slave, but I know his master well. He won't mind letting the boy help me out for a couple days. He's a good, fast rider, and I trust him, so I believe he'll be the perfect one to ride out and look for your friends. Perhaps you can write a note for him to take, and tell me what your friends look like so I can give him the information."

Makilien swallowed a bite of toast, eager to do whatever she could to get her friends here. "I can do more than that. If you can get me some paper and small bits of charcoal, I can sketch pictures of them. I can sketch one of Sirion too."

"Excellent."

They concluded breakfast in high spirits, and once the dishes had been cleared, Beregon found the supplies Makilien needed. For the next while, she sat and sketched those she knew would have come after her. She finished with the sketch of Sirion. Pausing for a moment, she stared at it, praying Beregon would be able to find him. She then gave the sketches to him and the note she had written for her friends. The blacksmith tucked them safely into his jerkin.

"Elohim willing, your friends will soon join us."

Taking a deep breath, Makilien nodded, praying it would be so.

When Beregon left the house, Makilien offered to help with the dishes again. She laid them all in the washbasin and started scrubbing while Sophine put the clean ones away. They talked of various things until Makilien finally worked up to asking a question that kept coming to mind.

"Have you always been blind?"

Sophine's movements slowed as she wiped a bowl dry and set it on a shelf. "No, not always."

Makilien wondered what had happened but didn't have the heart to ask. However, Sophine went on to share her story.

"My parents were slaves, so naturally, I grew up as one. A few years ago, I was sold to a cruel man named Halen. He would have me bring his horses here to be shod. That is how I met Beregon." A wistful smile softened her expression and her tone. "I guess you might say it was love at first sight. A couple months later, Beregon went to Halen and offered to buy my freedom. Halen refused, but Beregon continued to press him. At last, Halen agreed, but only to a very high price.

"For two and a half years Beregon worked, saving, doing any extra jobs he could find. The day before he bought my freedom, Halen beat me nearly to death just to spite him." Sophine bit her lip, tears in her eyes. "That's when it happened. When I returned to consciousness, my sight was gone."

She shook her head and touched one of the scars on her cheek. "I can't imagine how I must appear now, so scarred and such a burden. But Beregon paid Halen in full. He nursed me back to health and never once considered leaving me."

Makilien wiped a tear from her cheek and couldn't speak for a moment, throat tight with the emotion of the story. "I'm so sorry about your eyes. You and Beregon both are remarkable people."

Sophine smiled widely, her sadness over the past disappearing. "Beregon is one of the greatest blessings in my life." She paused a moment, but then said, "I hope Sirion would do the same for you."

"He would," Makilien murmured, and nodded to confirm it even though Sophine could not see it. "That is why I must do everything in my power to find him."

Sophine came close and touched Makilien's shoulder. "I'm sure you will. And I know my husband will do whatever he can to help you."

Outside the city walls, Beregon crossed the bridge and came before the forbidding fortress. Squinting in the sun, he eyed the jagged, half-finished walls. His gaze then dropped to the two guards blocking him from entering. He stopped, his eyes settling on one.

"I'm here to see Vayzar."

"What for?" the guard demanded shortly.

"I've reconsidered his request for me to do the metalwork for the fortress."

The man peered at him, eyes narrowing, and then inclined his head. "Come with me."

He pushed open the gate and led Beregon through the courtyard. Along the way, Beregon studied the surroundings, keeping a watchful eye for anyone who matched Makilien's sketch until they entered the fortress. After a silent march through the halls, they came to Vayzar's throne room where the guard left him standing momentarily at the door. When he returned, Vayzar was with him.

"Beregon," the man said, eyeing him with an air of suspicion. "This is a surprise indeed. Whatever possessed you to come see me?"

Beregon held his gaze and said simply. "I've changed my mind. I will do your metalwork."

Vayzar lifted an eyebrow. "Ah, so you've finally decided my offer is too good to pass up." He turned and strode up to his throne, draping himself across it. Now, his voice took on a bored tone. "The thing is, I'm not sure you're worth that much to me anymore . . ."

Beregon just stared at him for a moment. He had no interest in the money Vayzar had offered, but he knew Vayzar was now trying to back out of the deal by faking disinterest. Playing along with the treacherous little game, he shrugged. "If you no longer have need of my services, then I'll go."

He turned for the door.

"Wait."

Beregon smirked to himself, though he hid it before facing Vayzar. The man's eyes narrowed, peering at him shrewdly.

"There is a forge in the courtyard outside," he said, all pretense gone. "It hasn't been used in a while. The last smithy did not work out." He paused here, letting the import of that sink in. "My men will show you where it is so you can get to work."

Beregon inclined his head just slightly. "Very well."

He turned to follow the guards. Once he was out of earshot, Vayzar motioned to another of his men.

"Have him watched. I don't trust him."

Outside, Beregon found the small forge in need of repair. Resigned to the task, he got to work, but while he did so, his eyes searched the compound. He took note of the stockade across from him, and the two other large buildings at the farthest end of the courtyard.

Working at an easy pace, it took most of the day to make the necessary repairs. Soon, the hot afternoon sun beat down overhead, but a plank roof offered some relief from the heat. By evening, he had the forge workable.

As the darkness of night crept in and he prepared to return home, commotion from the unfinished rear gate caught his attention. One by one, pairs of chained men filed inside, marching wearily across the yard to the stockade. They passed close by the forge, and Beregon took in each of their sweaty, miserable faces, sympathy rising in his heart.

His eyes then caught on one man. The flickering torchlight made it difficult to see, but he was certain. This man was Sirion. Joy at this discovery filled him, but he was careful to hide it. He glanced over his shoulder, gaze catching on the guard who had stood watch over him all afternoon. The man's eyes narrowed. To throw off suspicion, Beregon pretended to see to a few final things, but his eyes found Sirion one last time before he disappeared into the stockade.

Sirion took the bowl of stew offered to him at the gap in the palisade and turned. Jered stood nearby with Ren and Tavin. He and Sirion had barely spoken all day, still affected by what had taken place the night before. Jered looked at him and motioned for him to follow. The four of them gathered at the far end of the stockade and Jon soon joined them.

Too worked up to bother with his supper, Jered peered at each of them, his eyes alight with determination. "The time has come to do something. I refuse to go on slaving for Vayzar day after day, wondering who will be next to be hauled off to the grinding house, and I will not just wait to be slaughtered once he is through with us."

The men glanced at one another.

"What do you propose we do?" Ren asked.

Jered spread his arm toward all the men inside the stockade. "There are over fifty of us. I say we rise up together and put an end to this."

"We have no weapons," Jon pointed out.

But the fire in Jered's eyes only intensified. "We have our hammers. They may not be as effective as a sword, but they'll do enough damage."

Ren shook his head, his voice rising, but only a little. "We're not fighters, Jered. How are just fifty of us supposed to defeat trained soldiers?"

"We have Elohim. And by working together with pure determination, I believe we can do this. What's the alternative? Would you rather die here like cattle bound for slaughter?"

They shook their heads.

"Good, because I won't. Now, all we need is a plan and to convince everyone else to act, because if we don't do this together, we'll fail. We have to be careful though. Word of this cannot leak out to Vayzar. I know I don't have to warn you of the consequences."

Their answer came in solemn expressions.

"What I need you to do right now is listen," Jered instructed them. "I want to know who else might be thinking of taking action so I can talk to them. If you hear anything, let me know. Once we're sure everyone is in agreement, we'll make our plans."

Sirion and the others nodded, and they all fell silent as their attention turned to their food. After they finished and parted, Sirion followed Jered to their spot in the shelter. Before they reached it, Jered stopped and pulled him aside. Lowering his voice, he said, "I'll need you to help me talk to the men. This is where the whole thing could fall apart. If even one person panics and turns on us, it's over. I trust you more than anyone in here to help me keep that from happening."

Sirion gave a firm nod. The gravity and danger of the situation, as well as the importance, was just as clear to him as Jered, if not more so. "You can count on me to do whatever I can."

Makilien looked across the table to Sophine who hadn't yet touched her supper. Her own food lay half eaten on her plate. Both were concerned about Beregon being so late. It made Makilien sick to think of something happening to him for helping her find Sirion. The couple had already suffered enough.

At last, the door opened. Makilien and Sophine rose eagerly as Beregon entered the kitchen.

"Sorry I was so late," he apologized, not even having to hear his wife's voice to know she'd been worried. He drew her into his arms and gave her a kiss.

"Did everything go well?" she asked once she could speak.

"I got in just fine. Vayzar still wanted my help, but he had a guard watching me all day." Letting his wife go, Beregon turned to Makilien, meeting her hopeful eyes. "I saw him."

Makilien's heart missed a beat. "You saw Sirion?"

"I did."

Shaking a little at the rushing flood of emotions, Makilien gripped the edge of the table and her voice broke as she asked, "Where was he?"

"Vayzar has a large group of men working in the stone quarry near here. That is how he is building his fortress. Sirion is one of them. At night, they are locked up in a stockade inside the courtyard. They came in from work just before I left."

"And how was he?" Makilien asked, still a little breathless. "How did he look?"

"It looks like they are worked hard, but he appears to be faring well under the circumstances."

Makilien breathed deeply and sank into her chair as her legs gave out. Overwhelming joy and a desperate desire to see him washed over her now that she truly knew, at last, he had never left this world. Not only that, but he was only a couple of miles away. Two tears rolled down her cheeks. She wanted more than anything to run out to him, prisoner or not. *Give me patience, Elohim.*

:Chapter Fifteen:

Infiltration

Makilien sat at the table, bent over a stack of paper and a small pile of charcoal. Sketching had been her favored way of passing time for years. She wished she could go outside, but Vayzar's men could be lurking anywhere. It only took one to catch a glimpse of her for everything to fall apart and endanger not only herself, but Beregon and Sophine as well.

Across the table, Sophine mended one of Beregon's shirts, surprising Makilien again with her skill. The two were quiet for a while, the only sound coming from the scratch of Makilien's charcoal and the pounding of Beregon's hammer as he served his regular customers.

After a moment, Sophine requested, "Tell me what Elimar is like. I always dreamed of living in an Elven city."

Makilien smiled, understanding such a dream. "There's a particular beauty and elegance about it, something only Elves can add to a place. It's all in the forest, filled with maple trees, and oaks, and beautiful white birch. Actually, it seems rather small for being a thriving city, but it's a very close community. Everything is beautiful, especially this time of year. There aren't really roads, just paths, and there are little rivers and ponds branching off..."

Sophine frowned when her voice died. "What is it?"

Makilien tipped her head toward the hall, her own brows lowering. "Do you hear someone talking?"

They both sat silent.

"Yes, it sounds like Beregon has a customer," Sophine said finally.

Makilien rose, straining to hear better. Something about that voice had sparked recognition.

"Is something wrong, Makilien?"

"No, it's just..."

With caution, she worked her way down the hall toward the partially open door into the shed. The voices came clearer now, and at once, Makilien's heart leapt for joy. She pulled open the door. "Aedan!"

He spun around, eyes rounding. Makilien didn't even allow him a chance to finish processing her presence before she had him in a tight embrace. He returned it awkwardly, still trying to figure things out.

"How... what?" He shook his head as she backed away. "What in Dolennar are you doing in Carel?"

Makilien gave a short, dry laugh. Where did she even begin? "You have no idea what you've missed. It's going to need more than a quick explanation."

Aedan glanced past her. "Are you here alone?"

"For now." Makilien's eyes switched to the Shaike standing behind him and smiled. "Hey, Tanzim."

"Makilien," he greeted, face stern, yet she caught the fondness in his gaze.

Finally, she turned to Beregon who stood by, quietly curious. By this time, Sophine had joined them. Makilien explained her friendship with Aedan and Tanzim and made introductions before turning her full attention back to her friend who still looked a bit thunderstruck. Out of all she had to tell him, one bit of information bubbled out first.

A big grin breaking across her face, she announced, "Sirion is alive."

Aedan did a double take. "Wait, what?"

"Sirion is still alive, and he is here in Carel. Beregon has seen him."

Caught in a spinning mix of confusion, shock, and joy, Aedan opened his mouth, but no words came. Finally, he said, "I think you need to start from the beginning."

Makilien could not help but chuckle, and nodded in agreement.

"Why don't we all go inside," Beregon suggested. "I'll help Sophine with lunch and you can explain."

The five of them gathered in the little house. Tanzim scrunched into the corner at the table and Makilien and Aedan joined him. Securing their full attention, Makilien went over all the dramatic events of the past weeks. Aedan was easier to read than Tanzim, but both were clearly surprised and exchanged glances and raised eyebrows. Makilien ended the tale with Beregon's sighting of Sirion the night before. By this time, they were well into their meal.

"Now we just have to figure out how to rescue him," Makilien said, hardly having touched her food. "Problem is, Beregon will no doubt be watched constantly, and Vayzar has the fortress well-guarded."

Aedan sat back, sorting through all the information. After a moment, he looked down, thoughts forming. He frowned a little, but then seemed to make up his mind as he loosened the laces of the vambrace on his right arm and pulled it off. Resting his arm on the table, all eyes fell on the black snake tattoo his father had branded him with.

"If that can get me inside, maybe I can get to Sirion."

A surge of hope coursed through Makilien. She had almost forgotten about Aedan's tattoo. Her eyes jumped to Beregon. "Do you think they would let him in?"

"I don't see why not." With a serious gaze, he focused on Aedan. "However, you must be prepared. You may be forced to meet with Vayzar."

Makilien hadn't thought of that. Vayzar would surely recognize him after all the trouble they'd caused in Reylaun. She looked at her friend, eyes filling with concern.

Aedan rubbed his hand along the raised scar tissue of his arm, but had already made his decision. "It's worth it to me to find out. Perhaps this is exactly the reason Elohim has allowed me to bear this shame, to help rescue Sirion."

His gaze turned to Makilien. "I also have another particular reason for wanting to get inside. My father is here in Carel. That's why I came. He should have arrived only two days ago to join up with Vayzar. I can't let him slip away again."

This added a new level of danger to the mission, but Makilien knew how important it was to him.

"Any chance they'd let a Shaike inside?" Tanzim joined in the conversation.

Beregon shrugged. "I don't know. I haven't seen any Shaikes around the city or the fortress."

Tanzim grunted in disappointment. "Best not 'rouse suspicion then."

It would have been nice to have the Shaike with him, but taking a deep breath, Aedan said, "I guess it's up to me."

"When would you like to go to the fortress?" Beregon asked.

"I've got no reason to wait," Aedan answered. "It just puts Sirion there longer."

"Well, I'm heading there this afternoon. I can show you where it is. First, however, we need to make sure you have the best chance of making it in and don't get grabbed for a slave."

"How can we do that?"

"Clothes." Beregon pushed back his chair and rose. "I'll see what I can find. I'll be back shortly."

While he was gone, Makilien questioned Aedan about his search for his father and his journey the last couple of months. Aedan was just as interested in all the news from Elimar. They had only covered the important things before Beregon returned a half an hour later with an armful of clothing.

"These should help you look the part and draw less suspicion."

"Thanks," Aedan said, and took the clothing into the living room to change. When he returned, he was dressed all in black from the linen pants and shirt to the leather jerkin and long black cloak. Between the clothing, his dark hair, and stern jaw line, he fit the appearance of Zirtan's former men, though Makilien knew better.

Beregon nodded in approval. No one in Carel was likely to mistake him as a wandering traveler to be captured and sold. "Are you ready for this?"

"Yes," Aedan answered without hesitation.

Now that they were about to leave, fear gripped Makilien. What if the fortress guards forced Aedan to see Vayzar? The consequences of that were too horrible to contemplate. Swallowing hard, she looked up into his eyes. "Be careful, Aedan."

With an understanding expression, he nodded. "I will."

Makilien drew in a breath, though her chest felt heavy, and it trembled a little. "You've been away for so long, it's hard to see you go off into danger again right away."

"I know." Aedan gave her a hug, hoping to ease her fear. "I'll try to be back tonight. If not, then tomorrow." Before turning away from her, he placed something in her hands. "Take care of this for me, will you?"

She looked down at the vambrace Vonawyn had made him to hide the tattoo. "Of course." With a smile, she added, "She misses you. Make sure you stay alive to return to her."

A grin broke out on Aedan's face, though he looked down bashfully. "That's good incentive." Looking at his hand, he said, "You better take this too." He pulled the ring from Darian off his finger.

Makilien nodded and took it, squeezing it tight. "I'll keep them safe." With another deep breath, she told him, "I'll be praying for you."

Aedan smiled. "Thank you."

With reluctant goodbyes, he stepped outside after Beregon.

Even with his new clothing, he eyed the people warily on their way through the city. He couldn't imagine the horror of passing through such a place unaware and finding yourself enslaved. Few times had he been more thankful to have

Tanzim as a traveling companion than he had when entering the city that morning.

These thoughts moved to the back of his mind when Beregon spoke, offering him suggestions for entering the fortress. "I would try to be assertive with the guards. Perhaps portray yourself as someone of importance. I've found many of the underlings are easily cowed."

Aedan gave a nod. His own experiences supported this. The enemy's men were used to being ordered around by someone higher and crueler.

In a few minutes, they arrived near the rear gate of the city, giving Aedan a glimpse of Vayzar's fortress. It didn't inspire awe as some might, but it was intimidating and suited what he knew of the man.

"We probably shouldn't be seen together," Beregon said. "Vayzar suspects I'm not fully on his side. I'll go in first and you can follow." He turned to Aedan. "I too will be praying for your safe entry."

"Thanks."

Aedan watched Beregon walk off and leave the city. Standing out of sight at a corner, he waited for his turn to approach the fortress, praying. A lot rode on successfully infiltrating, not merely his own welfare.

After allowing a good fifteen minutes to pass, he left his vantage point and walked toward the gate. The guards watched him, but said nothing. He crossed over the bridge and approached the fortress. The two men at guard here eyed him with more suspicion.

"What is your business?" one snapped.

Aedan held up his arm, allowing the tattoo to show.

The guard's expression changed. "You're here to join Lord Vayzar?"

Aedan snorted in mock disgust. "I didn't travel all this way just to say hello." The guards glanced at each other, and he added in a tone of impatience, "I've been under Lord Vayzar before. Now, will you let me in?"

He planted his fists on his hips and fixed them with a hard and intimidating gaze, no doubt something he had inherited from his father. They hesitated, but then one reached to open the gate.

"Report to Roark. He'll show you around."

Aedan nodded curtly and stepped into the courtyard. He strode toward the fortress until the gate closed behind him. Only then did he look over his shoulder and slow to take in his surroundings, but he did not linger too long. When he reached the fortress door, he pulled it open, cool, damp air drifting past his face as he stepped into the darkness. He slid the door closed behind himself and stood in silence, his heart thudding.

A long, dim hall stretched out before him, random torches casting eerie circles of orange light. He had a choice now— find this Roark or discreetly blend in with the men. Both options had their risks. Meeting with Roark would make him less suspicious, but what if he recognized Aedan as Jaeson's son or insisted on him meeting Vayzar. No, too many risks. He would blend in and deal with questions or suspicions as they came.

Adjusting his sword belt, Aedan took the silent hall. His footsteps, though soft, were amplified by the empty space, as was his breathing. Nothing stirred anywhere around him. A chill skittered down his back. The place had a way of making him think of suffering and death. It was as though he were the only living person within miles, just waiting for some frightful beast to descend on him. He shook his head and reined in his mind. Such thoughts would do him no service.

Several yards down the hall, he arrived at an intersection. More torches lit the way ahead than the halls to his right and left. Down these narrower corridors, he could only spot one torch far off. Contemplating, he decided to continue on the main path and return to these later.

A hundred feet ahead, he stopped where the hall again branched off to either side, but just in front of him stood a double door. One stood open a crack, and the murmur of voices filtered through. He stepped up to the door and peered in. Darkness filled the room except for one end where two torches flickered on either side of a throne. His eyes narrowed when he saw Vayzar reclining there. A little off to the side, he noticed the silhouette of another man, though he was almost hidden in shadow.

"How is the shadelin coming along?" Vayzar asked. "When will we have enough?"

"In a couple of weeks, we should be up to fifty barrels."

The voice of this other man rasped from the darkness, making goose bumps rise along Aedan's arms and his hair stand on end.

"Good," Vayzar replied, nodding in pleasure. "It's all coming together exactly as I planned. By that time, the fortress should be nearly complete, and I'll have no more need of this lot of troublesome, whiny, malcontents. They'll be all yours after that to perform whatever experiments you desire."

"You're too kind, my lord."

"Of course, there are one or two I will deal with personally, or rather personally watch you deal with, but you'll have all the test subjects you need for a good long time."

The other man shifted, and Aedan thought he caught the glint of torchlight in his eyes. "And I'm sure, in the future, you could benefit highly from my findings."

"Indeed," Vayzar agreed with a wicked grin.

"Then, if you have no more need of me, my lord, I will take my leave."

Vayzar waved his hand, and the man turned toward the door. Aedan backed away, eyes searching the surroundings. He had no place to hide. Taking a deep breath, he turned and walked back the way he'd come, resisting the urge to go faster. This was his first test at blending in. A moment later, the door opened and closed behind him. He held his breath and waited a moment before glancing over his shoulder just in time to see the man disappear down the hall to the right.

Aedan stopped now, breathing out. The man put a knot of dread deep in the pit of his stomach, but something pressed him to find out what part he played in Vayzar's schemes. Praying this wouldn't be a foolish action, he turned back again. He peeked around the corner. The man was barely visible up ahead.

With complete silence, Aedan trailed him from behind, keeping to the shadows. After two turns, the man descended a dark stairwell. Approaching with extreme caution, Aedan peered down, seeing the faint glow of torchlight. Dank air wafted up, carrying with it the sickly sweet smell of death. The knot in his stomach jerked tighter. Common sense urged him not to go any farther, but he pushed on. One carefully placed step at a time, he descended into the bowels of the fortress. A growing stench of rot assailed his senses, burning his eyes and nose. He put his arm over his nose and mouth, holding back the need to cough.

At last, he reached the bottom and found the torchlight coming from the end of a hall, which took a sharp turn to the left. He took a step and realized on either side of him were dark cells. The light wasn't bright enough to tell if any contained prisoners, but Aedan swallowed hard, his apprehension rising.

Steeling himself, he moved on toward the bend in the hall. When at last he reached it, he peered around a corner into a massive circular chamber, more like a cave than a room. Dozens of candles burned from a large chandelier hanging in the center and several tall lampstands. The right side of the room held tables and shelves piled high with parchments, books, various sized bottles and bowls, and a stunning array of plants and vials.

It didn't appear all that threatening until Aedan's eyes took in the fixtures at the opposite side of the chamber. Multiple devices used for torture loomed ominously. Along the wall hung various whips, chains, blades, and other pain inflicting instruments. Aedan's heart lodged in his throat and his tongue stuck to the roof of his mouth. Cold, numbing fear speared through his body when he imagined what took place here.

His eyes pulled away from the torturous machines and locked onto movement. The man he'd followed stood at one of the tables, meticulously measuring out unidentifiable substances into a large vial. The mixture bubbled and hissed as he held it up to the candlelight. An acidic odor filled the room.

The man's back was to Aedan, but he turned suddenly. Aedan pressed himself against the wall and held his breath. Utter silence surrounded him. His hand went up to the hilt of his sword, his heart about to break through his ribs. He bit down hard, praying with all his heart he hadn't been seen.

At last, he heard the man mixing his concoction and barely held back a sigh. Feeling he'd pressed his luck as far as he was willing to, Aedan turned and fled the nightmarish dungeon. But the scene had left an indelible mark on his mind, and he knew that it was likely his fate if things went awry.

:Chapter Sixteen:

The Meeting

Adding more shading to her sketch, Makilien glanced at Tanzim and grinned to herself. The Shaike was even more bored than she was so he'd decided to try his hand at sketching. He hunched over his drawing, shielding it from view with his massive forearm as he scribbled away. Makilien had tried to peek once, but he grunted in protest and pulled the sketch closer. His thick, black brows crunched low in deep concentration, making him look especially fierce.

Makilien refocused on her sketch, still smiling. The quiet around them continued until Tanzim let out a sudden growl and crumpled his paper. His yellow eyes turned to Makilien.

"I can't do it," he complained with a pout.

Makilien fought back a rising giggle. "It's all right, Tan." She tried to keep the mirth out of her voice. "It takes a lot of time and practice."

With a grin, she slid her drawing around in front of the Shaike—a drawing of him. Tanzim picked it up gingerly with his fingertips and studied it.

"Hmm," he rumbled. "This is good."

"Thank you. You can keep it if you want."

Pleased, the Shaike carefully rolled up the sketch.

Now Makilien glanced at Sophine who just sat listening with an intrigued expression. Hearing the pause in their conversation, the woman asked, "Tanzim, I'm sure this will sound very strange, but may I . . . well . . . touch your face?"

Tanzim cocked an eyebrow and gave Makilien a confused and rather comical look. Makilien had to bite her lip to keep from laughing out loud.

"You see," Sophine went on, "I never saw or met a Shaike before I was blind. Touch is the only way I can get an idea of what someone looks like."

Still perfectly perplexed, Tanzim muttered, "I guess . . . if you want to . . ."

Smiling, Sophine rose and moved around the table. She put her hand out, moving it through the air until she found Tanzim's face. With a light touch, she ran her fingers over his distinct features. Tanzim sat like a stone statue. His gaze followed her movements, eyes wide as if something terrible were about to befall him.

Makilien couldn't hold back any longer and burst into laughter. "She's not going to bite you, Tanzim."

Sophine stepped back, chuckling, and Tanzim glowered at Makilien.

"No indeed," Sophine said. "You have nothing to fear from me."

Tanzim sat, a little embarrassed, but Makilien saw a smile threatening to break out. Sophine moved back around to her chair, still chuckling softly.

A hard knock at the door startled them. Their mirth vanished. Makilien's eyes jumped from Sophine to Tanzim in alarm. The knock sounded again.

"Open in the name of Lord Vayzar!"

Makilien gasped, blood running cold. Had they discovered she was hiding here? What if something had happened to Beregon?

Her panicked thoughts were cut short when Sophine urgently instructed, "Get down in the cellar, quickly."

"But you'll be all alone," Makilien replied.

"If they don't find you, I'll be fine," Sophine said. "Now go before they come in."

They had no time to argue. Makilien hurried to the center of the kitchen floor and threw back the rug. Lifting the trap-door, she motioned for Tanzim.

"Come on."

The Shaike, eyes narrowed, glanced toward the hall at another demanding knock, but followed Makilien. Once they were both in the cellar, Makilien pulled the door closed. The thin shafts of light that streamed through the cracks disappeared when Sophine pushed the rug back into place. Her light footsteps creaked overhead and disappeared down the hall.

Perched on the steps, Makilien pressed her ear against the door, praying desperately for Sophine's safety. She'd be devastated if anything happened to the woman on her account. She and Tanzim sat still in the darkness, holding their breaths. Makilien caught the sound of the door opening and voices. Her heart raced, though she tried to calm it in order to catch the spoken words.

". . . looking for a girl. She escaped one of Lord Vayzar's men two days ago."

"What do you want here?" Sophine questioned.

"We've been ordered to search everywhere she could be hiding. We need to search your house."

"Please, can you wait until my husband returns?"

"No."

Heavy footsteps entered the house. Makilien gulped and ducked low as they came into the kitchen. The slight metallic ring of Tanzim's sword hissed in the darkness. Makilien's heart beat into her ribcage, her eyes going to where the other sword lay. Her muscles tensed, ready to lunge for the weapon if the door opened. Painfully long seconds passed. Another set of footsteps entered the kitchen.

"Find anything?" The voice came from right above.

"No."

The footsteps shifted. "Whose horses are in the shed?"

"My husband was re-shoeing them. He left a short time ago to help with Lord Vayzar's fortress."

Silence followed. *Please, let them leave,* Makilien pleaded. At last, the footsteps left the kitchen and deafening silence came again. Worry was beginning to creep in, but then Sophine opened the cellar door.

"They are gone."

Makilien breathed a great sigh of relief and climbed out. Tanzim followed, returning his sword to the scabbard.

Aedan couldn't have been happier to find the rear exit door. The winding halls and passages of the huge fortress were confusing, but, after wandering around all afternoon, he had a good layout of the structure in his mind. He had not come across his father in all his searching, but he had passed several men who paid him no heed.

Easing open the door, he slipped outside. Dusk had settled over the courtyard. The ringing of a hammer came from up ahead where Beregon was at work in the forge. Before moving from the door, he surveyed the area. He found the man assigned to watch the blacksmith, but his back was to Aedan. Other guards lazed around nearby, but had no interest in him. He looked to the wall and the men there under guard. Finally, his eyes shifted to his right and found the stockade.

Glancing once more at Beregon's guard, he headed off toward the structure, though he did not make it apparent that was his destination. Once past it and out of sight, he veered around behind the enclosure. Here he took note of its construction. The gaps in the palisade were not wide enough to escape through, but they would be wide enough to have a conversation with someone inside. He walked closer and peered through one of the gaps. It was quiet and empty, but likely wouldn't be for long as the sun neared the horizon. He tested one of the stakes, but it was solid.

Working his way back around, Aedan found a spot where he could remain out of sight, but still watch the gate where the men would come through. Crossing his arms, he leaned back against the wall of the fortress, appearing like the others who were whiling away their time.

Darkness grew. Before the sunlight disappeared entirely, Beregon left the forge. He glanced once at Aedan, but did not let his gaze linger. Once he was gone, the courtyard was quieter, though the sounds of nighttime bugs had set in.

Aedan stayed on alert and soon his vigilance paid off. The sound of dozens of footsteps and chains approached the fortress. In a moment, the men entered through the gate. Aedan stood up straight, his heart beating more rapidly. With eager eyes, he searched the faces of each man. He waited and waited for a familiar face. Then, near the end of the line, Sirion came into view.

Aedan drew in his breath. He hadn't doubted Makilien, but seeing Sirion alive, in the flesh, made it real. Scanning the entire area, he took a deep breath and strode forward. Keeping his head down, he walked along the line of men as they made their way to the stockade. Just before he came to Sirion, he looked up. Their eyes met for just a moment. He kept moving, but glanced back as Sirion did. Aedan gave him the slightest nod before staring straight ahead as he made his way into the shadows at the base of the wall.

Mind racing and heart pounding, Sirion could barely believe what had just taken place. Joy and hope rushed in so fast he wasn't sure if he could trust what his weary eyes had seen, but he couldn't help himself. For the first time in all these months, he had real hope of escaping this, and he had difficulty keeping a smile from his face.

Inside the stockade, he and Jered were unchained and guards passed out supper as usual, but Sirion's mind was far from eating. Taking the forgotten food with him, he moved to the far side of the stockade. Here, at one of the gaps, he waited to see if his eyes and mind weren't just playing cruel tricks on him. Jered followed and gave him an odd look, but asked no questions.

At last, almost an hour after they'd arrived back at the fortress, Sirion caught a whispered voice through the gap, almost too low to detect.

With joy coming anew, Sirion's gaze swept the stockade, and then he motioned Jered closer.

"Make it look like we're talking."

Many of the men had already settled in for sleep, but Sirion didn't want to jeopardize Aedan's safety. Jered gave him another odd look, but Sirion focused again on the stockade wall.

"Aedan," he murmured.

Following a brief silence he heard, "I'm here."

Sirion breathed out and thanked Elohim.

Jered's eyes grew round and questioning.

"A friend," Sirion told him, a smile finally breaking free.

Jered looked to the dark gap in the palisade and back to Sirion. "You have a friend here?"

"I do now." Sirion glanced to the gap, barely seeing the glint of Aedan's eyes. "When did you get here?"

"Just today. I came with Tanzim." He paused. "Makilien is here in Carel too."

Sirion's heart slammed against his chest, robbing his breath for a moment. She was alive! Relief washed through him, but then something else occurred to him. "How did she get here?"

"Your brother."

Fear stole away the relief, wrapping cold around Sirion's heart, and choking his voice. "Ryelan brought her here to Vayzar?"

"Yes, but she escaped him in the city before they reached the fortress. Don't worry. She's safe," Aedan assured him, knowing how he'd feel if he received similar news concerning Vonawyn. "She is staying with a couple who has been helping her, and Tanzim is with her now too."

Grasping one of the stakes, Sirion released a great sigh and bowed his head, thanking Elohim with all his heart that she was safe. Still, it sickened him to know what Ryelan had done.

"They've been doing everything they can to find a way to get you out of here," Aedan told him. "Others from Elimar should be here soon."

Sirion looked up, wishing he could better see Aedan's expression. With trepidation pounding inside, he asked, "Who survived the battle?"

He heard Aedan sigh and steeled himself.

"Lord Darand and Arphen are dead."

Sirion closed his eyes, tears rising up against the lids as he thought of how devastating this must have been to Eldor. But Aedan's next words brought comfort. "Everyone else survived."

"My uncle and Gilhir?"

"Yes."

Again, Sirion thanked Elohim, filled with both joy and sorrow. Aedan let him have a moment and then asked, "Any ideas on how we can get you out of here?"

"Unfortunately, no," Sirion answered with keen disappointment. The knowledge that Makilien was so close filled him with a gnawing desperation to be free, stronger than any he'd experienced in all these months. He looked at Jered and reality set in once again. "But I can't leave unless we get everyone out."

Aedan said nothing, though Sirion knew he understood.

"Do you know what Vayzar has going on here?" Aedan questioned.

With that prompting, Sirion shared everything he knew about Vayzar's operations, relieved to get the information out to someone who could do something about it.

"I followed Wormaw down to his dungeon today," Aedan said when he finished. "I certainly wouldn't want him loosed on Minarald."

"You must get warning to Darian," Sirion urged him. "He can't let anyone with barrels of strange powder into the city."

"I'll be sure to find a way to get word to him. I'm going to try to get back to Makilien tonight. She'll be anxious for news."

The intense longing to see her filled Sirion's heart once more—longing to see her face, to hear her voice. His memories of her were sadly faded after all this time. With emotion thickening his voice, he said, "Tell her . . ." He paused. Where did he start? "Tell her I miss her . . . more than I can say. And, if I don't see her . . . I still love her with all my heart."

"I will," Aedan replied in a low voice. A moment of silence passed before he spoke again. "She's been grieving for you. We thought you were dead. It nearly crushed her."

Sirion drew in a deep breath, his chest heavy, hating that Makilien had endured such sorrow.

"I'm afraid I don't have much to offer other than the loft in the shed," Beregon told Tanzim apologetically.

Tanzim grunted. "The loft is fine. It's dry. That's all that matters. And I can watch for intruders from there."

Makilien smiled at this. She could only imagine the welcome any unwanted guests would receive. Watching the two of them move down the hall, she sighed. She knew she needed to go to bed too, but she didn't think sleep would come easily knowing Aedan was in the fortress.

She'd barely closed the door to the living room when Beregon called her. She opened it again and looked out. Joy leapt inside her when she saw Aedan on the other side.

"You made it out!"

"Yes. I walked out with some of the men coming to the city looking for entertainment."

Since the hall was now quite crowded, everyone gathered again in the kitchen.

"Were you able to see Sirion?" Makilien asked, eyes bright with hope.

"Yes," Aedan told her. "I was able to speak with him through the palisade."

Makilien put her hand to her mouth and tears sprang to her eyes. Drawing a shaky breath, she lowered her hand and asked, "What did he say?"

"He told me what he knew about Vayzar. The man has quite a scheme to destroy Eldor and assume control."

"Seriously?"

Aedan nodded, and they sat at the table. For the next hour, they discussed everything he had learned from Sirion and what he'd seen in the fortress. One thing they knew for certain, word needed to get to Eldor.

"I would think your friends should arrive here any day," Beregon said. "I'm sure one of them will know how to send a warning."

"I'll go if I have to," Tanzim said, determination adding a little growl to his voice.

"We'll see what they have to say when they arrive," Makilien replied. "It would be best to send more than one person. At least it doesn't seem that Vayzar has sent any of this powder yet."

The others nodded.

Wearied and with nothing more to discuss, everyone rose to head to their sleeping quarters. At the living room door, Aedan paused with Makilien and let Tanzim go on out to the shed. Makilien stared up at him, waiting for what more he had to say.

Resting his hands on her shoulders, he looked down into her eager face, knowing how deeply his words would affect her. "Sirion had more he wanted me to tell you. He wants you to know he has missed you more than he can say and still loves you with all his heart."

Makilien's breath caught in her lungs and tears flooded her eyes, spilling over her eyelids. After everything she had been through with Ryelan, those words meant the world to her. A quiet sob broke free, aching to see him. Aedan drew her into a comforting embrace.

"I want to get him out so badly, Aedan," she cried softly.

"We will, Elohim willing."

:Chapter Seventeen:

Ultimatum

"I'm going to look for my father today," Aedan said, finishing the last of his breakfast. "He has to be in the fortress somewhere."

Makilien speared a bite of eggs with her fork, but didn't bring it to her mouth, concern obvious in her expression. "You don't think he'll turn you in to Vayzar, do you?"

"I don't know," Aedan answered honestly. "I seemed to get through to him once. I only hope I can again."

Makilien exchanged a worried glance with Tanzim. Neither one was comfortable with the situation.

"I shoulda been with you when you confronted him," the Shaike said.

Aedan gave him a half smile. "I know, but this is how it has to be. And this is something *I* have to settle between the two of us."

Tanzim let out a low rumble of displeasure in his throat, but said no more.

Aedan pushed back his chair. "I'll see Sirion again tonight and try to come back here."

With purposely optimistic goodbyes, he left the house, and those who remained continued their breakfast. Makilien, however, had lost her appetite.

Just before the others finished, a knock sounded at the door. Everyone stilled. It was a firm knock, though not as hard and demanding as the one the day before. Beregon looked around the table, noting the apprehensive expressions, and pushed to his feet. "Stay out of sight. It's probably just a customer."

He walked down the hall and Makilien, Tanzim, and Sophine sat and listened. The door opened.

"Can I help you?"

"Are you Beregon?" a male voice replied.

Makilien gasped. "Halandor!" she exclaimed before Beregon had a chance to answer.

She jumped up from the table and hurried around the corner. Through the open door, she caught sight of beloved faces. She raced out of the house, right into her father's waiting arms.

"Makilien! Thank Elohim you're safe," Néthyn breathed in her ear, embracing her tightly. Holding her at arm's length, he looked her over, assuring himself that she truly was unharmed.

Makilien beamed a smile up at him. She then gave Halandor a hug as well, and greeted everyone who had come to rescue her. With her father and Halandor were Torick, Loron, Elandir, and Elmorhirian.

"I am so thankful you are here," she said. "There is much I need your help with."

"Please, everyone come inside," Beregon invited and led the way.

Stepping into the hall, Makilien's friends noticed Tanzim at the far end.

"Tan, what are you doing here?" Halandor asked in surprise as he stepped into the kitchen.

"Me an' Aedan got here yesterday. His father's here in Carel. We came to get the horses re-shod and Makilien came bursting outta the house like she did just now."

Makilien chuckled. "Well, you can hardly blame me." Then, she immediately turned more serious, casting anxious eyes on her father. "Is Leiya all right? Did she make it back to the city safely?"

"She's fine," Néthyn assured her. "She is terribly worried about you, but she is safe."

Makilien breathed out a deep sigh. Now her gaze fell on Halandor. "What about Darian? He was still all right when you left?"

Halandor nodded. "Yes, he was fine."

Now that Makilien was assured everyone was safe, her friends had their own questions to ask.

"So where is Aedan now?" Torick wanted to know.

"He's looking for his father, but that's only half of it. We've discovered now who is responsible for the attacks in Eldinorieth." Makilien paused for only a moment. "Vayzar."

"The man who was going to kill your family in Reylaun?" Torick asked.

She wrinkled her nose in disgust. "Yes, him. He's behind all of this, and he wants to gain control of Eldor. He's working on a secret weapon to do just that."

Brows rose at this, and as soon as the necessary introductions were made, everyone found a place in the kitchen, eager to hear all Makilien had to tell.

Voices carried from around the corner, echoing off the stones. Aedan crept down the hall, cautious should it be someone he'd rather not meet. Closer now, he recognized Vayzar's voice, and was glad of his caution.

"You're familiar with Eldinorieth," the man was saying. "Perhaps I'll send you there."

"Whatever you wish, my lord."

Aedan froze. It was his father—he was sure of it.

"Then again, perhaps I should send a couple of the others . . . yes, that would be better. I swear, some of these men don't have brains in their skulls. Best not waste any who can actually think, like you." Vayzar paused. "Go find Roark. I need the two of you to find something for the men to do. Put them to work on the wall if you have to. Lazing around all day is going to make them soft."

"Yes, my lord."

Footsteps drew near. Aedan hurried back, slipping into a dark doorway. Only a moment later, his father passed by. Breathing deeply in and out, Aedan waited to be sure Vayzar had not come this way. When he was sure, he stepped out and followed his father. Halfway down the long, dim hall, he had almost caught up. His heart pounded. He'd waited almost a year for this. Taking another deep breath, he spoke.

"Father."

Jaeson halted mid-stride and spun around. Torchlight flickered in his wide eyes. Aedan's emotions flooded up at seeing his father's face once again, but so did his determination. He would not let his father slip away this time.

Things needed to be settled between them, one way or another.

"Aedan," Jaeson gasped, eyes darting back up the hall before landing on his son. "What are you doing here?"

"I've been looking for you," Aedan answered, approaching him slowly, but deliberately.

His father took one step back, hand rising to grasp the hilt of his sword. "So you're the one who's been following me these months."

"Yes." Aedan stopped now, keeping his hands firmly at his sides. This was it, the moment he had gone over so many times in his mind, yet anything he had rehearsed or planned escaped him.

Jaeson shook his head in regret. "You shouldn't have come here." He slid his sword from the scabbard, the hiss of the blade especially menacing in the dark hall. "I'm going to have to take you to Vayzar."

Aedan glanced at the glinting blade, but did not move, eyes rising to hold his father's gaze. "You know what will happen to me if you do. I'll be made to slave away in the stone quarry until Vayzar is finished with me, or I'll be sent straight down to the dungeon. Either way I'll end up tortured to death by Wormaw. Is that truly what you want?"

He reached back now and withdrew his sword. Jaeson raised his defensively, but Aedan took his own by the blade and extended the hilt toward his father. "Would you really deliver your son into the hands of a monster like Wormaw? If so, take it. I will not resist you."

He held the sword, unmoving. His heart hammered with each second as he awaited his father's choice. He had never planned it this way, but this was what it had come down to. His father had to choose.

Jaeson stared at the hilt and then into his son's eyes. A million conflicting thoughts raced through his mind and played on his face. Which would win out? His loyalty to Vayzar or some small bit of caring for his son, buried deep down, but still just within reach.

Jaeson reached out and grasped the hilt. Aedan's jaw clenched and his heart seized a moment, but he forced himself to remain still. Eyes locked on his son's, Jaeson just stood for a moment. Finally, he let his fingers slip from the sword.

"Do you have any idea the risk you've taken by coming here?" he demanded in a sharp whisper.

Aedan released a great breath. "Yes, I know."

Jaeson scowled. "You are a fool for coming after me."

"You are my father. I needed to speak with you."

Jaeson's expression softened for a fleeting moment before hardening again as he jerked his head. "This way."

Returning his sword to the scabbard, Aedan followed him down the hall. At a door, they stopped. Jaeson reached for a torch and pushed the door open.

"Inside."

Aedan stepped into the dark room. His father looked up and down the hall before walking in after him, closing the door. He turned to Aedan, the torch casting a circle of light around them while everything else lay in darkness.

"Why would you need to speak with me?" Jaeson asked, expression guarded.

Aedan put his hands on his hips. "The night on the battle-field, you were considering what I said. I could see it."

Jaeson shook his head and wouldn't look Aedan in the eyes. "That was almost a year ago."

But Aedan wouldn't take that as an answer. "Don't try to tell me you haven't thought of it since then, at least once."

Jaeson threw his hand out in a frustrated gesture. "What difference does it make?"

"Just because you served Zirtan doesn't mean you have to continue on this path," Aedan told him. "You can turn from it."

"You don't know what you're asking," Jaeson replied, once again avoiding his son's eyes.

"I'm asking for my father," Aedan said, voice suddenly raw with emotion. "I know you see the evil in this. I know you know it's wrong. You—"

"Enough." Jaeson looked at him, eyes intense, but mixed with pain. "You're asking too much. Now, you need to leave immediately. I can't guarantee your safety."

Aedan shook his head stubbornly. "I can't leave."

"Why not?"

"I have my reasons."

"Then your fate is of your own making."

Jaeson turned away and reached for the door.

"I won't give up on you."

Aedan's father paused, hand resting on the knob, but he did not turn back. Two heartbeats later, he opened the door and walked away without a word.

"We have to find a way to stop Vayzar and get Sirion and the other captives out of the fortress," Makilien said, voice firm with determination. "We also must get a warning to Darian as quickly as possible. Who knows when Vayzar might send some of the shadelin powder."

Halandor nodded and replied, "The warning will be the easy part. Carmine came with us. He's staying out of sight a couple miles from the city. We can send him back to Eldor with the news."

Makilien breathed a sigh of relief. "Perfect. He'll be able to get word to Eldor in only a couple of days." She rested her elbows on the table, looking at her friends, eyes searching. "Now, what do you think we can do about Sirion?"

Halandor considered this question and how best to answer, knowing the emotion behind it. "We will have to scout the area around the fortress and get an idea of where an escape might be possible."

"Aedan said he has a pretty good idea of the fortress's layout. Maybe when he returns, he could describe it and I can draw it," Makilien suggested.

"Good idea. And maybe he can search for any weaknesses in Vayzar's defense."

"I'm sure he will do that."

"You'll have to be careful to stay out of sight," Beregon warned them. "If Ryelan sees one of you, he and Vayzar will take measures to counter any rescue attempts."

They agreed. Secrecy was critical.

"Looks like we'll have to rely heavily on what you, Aedan, and Sirion can tell us," Torick said.

Ryelan squeezed his fists so hard his knuckles whitened. "Answer, man, or I'll personally drag you off to Lord Vayzar myself."

The grubby old shopkeeper peered up at him through half-closed eyes.

"'Aven't seen any young women," he said finally, proving he truly could speak after uttering a bunch of unhelpful grunting and shrugging. "Ain't been that lucky."

Ryelan growled. He had a good mind to hit the man for his trouble. Turning, he stormed out of the dingy shop and halted in the street, about ready to plow his fist into the first thing unfortunate enough to cross his path. He muttered under his breath. *Where is she?* At this point, he would have gladly given up the frustrating search had Vayzar not once again threatened Irynna.

He glared at every person and building within sight, mentally demanding that each one of them to give up Makilien's location. He was running out of places to look, yet she had to be somewhere in the city. The gate guards had reported no sign of any women attempting to leave. *Someone is harboring her*, he thought, gritting his teeth. *And when I find out who. . .*

His eyes caught on Derrin coming up the street. Though he doubted it, Ryelan asked, "Did you find her?"

"No," Derrin mumbled.

Ryelan looked at him hard. He wasn't so sure anymore that Derrin would tell him if he did. Catching the Half-Elf's glare, Derrin said more firmly, "No, I did not find her, and I didn't find anyone who has seen her."

Ryelan blew out an angry breath. "She can't have just disappeared."

He turned and marched down the street toward the fortress. Derrin followed.

"You're doing this to protect Irynna, aren't you?" he asked. "And you do realize how your brother would feel if he knew you're trying to hunt down the woman *he* loves?"

Ryelan caught Derrin by the arm and jerked him to a halt. "Do not talk to me about my brother. *I* am the one who stopped *you* from killing him, remember? So don't press your luck with me."

With a final glare, he marched on, his face set in a scowl, cursing Derrin for reminding him of his already sorely bothered conscience.

Back at the fortress, Ryelan came across Irynna on his way in.

"I take it you didn't find anything," she said, expression drawn.

Ryelan shook his head, stopping to face her.

"We have to do something, Ryelan." Desperation leaked out in her tone. "I will not be made a slave again."

"I know. I'm doing everything I can," he replied, voice clipped in frustration and concern over the situation.

Irynna gave him a disbelieving look. "Not everything."

Ryelan opened his mouth to dispute that, but Irynna stepped closer, her voice lowering cautiously. "The two of us could leave here. Run away. Leave Vayzar and live our own lives."

Ryelan released a heavy sigh and shook his head. "I can't."

Irynna's brows drew together. "Why not?"

"I . . . I just can't."

The look of hurt on Irynna's face nearly killed him.

"Makilien was right, you know," she said, the hurt coming out in her voice. "You don't owe anyone anything. And men like Vayzar, they just want to use you."

Ryelan shook his head and looked away from her. How did he explain that he felt trapped, unable to escape this web of cruelty, lies, and evil he'd been a part of all these years?

When he did not speak, Irynna's disapproving frown deepened, further wounding him. Voice still low, but edged with frustration, she said, "Someday, Ryelan, you are going to have to decide where your loyalties lie—with those you care about or with men like Vayzar." She backed away. "Know this, I will not wait around to be enslaved again. If I have to, I'll go . . . with or without you."

Her last words were spoken with a slight tremor, but she didn't wait for a response before turning and walking away. Ryelan stood silent as her footsteps faded and felt the weight of everything crushing down on him.

Silver moonlight illuminated the streets as Aedan made his way back to Beregon's shop. It would have been a peaceful night if not for the raucous laughter that erupted every so often, and the wicked nightlife roaming the streets. Alert for anyone who might want to make trouble, Aedan was confident in his ability to defend himself, but his trip was still a tense one.

At last, he arrived at the house, welcomed by the warm light of the small windows. He went to the door and knocked quietly. As soon as Beregon let him in, familiar voices came from the kitchen, drawing him deeper into the house.

"You made it," he said, walking in and smiling at his friends.

"Aedan," Torick replied with pleasure, "Good to see you."

Smiling a little wider, he said, "Good to see you too. When did you get here?"

"They showed up just after you left," Makilien told him.

Elmorhirian rose. "Here, Aedan, sit."

"I won't take your spot."

"Please. I've just been sitting around most of the day anyway."

Aedan smiled and sat down.

"Any news?" Makilien asked.

"I found my father and was able to speak to him."

Everyone looked at him with interest, and Torick asked, "How did that go?"

Aedan shrugged, wishing he had better news. "He's conflicted, I know he is, but he won't turn from Vayzar, yet. But I don't believe he will turn me in. I'll keep trying to get through to him, if I can."

"Well, at least he let you go," Torick said, and the others agreed.

"What about Sirion?" Makilien wanted to know. "Were you able to talk to him again?"

Aedan nodded

"How is he?"

"He was tired," Aedan told her, debating how specific to be. He hated to burden her further. "I guess it was a long day. The sun is brutal on the men."

He could see the hurt on her face to think of Sirion slaving away so hard every day.

"He told me that he and the other men inside the stockade have been planning an uprising," Aedan went on.

"How many men are there?" Halandor asked, interested with this bit of information.

"About fifty. They wouldn't be able to get weapons, but they have the hammers they use at the quarry."

Halandor settled back in his chair, expression thoughtful. "We could work together with them to overthrow Vayzar. Obviously, we can't attack Vayzar's fortress alone, but if we join the captive men, we might be able to pull it off. How many men does Vayzar have?"

"I'm not sure, but there doesn't seem to be many. Around a hundred, I'm guessing."

"Maybe tomorrow you can discuss it with Sirion. If you can, you'll need to scout out the fortress for us, and let us know of any potential weaknesses."

Aedan nodded. "I'll do whatever I can. No one seems to take much notice of my presence."

"Do you think you can describe the layout of the fortress well enough for me to draw?" Makilien asked.

"Roughly, sure."

Beregon brought Makilien a piece of paper, and Sophine was dishing up a plate of supper for Aedan when someone tapped on the door. They paused. Makilien was getting quite paranoid about all these unexpected interruptions, but she felt a little better now that her friends where here and prepared to fight if need be. Beregon went to the door.

"Come in," he said quietly.

A moment later, Jorin entered the kitchen and came to an abrupt halt, not expecting the group that met him. No one said a word. Jorin eyed each of them, uncertain of their reactions, and Makilien sensed the rising tension and suspicion in the room.

Beregon came in behind, and Jorin turned to him, finally breaking the awkward silence. "I came to see if you'd been able to get Makilien out of the city."

"Things have turned out a little differently, as you can see. We're discussing how to stop Vayzar . . . if you'd care to join us."

Jorin's eyes darted around the room once again, taking in the guarded stares. "I'm not sure I'm welcome."

Feeling for him, Makilien looked at her friends. She couldn't blame them for their mistrust, but she tried to convey her own acceptance of the man. Her gaze met her father's, holding it for a moment. Understanding the message, he looked up at Jorin. "You saved my daughter. That's enough for me."

With these words, the others nodded their agreement.

"Very well," Jorin murmured and joined them at the table, though he didn't appear completely at ease.

Silence fell again. Makilien was unsure what to say. To see her once bitter enemy sitting amongst her friends was a sight to behold.

She was relieved when Beregon got things going. "Jorin, have you ever been inside Vayzar's fortress?"

"No."

"We're trying to figure out as much about it and its weaknesses as we can. Both Aedan and I can get inside, but I'm watched and Aedan has to be cautious not to be seen by Vayzar."

Jorin stared at the table as if debating for a long moment. When he looked up, Makilien caught a look of cunning in his eyes, though not one of evil intent. "Maybe I can help. If I could get in and speak with Vayzar, he might think it worth it to have someone who worked so close to Zirtan."

Glances were passed around the table, but it was Halandor who said, "The more eyes and ears we have inside, the better. You might be allowed to roam freely and could learn even more than Aedan if Vayzar were to include you in his plans."

Jorin agreed. "Get me out of the city and I will see what I can do."

:Chapter Eighteen:

A Valuable Asset

"**A**s soon as you have an opening, go. I'm not sure how long I'll be able to keep their attention."

Beregon glanced over his shoulder at Jorin who nodded. He took one last look around the corner, eyeing the guards at the gate before facing the other man fully.

"This is a good thing you're doing."

Jorin said nothing in response, and neither did his expression change. Beregon knew he should get going, but lingered a moment longer, putting a hand on Jorin's shoulder. "Remember our conversations. None of us knows our end, especially in circumstances such as these. Once it's over, it's too late to consider the things we always pushed from our minds while we were here."

Still, Jorin did not respond, but Beregon prayed he listened. Leaving it at that, he walked on, around the other side of the building. When he reached the main street, he approached the gate, but instead of passing through, he walked up to one of the guards and motioned for the other. They frowned, giving each other a questioning look, before the farther one came closer. Beregon lowered his voice to force them to pay close attention to him.

"On my way here, I saw a suspicious group down one of the streets."

"What do you mean, suspicious?" one of the guards asked, frown deepening.

Beregon shrugged. "They just seemed suspicious. I know Vayzar is searching for a girl, and one of them could have been a woman."

"Which street?" the guard asked more enthusiastically.

Beregon turned and pointed. "About three streets back that way."

Glancing past the men, he caught a glimpse of Jorin sneaking through the gate.

Beregon gave another shrug. "It was probably nothing, but I thought I'd let you know so you can keep an eye out."

"Thanks," the guard said, their attention still focused down the street.

Pleased, Beregon went on through the gate, though he lingered to give Jorin time to get inside the fortress.

There would be no sneaking past the fortress guards so Jorin squared his shoulders and approached them directly. After all, he'd once commanded men like this.

"I am here to see Vayzar," he said straight-out.

He met their suspicious gaze with a cold look. One guard withdrew his sword and used the tip of it to push back Jorin's hair. The man snorted. "I thought I'd seen you before. You're a slave," he said scornfully. "Where's your pass to leave the city?"

Jorin glared at him in disdain. "I don't have one."

"Then how did you get out?"

"Doesn't matter. This should be enough to get me inside." He yanked down his sleeve to show his tattoo. "I was one of Zirtan's right-hand men. My brother led his army. I'm offering Vayzar my expertise. You can either take me to him or explain to him why you turned me away."

The guard contemplated this. Either way presented the chance of angering his master. At last, he scowled and ordered the other guard, "Watch the gate. I'll take him inside."

Jorin followed his escort into the fortress. In a few minutes, they arrived in the throne room. Vayzar looked up when they entered. Irritation flashed across his face at being interrupted while meeting with a group of his advisors.

"Excuse me, my lord, but he insisted on seeing you," the guard said apologetically, gesturing back.

Vayzar's eyes swung past him, widening a little. "Jorin. What are you doing here?"

He stepped past the guard. "I came to offer my service."

"Is that so?" Vayzar replied, an eyebrow rising. "And what makes you think I would want it? You've already proven unreliable, which is why I never sought you out in the first place."

"My lord, I served Zirtan loyally for many years," Jorin responded heatedly. "Makilien may have escaped me—"

"Twice," Vayzar inserted.

"And both instances were entirely out of my control," Jorin stood his ground. He had no intention of backing down, dangerous or not. "We were attacked by surprise, and the second time I only just escaped with an arrow in my back. What do you propose I should have done differently?"

Vayzar narrowed his eyes. No one dared talk to him like that, and he wasn't sure what to think of it. "Very well, point taken." He considered this for a moment, sizing Jorin up, and realized the benefit of having the man around. "All right, I'll give you a second, or should I say, *third* chance? You could be useful to me." He looked to the guard who had brought Jorin in. "Inform Jorin's master I have need of him and that he is therefore no longer his slave. If he has a problem with that, convince him it's not worth pursuing."

"Yes, my lord."

The guard left, and Vayzar's attention returned to Jorin, a cold light of satisfaction in his eyes. "Actually, I already have an assignment for you. After you get changed, I want you to find Ryelan and join in the hunt for Makilien. She got loose somewhere in the city, and I want her found. At least you know what she looks like and whatever you lacked in your ability to follow through, you made up for in your zeal to catch her." He paused, looking at Jorin closely. "I'm sure you get around and hear things. You haven't heard or seen anything about her that I should be aware of, have you?"

Jorin stood silent for two heartbeats. "No."

"Too bad." Vayzar turned to a burly, dark haired man at his side. "Roark, show him around and get him some more suitable clothing."

The man nodded. As he and Jorin turned to leave, Vayzar had a few last words for Jorin. "Bring me Makilien and you'll prove yourself to be a very valuable asset to me. One deserving of a place among my inner circle once I have control of Eldor."

Jorin looked over his shoulder, contemplating these words. With a nod, he continued after the other man.

Derrin skulked down the hall, half hoping Ryelan wouldn't find him. No doubt the Half-Elf would want to resume the search for Makilien immediately. But even if Derrin managed to avoid him for a short time, it would only make Ryelan more ill-tempered. He sighed. Since when had he become Ryelan's dog to be ordered and kicked around and expected to obey? He grumbled under his breath. So much for the power and respect he had been promised.

A glint of light flashed at the corner of his eye. In an instant, a sharp blade pressed against his throat. He froze, staring down at the sword. Swallowing, his eyes rose to the holder. His mouth opened, but it took a moment for his voice to follow.

"Aedan?"

Aedan moved around in front of him, the point of his sword still hovering around Derrin's chest.

"Wh-what are you doing here?" Derrin stammered eyes searching the shadows to see if he was alone.

"If I believed I could trust you, I might tell you . . . but I don't."

Derrin winced. For some reason, that declaration cut unexpectedly deep. "Is it for Sirion?"

Aedan did not answer, his face hard, and Derrin caught the threat in it. He shook his head. "I won't tell Vayzar you are here."

"Why not?" Aedan questioned, voice cold. "Wouldn't your new master be pleased with you for bringing him that kind of information?"

Derrin let out a deep sigh. "I never had anything against you, Aedan." Truly, he was the only one Derrin had ever counted a friend.

Yet, Aedan shook his head, expression never softening. "But you want to hurt the people I care about. What hurts them, hurts me."

Derrin dropped his gaze and nodded slowly, realizing just how big the gap between them had grown since the last time they had been face to face—since Aedan had fought to save his life in the cave.

"Is it as you thought it would be?" Aedan asked, and Derrin's eyes jumped back to his face. "All the killing, and the torture, and the suffering? Has it made you the man you wanted to be?"

Derrin swallowed hard, his stomach convulsing at the very thought. "No," he said, barely loud enough for Aedan to hear.

Aedan lowered his sword, only now believing the regret he sensed in the other man. Before he could say anything, someone approached. Aedan looked up the hall and slid his sword back into the scabbard. With one final look at Derrin, he walked away.

Derrin watched him go. Something inside him cried out as if his one-time friend held the key to escaping this entire mess. He wanted to go after him, to ask—no *beg*—for help, but he stayed frozen in place. Could he escape this? Or was he in too deep? He realized in a far corner of his mind, he was afraid. Afraid of what would happen if Vayzar caught him turning.

Coward. The biting word cut through him.

Derrin ground his teeth together. Adding to the miserable situation, someone barked his name. He looked over his shoulder as Ryelan marched up to him.

"Where have you been?" he demanded, voice like ice.

Derrin didn't answer.

"You know we have to keep searching for Makilien, now come on."

Shoulders sagging, Derrin followed obediently. He glanced back once, but Aedan was gone.

Aedan slipped out the back door just after darkness had fallen. Easing it closed, he scanned the courtyard. All was quiet and shadowed. With great caution, he snuck around the stockade. Sirion and Jered were waiting for him. They greeted each other quietly, and Aedan said, "Good news. Halandor showed up yesterday with Torick, Loron, Néthyn, and Elandir and Elmorhirian. That brings the total to thirteen of us now."

Sirion mentally tallied everyone. "Who is thirteen?"

"Jorin."

"What?" Sirion said in surprise.

"Yes," Aedan replied. "He came last night and offered to get inside the fortress to gather information for us. I think we can trust him. He did save Makilien after all."

"Well, it's one more person, and I'd far rather have him on our side than Vayzar's."

Aedan agreed. "We talked for a while last night. If you can get the men on board, it seems working together to overthrow Vayzar is our best plan."

"We'll get them on board," Jered said confidently. "What's the alternative? Escape is the only option that doesn't present certain death."

"How soon are we going to act?" Sirion asked.

"I'm sure the sooner the better. Every day Vayzar gets more and more of that shadelin powder and those in the grinding house are that much closer to death. I've been able to explore most of the fortress. I'll bring that information back to everyone and be able to tell you more tomorrow."

"All right. We'll talk to the men tonight."

As they turned away from the wall, Sirion glanced at Jered. A fire of determination and excitement burned in his eyes. Sirion felt the same fire warming the blood pulsing through his body. For the first time, escape was within his grasp. At last, he could see an end to this nightmare. The thought of regaining everything that had been torn away from him made his chest ache with emotion and longing. *Please grant us success, Elohim. Success and protection.*

Just before reaching the shelter, Ren, Tavin, and Jon met them.

"Is something going on?" Ren asked, curiosity lighting his eyes. "You two have been very secretive these last couple nights."

Jered glanced at Sirion and focused on Ren, a wide grin slowly growing on his face. "Gentlemen, we've been given an opportunity to not only escape, but overthrow Vayzar."

The men looked at each other, surprise and excitement now filling their expressions.

"What sort of opportunity?" Ren wanted to know, voice hushed.

"I have a friend inside the fortress," Sirion told them. "And others in the city."

"They are going to help us out?" Jon asked, unable to hide the hope in his voice.

"We are going to help each other," Jered said. "We have to stop Vayzar for good or he'll just capture more men to take our place and continue what he is doing here. I'm not about to see that happen."

"How many friends do you have here?" Ren asked Sirion. "Are there enough to defeat Vayzar?"

"There are quite a few, but it depends on us too. We must work together in this. Then there will be enough. We need everyone in agreement."

"How soon are we going to do this?" Tavin asked.

Face animated, Jered answered, "Probably just a matter of days. We'll know more tomorrow night once Sirion's friends can make more plans. In the meantime, it's up to us to prepare everyone in here."

Jorin's boots echoed in the hall as he strode toward the dining room to meet with Vayzar. For the first time in almost a year, he actually felt human, able to walk around freely and clothed in fresh clothing. He'd forgotten how good it felt.

When he entered, Vayzar was at the table waiting for him. "Did you find anything?"

"No."

Vayzar scowled, and Jorin added, "But rest assured, I will keep searching."

"At least I know you truly want to find her," Vayzar said around a mouthful of food. "I'm beginning to wonder about Ryelan, even after threatening him with the loss of his girl-friend." He motioned to a chair. "Sit. Eat. You must be starving."

Jorin accepted the invitation. After swallowing down a bite of savory chicken, he asked in a nonchalant tone, "What are your plans for Eldor?"

Vayzar ceased eating and settled back in his chair, eyeing Jorin as he decided just how much he wanted to trust him. Concluding he had no reason not to, he dove into the expla-nation with a good bit of self-satisfaction over his cleverly devised scheme. "A couple years ago, I came into contact with an alchemist—a truly frightful individual with my sense of vision. He told me he was working on a powder that, when burned, could wipe out an entire city if there was enough of it.

"Naturally, I searched him out after the battle and he agreed to partner with me. I am providing him with the materials to create the powder as well as test subjects for his various other experiments. As soon as he has created enough powder, I'll have it secretly delivered to Minarald. Once I've killed off their army, nothing will hinder me from taking over the city. From there, I can easily control the country. The only thing left to deal with is the Elves. They are sure to put up a fuss."

Jorin frowned. "Why not just bring the powder into their city to dispose of them as well?"

In the next moment of silence, an all-together evil smirk grew on Vayzar's face. "You know, Jorin, I believe Zirtan may have been too hasty in discarding you. I like your way of thinking. You're right, of course. The Elves are of no use to me.

They are far too stubborn to submit to my will, so the best way to deal with them is to eliminate them."

Jorin nodded his thanks to the acknowledgement, and both men focused again on the meal. Once Jorin finished eating, however, he rose. "If you'll excuse me, my lord, it's been a long day."

"Of course. Do as you wish. I want you to join Ryelan again in the morning to search."

Inclining his head, Jorin left the dining room, taking the halls to the fortress entrance. Outside, under the faint light of the moon, he crossed the bridge and entered Carel. This time he walked the streets as a free man. Shortly, he came to Beregon's house where he joined everyone in the kitchen.

"How did it go?" Beregon asked.

"It took a little persuading, but Vayzar realized I could be of value to him," Jorin answered. "He had me out searching for Makilien all day, but I was able to speak to him about his plans for Eldor before I left."

"What did he tell you?" Halandor wanted to know.

"He is going to use the powder to destroy the army in Minarald. The only hindrance to his plans is the Elves. I suggested he use the powder to eliminate them."

Elandir choked on the water he'd just swallowed. "You what?"

Jorin rolled his eyes at the Elf's reaction. "The more he trusts me, the more I'll be able to help you."

Elandir rubbed his forehead, horrified at the prospect of Elimar being wiped out.

"Besides," Jorin went on. "It's our plan to stop him before any of the powder ever reaches Eldor, is it not?"

:Chapter Nineteen:

Eve of Escape

"Oh ne more day and we'll be free of here."
Sirion smiled at Jered, barely contained anticipation flowing through him. Only hours lay between them and freedom. His gaze ranged around the shelter. An anxious energy permeated the air. Everyone was ready—ready to put an end to this.

Jered finished his supper and settled comfortably back against the wall. "I don't know about you, but as soon as I'm free, I'm looking forward to a bath, some clean clothes, and taking at least one full day to rest."

Sirion let out a long sigh just thinking about it. There were a million things he could look forward to right now, but what he wanted above all was to see Makilien. To reestablish her face in his mind, and to be reunited with his family and friends, those he cared so much about.

Jered nudged him and grinned. "I'm looking forward to meeting her. After everything I've heard and you've told me, she must really be something."

Sirion's answering smile reflected the deep love held in his heart for Makilien. "Yes," he murmured. Then, remembering it was growing late, he rose. "Aedan will be here soon."

The two of them walked to the palisade, leaving the other men talking quietly of the following day. A few minutes later, Aedan arrived.

"Everything is set," he told them, shared anticipation in his eyes. "Elandir and Elmorhirian will ride to the quarry about an hour after dawn. That is when you attack. As soon as you have taken care of the overseers and are on your way here, the others will attack from the front. Jorin and I will be inside by that time to let everyone in if Vayzar locks the gates."

Sirion drew in a deep breath, attempting to keep his heart from racing with his thoughts. "Sounds good. We'll be ready for Elandir and Elmorhirian."

"Good." Aedan glanced over his shoulder. "I'm going to take one more look through the fortress before I head back to Beregon's." He gave Sirion a quick smile. "I'll see you tomorrow."

Sirion nodded, his own smile coming easier than it had in many months. "See you tomorrow."

With that, Aedan left the palisade behind. He looked up at the pale slice of moon shining overhead and spoke to Elohim. So much rested on the success of their plans—so many lives.

As he'd become accustomed to, he slipped inside the dark, silent fortress for one last reconnaissance mission as he considered their plan of attack. The gate was never heavily guarded; therefore, he did not believe Vayzar could keep anyone out for long. For all the man's cunning, he'd left his main defense open to attack.

Right in the middle of these thoughts, something hard smashed into Aedan's back, shooting pain across his shoulders. Gasping, he fell to his knees.

Beregon set a large burlap sack on the table. "Here's what I was able to gather today. I didn't want to ask around too much. If word reached Vayzar that I was gathering armor, he'd know something was up."

Halandor opened the sack and pulled out two pairs of vambraces, a pair of pauldrons, and a leather breastplate. "This is good," he said. "It's better than no armor at all."

He handed Makilien one pair of the vambraces, which were rather small to be men's. "These should fit you."

Makilien tried them on and nodded. With these final items from Beregon, everyone would have at least some form of protection.

She looked around at her friends. Elandir, Elmorhirian, and Tanzim were sitting in various places sharpening their swords. The others were either inspecting their own weapons or armor. Anticipation tingled in her fingers as she rubbed them along her sword. She didn't know how she would ever be able to sleep that night.

Across the table, Elmorhirian lightly fingered the sharp edge of his blade and slid it into the scabbard with an audible snap. Makilien saw the same eagerness in his eyes.

"Vayzar's going to regret messing with us," he said.

Makilien smirked. Then she noticed Loron looking intently down the hall.

"What is it?" she asked.

"Someone is at the door."

All grew quiet. A slight metallic creak came from the door as the knob turned slowly, but the lock held it shut.

"Aedan and Jorin would have knocked," Halandor murmured.

Makilien's heart pounded with deep thuds, apprehension creeping up her spine. Everyone stood very still. Suddenly, something crashed into the door and the lock broke. The door flew open and men rushed into the house. Swords were drawn in an instant, and Makilien's friends pushed forward to meet them. The echo of blades clashing rang through the small house.

In the commotion, Makilien grabbed Sophine's arm and hurried her to the farthest corner of the kitchen. "Stay down."

Makilien crouched with her, sword drawn in case she had to use it.

"Please, Elohim, protect us," she whispered a desperate prayer for herself and her friends.

Most of the men couldn't even reach the fight because of the narrow hall.

Then Tanzim bellowed, "Move!"

With a roar, he disappeared down the hall and there came several pained and panicked shouts as he forced the fight outside. The rest of the men rushed out, meeting their foes. Makilien wanted to join them, but wouldn't leave Sophine defenseless.

The sound of battle raged, and she continued to pray that her friends wouldn't be overwhelmed, not knowing how many men might be outside. In the thick of it, a man burst into the kitchen. Makilien's heart jumped into her throat when his cruel eyes landed on her and Sophine. She jumped up as he moved toward them. Their swords met with a crash. Hands tingling, Makilien took another swing, but the man sidestepped, forcing her to do the same as she raised her sword to block his next attack.

She never saw it coming. The blunt hilt of another sword jabbed into her unprotected ribs. Sharp pain shot through her chest. She groaned and gasped for air, her sword lowering harmlessly. The man to her left yanked it away.

Sophine cried her name and rose, but the first man backhanded her and she fell to the floor against the wall.

"No!" Makilien cried and rushed toward her, but the other man grabbed her around the waist and clamped his hand over her mouth.

She struggled with all her might, kicking, clawing, doing whatever she could, but it was to no avail. She watched helplessly as the first man pulled a flaming log from the hearth and lit the curtains and tablecloth on fire. Makilien tried to scream, knowing that Sophine would be burned alive if she remained unconscious, but the muffled sound was not loud enough.

The men dragged her to the hall as smoke filled the kitchen. She continued to fight all the way. Her friends were still in the midst of a brutal fight outside, and she could not gain their attention no matter how hard she tried. Keeping to the shadows, the men dragged her away from the shed. Hot tears rolled down her cheeks as the sound of fighting soon faded away behind them.

At last, Halandor's opponent dropped and the remaining men, realizing they were now outnumbered, turned and fled.

"Fire!"

He spun around at Beregon's shout. Smoke poured from the door of the house. Fear gripped him. Makilien and Sophine were still inside. Beregon rushed inside. Néthyn and Halandor were right behind him, calling for the two women. Bursting into the kitchen, the heat and crackling of flames surrounded them. The air was so thick with smoke they could barely see or breathe.

Beregon gasped his wife's name and rushed to the corner. When he turned back to Halandor and Néthyn, his wife lay in his arms.

"Is Makilien back there?" Néthyn asked, eyes trying to see through the haze.

Beregon shook his head. "No."

"Get her out," Halandor told Beregon, and he and Néthyn continued their frantic search for Makilien. They searched all over the kitchen, cellar, bedroom, and living room. By this time, Halandor felt the lack of oxygen stealing away his strength and flames had nearly engulfed the house. He heard Néthyn coughing and took him by the arm.

"She's not here. We have to get out."

The two of them stumbled outside. Their friends waited for them and led them a safe distance from the burning house.

Hands on his knees, Halandor coughed and drank in the cool night air. His eyes and lungs burned from the smoke, but his mind was on Makilien. He looked all around for her.

Nearby, Beregon still held his wife waiting for her to wake up. At last, she began coughing, and in a moment, her eyes opened.

"Beregon?" she gasped.

"It's all right, love. I'm here," he said, gently touching her face.

"Is Makilien safe?"

"I don't know. We can't find her."

"They've taken her," Sophine said with sudden desperation. "Someone came in. I think there were two of them."

Beregon looked at the others, but already Halandor and Néthyn were moving. The rest followed.

Right on the edge of sleep, the sound of the stockade gate banging open woke Sirion with a jolt. He raised his head. A group of men bearing torches marched inside. Everyone sat up, watching their approach, and nervousness trickled through the group. Dread turned to ice in Sirion's stomach. He glanced at Jered, the flicker of torchlight dancing in his eyes.

Reaching the shelter, the guards moved deliberately through to Sirion and Jered's corner. Standing over the two of them, one of the men snapped, "Get up."

Sirion was slow to rise, limbs heavy with growing dismay. His heart pounded hard and painfully against chest, sickening expectation stirring up his stomach and running cold through his veins. On the very eve of escape, something had gone horribly wrong.

The guard grabbed his arm and twisted it around behind his back. A pair of shackles clamped hard around his wrists, bringing a dreaded feeling of helplessness.

"What is going on?" Jered demanded, as he too was chained.

The guards didn't favor either of them with an answer. They shoved them out of the shelter as the rest of the men looked on. Outside the stockade, they entered the fortress. Engulfed by the darkness and stone, Sirion felt all his hope collapse in a devastating heap. He hung his head. *Why Elohim?* his heart couldn't help but ask. *Why now? Why tonight?*

When they arrived in the throne room, the guards jerked Sirion and Jered to a halt in front of the throne. Vayzar sat there, his expression one of cruel amusement and pleasure.

"What do you want with us now?" Jered demanded in no attempt to hide his disdain for the man.

Vayzar chuckled deep in his throat. "You think you're so clever, don't you? So resourceful, so sneaky . . . my two schemers." His face morphed from amusement into an expression of utter contempt and ruthlessness. "But you should never have tried to engage in a battle of wits against me."

He nodded to his left. Sirion and Jered watched as two men stepped from the shadows. One of the men had a dagger pressed to his throat. A chill raced across Sirion's skin as his stomach sank even further.

"Aedan," he murmured.

Vayzar chuckled again. "You poor fools. You really thought you could plan an uprising and attack against me?"

Sirion's tongue seemed to have sucked away any moisture in his mouth, preventing him from swallowing. He breathed heavily at the stinging impact of defeat and the consequences it would bring down on them. But how could Vayzar have learned of their plans?

The man rose and slowly descended the steps, punctuating each icy word he spoke. "I will see that your attempt costs you dearly."

This time he motioned to his right. Sirion followed his gaze, intense fear rising up to claw at his heart. Two more people appeared from the darkness. Sirion's throat closed, the full weight of horror forcing the air out of his lungs as his worst fear was realized. His voice broke, and he managed only one word.

"Makilien."

:Chapter Twenty:

Protection and Sacrifice

Tears glimmered on Makilien's face and her lips trembled. Seeing Sirion right there in front of her, she could barely breathe. They drank in the sight of each other, and Sirion took a step toward her, but the guards yanked him back. Makilien jerked against her own captor, but they were cruelly held apart.

Smirking at this silent, but poignant exchange, Vayzar stepped between them, breaking their gaze.

"Reunited at last," he crooned. And all the deep blackness of his cold heart trickled out with a chuckle.

Sirion looked at him, his voice still raw and labored. "Please, let her go."

Makilien had never seen such deep fear in his eyes, fear for her.

Vayzar scoffed. "Let her go? Oh no, not when things are just getting interesting." He motioned to his guards who brought Aedan and Makilien in closer, but still held Makilien and Sirion just out of reach of each other. Eyes moving between each one of them, Vayzar went on, "No, I have far too much planned for the four of you."

He grinned at the apprehension they couldn't quite mask and ordered the guards, "Take them outside."

Jerking the four captives around, they led them through the fortress. Sirion fought to look over his shoulder and locked eyes with Makilien. Her eyes still held remnants of tears, but she was being brave now. Again, he was struck with the overwhelming desperation to get her out of this. Somehow, some way, he had to.

Outside in the courtyard, torches lit up the tall posts near the stockade. Sirion swallowed a reaction to the remembrance of what he'd seen take place here as they were each tied between the posts in a long row—Makilien first, then he and Jered, and finally Aedan.

Vayzar stood before them, his wicked grin and yellowed teeth lit eerily by the torches.

"Enjoy the night," he told them cheerfully, but his voice dropped to a more sinister tone, "because tomorrow, you will come to regret every action you have taken against me." He stepped close, looking each one of them in the eyes as he worked his way down the row. "If you think you know pain, think again. And escape is just a dream. Thanks to you, I know to have all my entrances more heavily guarded. You'd *never* get out and rescue would *never* get in."

With these words and a flaunting flourish of his cloak, he marched back to the fortress with the guards. All fell deathly silent as a heavy doom settled around them.

Snapping out of its grip, Sirion looked at Makilien, eyes searching her face. "Are you all right? Did he hurt you?"

Barely holding her emotion in check, she answered softly, "No, I'm not hurt."

"What happened?" Aedan asked, voice raised in frustration. "How did he get you?"

Makilien let out a long breath. "A bunch men attacked Beregon's house. In the chaos, they dragged me away."

"Are the others all right?"

Blinking at tears, she shook her head. "I don't know."

Sirion closed his eyes for a moment. "How did Vayzar find out about this?"

"Someone betrayed us," Jered said, tone hard-edged with anger.

"But who?" Sirion asked. "It had to be someone who knew everything about our plans."

"Jorin."

Everyone looked down to Aedan. "Who else could it be?" he continued, matching Jered's tone.

Makilien bowed her head in sadness. She'd been sure they could trust Jorin. He'd saved her life.

"I know how it seems," she said, "but we can't know for sure it was him, not until we see some evidence of it. And, if he is innocent, we must not say anything about him or Vayzar will know he's with us."

"You're right," Sirion agreed, though Aedan and Jered didn't seem as convinced.

Now Sirion's focus shifted to the rope around his right wrist, and he twisted his hand, pulling hard. The others joined in, testing their bonds for weakness. After some time of struggling, Makilien blew out a heavy breath, shaking her head in despair. "It's no use. Mine are too tight."

The emotion that had been building inside crashed in. Tears burned her eyes and numbing fear spread through her whole body. She'd been in bad situations before, but this felt different. She was terrified of Vayzar—terrified of his twisted cruelty, and terrified to see him hurt those she loved.

Hearing the tremor in her voice, Sirion looked over at her and saw the fear. His own lingered, but he thought only of comforting her.

"It's all right," he told her, voice quiet and reassuring. "It would only take one of us to get free. We have time. We'll keep trying."

Eyes wide with the prospect of such a bleak future, she whispered, "What if we don't get free?"

Sirion clenched his fists, feeling the tightness of the restraints around his wrists. If only he could reach Makilien, hold her hand, anything. He knew the answer, but wished he could do something to add more comfort to it. "Then it is Elohim's will that we face Vayzar tomorrow."

But it was enough. Makilien nodded. She'd let her fear get the best of her. *Help me trust You and have courage,* she prayed.

Halandor walked around the remains of the house and shed as smoke curled up into the pale sky and joined the others who stood at a loss. All their plans were destroyed, just like the house. A moment later, Beregon joined the group after taking Sophine to stay with friends where she'd be safe should Vayzar's men come to finish them off.

"Do we have a plan?" he asked.

Halandor shook his head, burdened by the weight of helplessness. "No. We have to get Makilien and the others out of the fortress, but it will be next to impossible now that Vayzar knows we're here."

"I'd like to know how he found out," Torick growled, eyes flashing.

"Do you think Jorin told him?" They all looked at Elandir. "I mean, now that he's a free man and has gained favor with Vayzar, what would stop him from joining him whole-heartedly?"

Beregon hung his head at this. "I want not to think he would do that, but I know I can't truly speak for him."

As if summoned, Jorin appeared through the smoke before them. Everyone tensed, some reaching toward their weapons. Jorin's face was hard set and intense, yet not hostile.

"I know what you are thinking," he said, not skirting the obvious. "You believe I am responsible for this, that I sold you out to Vayzar. I don't blame you, but I didn't do it."

"Then how did he find out about us and our location?" Torick demanded.

"I don't know yet," Jorin answered, trying to convey his honesty. "But I do know Vayzar is aware of everything, including your plans to start an uprising and attack."

Glances were traded. Besides Jorin, they were the only ones who knew of these plans and could have gone to Vayzar with the information. Suspicion flared in their minds again.

Aware of how it looked, Jorin put his hands out in innocence. "Blame me if you want, but I came to tell you that if you are going to make a move, you will have to do so soon.

Vayzar has Makilien, Aedan, Sirion, and Sirion's friend tied up in the courtyard. He wants to see them suffer, but he won't wait long to kill them."

"Is Vayzar going to send more men after us?" Halandor asked.

"No," Jorin answered. "He is waiting for you to come to him. He knows you won't just let Makilien and the others die."

"Do you have any suggestions for us?"

Jorin shook his head. "Vayzar has the entrances heavily guarded. I'll look for some other way, but I don't think there is one. It may be all you can do is force your way in, but that is exactly what Vayzar wants and is expecting."

Halandor sighed. "It seems to be our only choice."

A chill tingled along Makilien's skin. Dawn was cold in the dreary stone courtyard. She tipped her head from side to side, stretching the tired muscles in her neck, and opened and closed her fists. Her fingers and arms were numb, yet her wrists stung. She breathed deeply, but felt like she had a chunk of ice in the pit of her stomach.

Rays of light peeked over the wall, but they did not bring a sense of hope. Weary from the night, all struggles to free themselves were halted. They'd run out of time.

"We need to pray," Sirion said, breaking the silence.

The others nodded and bowed their heads.

"Elohim, You see where we are, and the hopelessness of our situation," Sirion spoke quietly, but his voice was empowered by knowing, no matter what, Elohim would never abandon them. "We are powerless against our enemies, but we know You are here, right now, in this courtyard with us. We are not on our own. We pray for deliverance, but if that is not Your plan for us, give us the strength to trust You and face our enemies. Help us endure whatever pain we must. We know that in the end this will all have a purpose. Thank You that we don't have to do this alone. Amen."

Makilien, Aedan, and Jered echoed him. By this time, the sun rose above the wall, bathing them in soothing warmth. It reminded Makilien of Meniah, and she did feel strengthened. The might of Elohim was far greater than that of any enemy, even greater than Vayzar's cruelty.

Only moments after the prayer, the fortress door opened. Vayzar strode out with a large group of followers. Among them were Ryelan, Derrin, Jorin, Jaeson, and Halen. Sirion had to swallow down an uprising of dread at the appearance of this last man. Crossing the courtyard, they came to stand in front of the captives. Makilien's eyes searched Jorin's face, but his expression was unreadable.

"Good morning," Vayzar greeted them, his voice making Makilien cringe. She'd so hoped, after leaving him chained up in Reylaun, that she'd never have to hear it again.

"Such long faces," he taunted. "Difficult night?" He chuckled at his own question. "Excellent. Now, how about we acknowledge the person responsible for your misfortune?"

They stared at him expectantly, and a few glances were cast at Jorin, but Vayzar looked off to his right. Following his gaze, they found two guards escorting a red-haired young man from the stockade. Jered's mouth dropped open.

"Ren!"

They watched, mortified, as he joined the group of on-lookers. The young man fidgeted and would not hold their gaze.

"Traitor," Jered ground out, straining against his bonds. "You betrayed us all."

Still, Ren would not speak, but Jered wasn't finished.

"We had a chance of escape, but you've doomed everyone. All who die here, all who die as a result of this, will be on your head."

Finally, Ren looked up at him and opened his mouth to speak, but closed it again and shook his head. Turmoil filled his eyes, and he turned to Vayzar, voice pained. "I've done what you asked. Can I go?"

Vayzar frowned. "Go? Go where?"

"You said I could go free in exchange for information."

"Did I say that?" Vayzar tilted his head as he pretended to think. "Hmm . . . I don't remember saying that. Guards, take this wretch to the grinding house."

The blood drained from Ren's face as his eyes rounded in panic. "No! You promised to set me free!"

The guards grabbed him by the arms and dragged him away despite his struggles and desperate pleas that continued until they'd disappeared around the fortress.

Jered glared at Vayzar, chest heaving. "You're an animal."

Vayzar smirked, eyes flickering in wicked amusement.

"Now, the next bit of business." He nodded to the other guards.

Without warning, two grabbed Jaeson and shoved him forward. Aedan jerked against his restraints, but they held fast. Facing Jaeson, Vayzar speared him with a withering gaze.

"Did you know your son was here?"

Jaeson glanced at Aedan and sighed as he gave a quick nod. "Yes," he admitted. "I did."

Anger flamed in Vayzar's eyes. "And why didn't you tell me?"

Again, Jaeson looked at Aedan, this time holding his gaze. "Because, he's my son."

Vayzar's fists squeezed tight. "Then, right here, right now, you are going to make a choice. Either him or me. I'm sure you're aware of how *unpleasant* things will become if you choose wrongly. If you still have loyalty to me, then go right now and kill him."

Jaeson paled, and everyone stilled at the magnitude of this choice. He looked from Vayzar to Aedan and back. It was the ultimate test. His life or his son's.

At last, Jaeson let out a heavy breath and shook his head. "I won't do it. I won't kill him."

Aedan breathed out in relief, but his expression remained taut with fear for his father. However, no fear was found in Jaeson's eyes. Standing tall and confident, he looked down on Vayzar and declared, "I'm done. I won't do this. Aedan helped me see the error of it and realize Elohim is real. If He will still have me after what I've done, then I trust my life to Him."

He looked at his son, sharing a moment of joy as a hint of a smile lifted his expression.

Vayzar was livid.

"Fool," he spat. "If that is what you choose, then you will remain here to witness the pain inflicted on your son, and after that, you'll be thrown down into the dungeon to be one of Wormaw's next test subjects. And there you too will experience more pain than you can imagine."

Unmoved, Jaeson said, "Do what you will."

Caught somewhere between self-restraint and wanting to murder the man himself, Vayzar barked, "Halen!"

The man strode forward, towering over Vayzar who now found his anger appeased by the anticipation of what was to come. "Some of you haven't met Halen, but Sirion knows him very well, don't you?"

Makilien looked up at Sirion, seeing how every muscle in his body tensed, and the look in his eyes was a mix of fear, repulsion, and dread. Fear ripped through her too at his reaction and the realization that this was the same cruel man who had blinded Sophine.

"As I'm sure Sirion can attest to, Halen is a master at inflicting pain," Vayzar went on, voice rising with an all too evident pleasure. "And that is exactly what I want."

Halen took the whip from his belt, and panic overwhelmed Sirion. Vayzar was right, he knew too well the kind of pain and injury Halen was capable of. To think of that brutality unleashed on Makilien, a woman, was something he could not bear.

"Vayzar," he called out, begging Elohim that the man would listen.

Vayzar looked at him, and Sirion held his eyes. "Leave Makilien out of this."

"Ha!" Vayzar scoffed.

But Sirion cut him short. "Leave her be. I will take her beating and my own."

Makilien gasped. "No!"

Vayzar's eyes lit up upon seeing the horror on her face. "No, I think he's right." He chuckled deeply, thrilled over this turn of events. "Oh, yes, this is good. It will hurt you far more this way, to see him bear the pain that should have been yours."

Makilien yanked against her ropes, feeling her heart already tearing in two. "You heartless monster!"

"Oh, I am heartless, aren't I?" Vayzar only chuckled again. "Proceed, Halen."

The man strode toward the prisoners, letting the whip uncoil. Sirion's eyes locked with those of his nemesis. A wicked grin stretched across Halen's face, a look Sirion had seen far too many times.

"Start on the end," Vayzar instructed. "I want to give Makilien a good long time to consider what her boyfriend will endure, only double thanks to her."

Tears of pain and anger burning in her eyes, Makilien glared at him, hating him with every fiber of her being. She shook with the intensity of the pain ripping at her soul.

Halen marched down to the end of the row where Aedan was tied. He walked behind and tore open the back of Aedan's shirt. Aedan clenched his fists, body tensing, heart racing. He'd experienced this sort of pain before, but somehow knew this would be worse. Yet, he was determined to fight it. He breathed in deep, preparing.

The whip snapped. His skin split low on the right side, taking his breath away. He gritted his teeth together, but made no sound. Again and again, Halen's whip descended, tearing viciously at his back. Sweat beaded on his forehead and his clenched jaw ached. Finally, after over a dozen lashes, Aedan grunted in pain. With one more burning lash, Halen stepped back. Bowing his head, Aedan breathed heavily, wincing as pain throbbed throughout his body.

Halen moved on to Jered who stood stone-faced. He received the same, though like Aedan, the young man didn't give their audience the satisfaction of a reaction. Vayzar looked thoroughly annoyed by this, and Jered almost laughed at him.

Now, Halen came to Sirion. All eyes shifted to the two of them, and a deep, suffocating dread settled on the four companions. With rough hands, Halen ripped open Sirion's shirt, revealing the scars of wounds he'd already inflicted. Sirion pulled in a deep breath, praying for strength and resistance to the pain, aware it would surely rival any he'd faced in the past. The fiendish anticipation in Vayzar's expression assured him of that. He bit down hard, and, in that moment, his eyes locked with Ryelan's—his brother, his best friend as a child. Uncertainty flickered in the depths of those dark eyes, and with his gaze, Sirion pleaded with him to turn from this choice he'd made, to remember his family love and loyalty.

White-hot pain seared across Sirion's back at the vicious crack of the whip. He flinched, muscles jerking taut. No matter how many times he experienced it, he never grew used to the pain. One after another, every brutal lash left behind deep, burning wounds, yet with each he remained steadfastly silent, willing himself to endure the pain.

Soon, they reached the number Aedan and Jered had received and surpassed it. Sweat ran down Sirion's face, and his body shuddered at the ferocity of each cruel strike. All his effort channeled into hiding the pain so Makilien would not have to see his suffering. His legs shook, and he could barely take in a breath before it was torn from his lungs. Tears of pain mixed with the sweat on his cheeks. He fought desperately for control of the agony rising up in his throat. *I must endure*, he told himself. But, at last, his willpower slipped. At the next lash, a deep, agonized groan broke from his chest. He tried to regain his control, but his strength was spent. With each of the following lashes, he cried out in pain, powerless to hold it back.

Makilien screamed. "Stop, please!" she begged, sobbing.

But her pleading and crying only added to Vayzar's satisfaction.

Halen continued on, going well beyond double that of Aedan and Jered's beatings. Sirion barely even heard Makilien. Now only blinding pain consumed him. *Please let it end*, he cried out to Elohim.

"Stop!" This time it was Ryelan's voice that cut in.

All eyes fell on him. He spoke firmly, but desperation mingled with his tone. "He's had enough."

A moment of complete, heart-pounding silence followed. At last, Vayzar said, "Leave him be . . . for now."

Recoiling the bloodied whip, Halen joined Vayzar as the men dispersed.

Sirion hung limp between the posts. Head bowed, the ground faded in and out beneath him, and he closed his eyes as he dragged in one ragged breath after another. His torn back pulsed with agonizing intensity. He wanted to let go, to slip into the welcome relief of unconsciousness, and escape the pain, but hearing Makilien's deep sobs, he resisted.

Gathering whatever little strength he could manage, he straightened, raising his head. The movement ignited fire in his nerves, and he barely suppressed a groan, gasping for breath. For several moments, he just stood, trying to take normal breaths, dazed by the pain. Finally, he turned his head to look at Makilien. The deep agony of her tear-streaked face tore at his heart. She met his eyes, weeping inconsolably.

"You didn't have to do that for me," she cried.

"Yes, I did," Sirion said gently. He looked her deep in the eyes. "What kind of man would I be not to protect a woman or to sacrifice for the one I love?"

Derrin stumbled down the hall, his face ghostly white in the light of the torches. The scene in the courtyard haunted his mind. Struck with a sudden wave of dizziness, he grabbed for the wall. At the same moment, his stomach heaved. Weakly, he rested his forehead against the cold stone and groaned. He squeezed his eyes shut. *You wanted this. You wanted to see Sirion suffer. Now you have. Was it worth it?* The thought nearly made him throw up again. *What kind of monster have I become?*

Vayzar and Halen's faces floated through his mind. He hit his fist against the wall.

"No!"

He didn't want to be them.

Suddenly, he sensed a presence. He looked up. Ryelan stood in the shadows a few feet away. The Half-Elf just stared at him, his expression utterly blank. Just seeing his face, so identical to Sirion's, made him shudder.

"I can't do this," Derrin gasped. He shook his head. "I *won't* do this. Turn me in to Vayzar if you must, but I have to find a way out. I will not become the monster he is."

He turned and walked slowly down the hall, head bowed. Ryelan remained rooted to the spot for a long time after, not knowing how to bear the crushing weight of emptiness and despair that devoured him from inside.

:Chapter Twenty-one:
The Only Hope

The soothing warmth of the sun from that morning now became their enemy. As it climbed higher, the heat grew stronger. With not a cloud to offer relief, it beat down on them mercilessly. Makilien's tearstained cheeks and lips dried out, but no physical discomfort could compare to the emotional pain.

Ever on the brink of tears, her gaze turned to Sirion when he shifted. His eyes were shut tight in pain, and Makilien bit her lip. *Why did he have to bear so much for me?* Her heart ached like never before. Two tears rolled down her cheeks, but they were soon dried by the breeze.

She glanced toward the stockade. Once in a while, she caught sight of the slaves watching them. All work on the fortress had ceased since the capture of her and the others— a precaution so their friends couldn't proceed with the uprising. It was a cruel reminder of how utterly they'd failed.

"Do you think this is it?" Makilien murmured. "After everything we've escaped in the past, do you think it's finally the time we won't?"

Sirion looked at her, squinting in the sun, and gave a slight shake of his head. "I don't know . . . but I will believe there is a way right to the end."

Makilien's throat constricted as she forced out words. "I'm not afraid to die, really, but I am afraid to see you die . . . again. I am so afraid to see anyone I care about die."

"So am I," Sirion barely more than whispered.

Makilien tried to swallow the lump in her throat, and silence came again. She prayed continually for their rescue, pleading with Elohim. She wanted to take comfort in knowing they still had friends who would not give up on them, but were they capable of successfully storming a fortress? *Oh, Elohim, what can any of us do?*

"Makilien."

She turned to the sound of Sirion's gentle voice. "Yes?"

His gaze was set out on the blue sky over the wall, but his deep brown eyes shifted, landing fully on her. "If we are delivered from this . . . will you marry me?"

Makilien's breath caught and a multitude of emotions flooded up inside her. Here, in the middle of one of the most painful trials they had ever faced, she had a ray of hope for a future she'd so recently thought lost. Tears overflowed, and she nodded quickly, her voice breaking as she said, "Yes. Absolutely, yes."

Sirion smiled that gentle, kind smile she had so deeply come to love, and for just that fleeting moment, they were able to forget the pain and the misery. She too broke out into a smile, moist eyes glowing.

Looking at her with all the love he had in his heart, Sirion said, "If I could, I'd marry you right here, right now, so that in whatever happens in the next hours, I'd know you were my wife."

Fresh tears trickled down Makilien's cheeks, though she laughed pitifully. "You're making me cry." She sniffed and nodded. "I would marry you now."

Sirion let out a quiet sigh, and she saw in his eyes the contentment of knowing that, despite their uncertain future.

"We'll live in Elimar, near your family," he told her, keeping the hope alive a little longer.

"What about Silnar?" she asked. "Don't you want to be near your uncle? Because, as long as I am with you, I will live anywhere you want."

"And I want that to be Elimar," Sirion answered. "We'll have a beautiful house near the river." Makilien closed her eyes, imagining it. "If there isn't one, I'll build one for us."

"Oh, Sirion, it sounds wonderful," she breathed, clinging desperately to the hope it wouldn't just be a dream.

Irynna searched the halls for Ryelan, but couldn't find him anywhere. She passed a couple guards and ducked her head away from their leering gazes that always chilled her. The lump growing in her throat increased. Her pace increased with it. Where was he?

At last, she came around a corner at the far end of the fortress and discovered Ryelan sitting on a bench halfway down the dim hall. He did not look up until she reached his side. Her stomach clenched. His eyes were darker and more anguished than she'd ever seen them. She sank down beside him, but he did not speak. She laid her hand on his arm, feeling the rock-hard tension in his muscles.

"Ryelan, we cannot stay here," she murmured, her sense of urgency growing more intense now that she'd found him. "Not after what Vayzar just did. You can't hold with the cruelty of what he did to your brother, or to any one of them."

His jaw shifted.

"Please, Ryelan, let's leave," Irynna pressed, wide eyes pleading.

Ryelan bowed his head and clenched his fists tight. "You don't understand. I'm in this too deep." His voice dropped to a hoarse whisper. "I don't think there is any escape for me now."

"Yes, there is." She gripped his arm, trying to make him understand. "Nothing is keeping you here."

Ryelan shook his head. "You shouldn't be with me, Irynna."

All the air left her lungs. "What?"

His haunted eyes met hers. "I am not a good man, and I've dragged you into being a part of this. You should have someone so much better than me. I'm no different from Vayzar and the other men here . . . no different from the men who killed your family."

"Ryelan—"

He cut off her protest and rose. "Go to your room and pack your things. I will get you out of here tonight, as soon as it is dark. I won't let you be dragged in deeper."

Irynna rose with him, her eyes filling with tears. "I can't just leave you here." She may have threatened to go without him, but when it came right down to it, she couldn't.

"You must," Ryelan insisted. Her pleading eyes cut deep into his heart, but he resolved to remain strong. Voice rough, he said, "Go. I will come for you after dark."

Irynna hung her head, hearing the finality in his tone, and slowly walked away. Tears trailed down her cheeks.

In her room, she did as she was told. Her hands trembled as she folded her clothes and tucked them into a leather pack. She brushed the back of her hand across her wet cheeks, but the tears still came fresh. She had lost everything—her home, her family, her freedom, and finally Ryelan. Now she would have to face the world on her own with no one to turn to, no one to guide her or comfort her. No one to protect and love her.

Despite her valiant effort to hold back, a weak sob broke from her chest, and she sank down on the bed, overwhelmed.

"If You're real, Elohim, where are You?" she cried. "I don't understand. Why is everything I love taken from me?"

She hugged her knees up to her chest and huddled against the wall, surrounded by shadows and stone. Her entire world was crashing down around her, and she could do nothing to stop it.

Derrin peered down the dim staircase. His unsettled stomach lurched at the nauseating stench drifting up from below. He looked down the dark hall he had come from. A heightening sense of apprehension urged him to go back, but he resisted.

Taking a fortifying breath, he only hesitated a moment longer before he took the first step down the stairs. Heart pounding with deep, powerful thuds, he took each descending step into the dungeon. The pale glow of distant torchlight faintly lit his path.

At the bottom, he paused. The dark cells yawned like cold tombs on either side of him. He swallowed hard but pushed on. Straining to see into the darkness, he checked each one. In a middle cell, the dark form of a man sat against the wall, head bowed.

"Jaeson?"

He looked up. "Derrin?" Pushing to his feet, he came to the door. "What are you doing here?"

Derrin cast a wary glance down the hall toward Wormaw's lair, fear worming around in his gut, but when his eyes returned to Jaeson, they were pained in desperation for answers. "Do you really believe Elohim could still want us after what we've done?"

Wrapping his fingers around the bars, Jaeson sighed. "I hope so. I want to believe it. What other hope do we have?"

"None," Derrin murmured, feeling empty inside. He hung his head and his eyes fell on the cell door's lock. He ran his fingers along the keyhole. "If I had a way, I'd let you out of here."

Jaeson gave a half-hearted shrug. "Whatever happens now is only what I deserve."

Derrin grimaced. *What I deserve.* The words echoed in his mind. He deserved a place in a cell right along with Jaeson. No, he deserved to be the one tied up in the courtyard with his back ripped to shreds.

"Derrin, will you do something for me?"

He looked up, meeting Jaeson's eyes.

"If you can, will you tell Aedan thank you for not giving up on me. I don't know if I'll ever get a chance to tell him."

Derrin nodded, wondering how he'd been so blind before. Aedan had tried so hard to help him see the truth. If only he'd listened. Then he wouldn't be in this mess. "He's a good man . . . I wish I was more like him."

"So do I," Jaeson said with a deep sigh.

Regret eating away at him, Derrin glanced down the hall again. His heart almost broke through his ribs. Wormaw stood a few feet away in deadly silence. Derrin stumbled away from Jaeson's cell, his mouth turning to cotton. He waited, breath trapped in his lungs, for Wormaw to make a move, but the man just pierced him with a look that froze Derrin's blood. When the man still did not move after several seconds, Derrin backed a few more steps and turned, making a hasty retreat from the dungeon. Though Wormaw did not follow, heavy doom settled on Derrin. This incident would never be kept from Vayzar, and he sensed his time was growing short.

As shadows crept upon them, the chill breeze of evening filtered through Makilien's sweat-dampened clothing and made her shiver. She licked her lips, but it would not quench the dryness. All the effort she'd put into trying to be strong all day left her exhausted. The last thing she felt she could handle was another confrontation with Vayzar.

Just as the last bit of pink in the sky disappeared, the detestable man strode out with his guards. Afraid her resolve might falter, she prayed in desperation.

Vayzar stopped and took inordinate time to study each one of them, a smirk soon growing into a malicious grin.

"Miserable yet?" he taunted. "Or has your God magically made you immune to the pain?"

Makilien closed her eyes and gritted her teeth, struggling with her hatred for the man. *Please just leave us alone,* she silently begged him.

"Vayzar," Sirion said, voice weary yet determined. "Makilien is a woman. Can't you find some small measure of decency in your heart and let her go?"

Vayzar scoffed. "Do I look like I care about decency?" He strode up to Makilien. "Woman or not, she was the start of all our problems." Grabbing her by the chin, he forced her to look him in the eyes. "This is your fault, you know. None of this would be happening if not for you. Perhaps it would have been better for everyone if you had just died and been forgotten long before you ever left Reylaun."

A welling up of sadness constricted Makilien's chest, and tears pooled in her eyes. She tried to look away, but he squeezed her jaw tightly.

"Take your hands off her," Sirion demanded, wishing for all the world he could get free of his bonds. "Don't listen to him, Makilien. Think of the thousands of people who would be enslaved if not for our victories, and you had a part in it."

"Yes, but at what cost, hmm?" Vayzar countered. He twisted Makilien's head around to face Sirion. "Look at him. Think of the pain *you* caused him."

This hurt her more than anything.

Sirion locked eyes with her. "Makilien," he said her name earnestly. "Don't listen. Don't give in to guilt or blame yourself. That's exactly what he wants."

Makilien fought hard to keep Vayzar's words from penetrating her heart. She knew it wasn't true, but it was little comfort amidst so much pain. Scowling, Vayzar released her with a shove. She bowed her head, breathing hard. This bombardment had left her emotional defenses significantly weakened.

Vayzar paced in front of them, looking for another to prey upon. At last, he stopped in front of Aedan.

"Your father is down in the dungeon at this very moment," he announced. "Wormaw already has plans for him. He will pay for his betrayal, a betrayal you obviously had a hand in."

Aedan stared at him, expression giving away nothing. "You may hurt him physically, but now that he believes in Elohim, he has nothing to fear." He leaned forward a little, looking Vayzar in the eyes. "And neither do we."

Face flushing, Vayzar's anger erupted, and he drove his fist into Aedan's ribs. Aedan groaned through clenched teeth.

"Well, you should fear," Vayzar spat. Encompassing them all, he warned, "You better say your goodbyes tonight. Tomorrow you will all die, and by the time death comes, you'll be begging for it."

He stormed off, his footsteps loud and angry, leaving his captives to anticipate their fate.

When a quiet knock came at the door, Irynna's heart nearly failed. *No,* she cried inside. Drawing a heavy breath, she tried to prepare herself for the pain she would have to face at this separation. Ryelan stood in the shadows outside her door. His expression was guarded, but his anguished eyes betrayed him.

"Are you ready?"

Irynna gave a weak nod and stepped out of the room.

After taking her pack from her, Ryelan handed her a heavy, dark cloak. "Put this on."

Once she'd secured it over her shoulders, she followed him. Both were silent as they made their way to the entrance. Ryelan was on edge, carefully checking every hall they traveled. Irynna's heart pounded hard and desperate against her chest, panic growing with every step. When they finally reached the front door, she grabbed Ryelan's arm, stopping him from opening it. He turned to her, his face shadowed in the darkness. Swallowing hard, she knew she had this one last chance.

"*Please,* Ryelan, don't make me go alone."

Even in the dim light, his eyes glittered with moisture. "I can't let you stay with me. I don't deserve you, and you deserve more than a man like me."

"But you're the man I want." She reached up, putting a hand on his cheek. "I love you."

Rising up on her toes, she pulled his head closer and kissed him, willing it to erase their troubles and convince him of the life they could have. But reality crashed in again when Ryelan pulled away. He stared down into her eyes, looking as if he were on the brink of rethinking everything. But then, without a word, he reached for the door and pulled it open. Shoulders sagging, Irynna followed him outside. In the courtyard, her horse was saddled and waiting. A sword hung from the saddle, and Ryelan secured her pack.

"There is food and plenty of money in the saddlebags," he told her, voice distant.

Without looking at her, he took the horse's reins and led the way to the gate. When the guards saw them, suspicion sprang to their eyes, and they would not open the gate on Ryelan's approach.

"What are you up to?" one of them asked.

"I'm sending her on an errand," Ryelan answered, his tone taking on a superior edge.

But the guard wasn't convinced.

Ryelan's eyes narrowed. "Go ask Vayzar if you want, just open the gate."

The guard hesitated a moment more, but finally obeyed. Giving him a hard look, Ryelan led Irynna through. On the other side, they went on a few yards before Ryelan stopped and faced her. He reached to pull her hood up over her head.

"Keep your face hidden. Don't let anyone know you're a woman unless you must."

Irynna just stared blankly at him, devastated that she hadn't been able to change his mind. Pulling his eyes from hers, he led her to the side of the horse and helped her mount. Irynna took up the reins, her eyes focusing on the bridge. Just before she could touch her heels to the horse's sides, Ryelan's hand clasped around hers. She looked down into his eyes, finding the mask of strength gone and all the emotion and pain laid bare.

"I will always love you," he murmured, voice raw. "That is why I'm doing this."

Before Irynna could reply, Ryelan stepped back and lightly slapped the horse's rump. The animal trotted off, leaving the fortress behind. Squeezing the reins, Irynna glanced over her shoulder, willing herself not to cry or turn back. Ryelan stood in the moonlight, watching her go. Choking on a sob, she faced ahead as the horse clattered over the bridge.

On the opposite bank, she looked back once more. This time, Ryelan was gone. A new wave of hopelessness and fear crashed over her. What would she do now? Where would she go? A single tear left a glistening trail down her cheek.

Fighting to breathe in the rising sea of despair, she turned her face away from the fortress and her eyes landed on the gate of the city. Her hands shook at the memories of that place. She could never go near it. She'd be caught and enslaved again with no one to save her this time. Yet, realization struck her in that moment that her only hope for help lay behind the walls. She shook her head, quailing with fear. She couldn't dare attempt such a thing, could she? But what more did she have to lose?

"If we are going to act, we must do so soon. We are running out of time," Halandor said, voice betraying the anxiousness growing in all of them. "We know Vayzar won't make any of the captives work the quarry until Makilien and the others are dead. Uprising is no longer an option. We have to do this ourselves."

"Vayzar will be expecting us to move tonight," Elandir reminded them.

"Even so, what choice do we have?" Torick asked, shoving a stick into the fire harder than need be. "If we wait much longer, Makilien and the others will be killed. We either have to make our move fully accepting that we'll likely fail or make peace with the fact that we can't save them. I, for one, would rather die trying than give them up for lost."

All around him, the others nodded in agreement.

"What about attacking just after first light?" Beregon suggested. "The guards will be tired and complacent by then, and less likely to expect an attack after a quiet night."

Halandor agreed and said decidedly, "First light tomorrow, we attack the rear gate. Loron, you, Elandir, and Elmorhirian will need to take out any archers while we face the other guards."

The Elves nodded, fingering their bows.

"If we can successfully get inside, we might still be able to free the captive men and gain their help," Halandor said hopefully. "We..."

He paused when someone on horseback approached the ring of light from the fire. The rider stopped in the shadows and slid off, tentatively walking toward them on foot. Reaching the light, the rider pushed back the hood of their cloak. Everyone stared in surprise.

"Irynna," Halandor said.

Her wide eyes darted between them, and she swallowed hard. She would be powerless against so many armed men, and it was not far from her mind that she'd played a big part in Makilien's abduction. With a tremor in her voice, she murmured, "I need help."

The men looked at each other, and Irynna found herself pouring out everything to them. She managed to keep from crying, but her voice was thick with tears.

"I'm sorry," she said, finishing with a pitiful shrug. "I never wanted to be part of this. I just had no choice." She shook her head in regret. "I'm afraid to be alone. I know it's crazy of me to think you would have any desire to help me, but you are the only ones I could turn to."

Halandor rose and walked toward her. She watched him and cowered a little when he came near, but he spoke to her in a gentle voice.

"We're not going to hurt you. Come by the fire. We need to ask you a few questions."

Irynna followed meekly. Once she was in their midst, Halandor asked about Makilien and the others. With reluctance, she told them what had taken place that morning. Witnessing their reactions and the deep concern for their friends, her regret multiplied.

"I am so sorry this happened," she told them. "I don't believe it's right, and I'm afraid it will only get worse. Vayzar plans to kill them tomorrow, and it will be through torture."

"Not if we can help it," Torick said with steely determination.

Irynna glanced at him, but her focus remained on Halandor. "I know you have to do something to save them, but I beg you, please don't kill Ryelan. He doesn't want to be part of this, I know he doesn't, he just doesn't think he can escape it."

"We will do what we can," Halandor promised. "We don't want to harm him, but most of it will depend on Ryelan."

Irynna hung her head, so desperately wishing he had come with her. The thought of him staying with Vayzar, of still fighting for the man and dying because of it, was almost too much for her to bear. She hugged her arms around herself, closing her eyes against a flood of tears.

Quiet surrounded them but for the popping and crackling of the fire as they all considered what had been done and what was to come.

Before anyone could speak again, a voice came from the darkness behind the group.

"Halandor."

Everyone spun around at the familiarity of the voice.

:Chapter Twenty-two:

Another Chance

The black night sky turned a deep blue, and a golden glow spread in the east. A little sparrow flitted into the courtyard and perched on one of the posts. Oblivious to the plight of the captives, it warbled happily. Makilien lifted her head from her shoulder, and her weary eyes trailed the bird as it flew away, disappearing over the wall. Oh, to be able to just fly away. Her companions shifted, trying to find a comfortable way to stand, but their arms and legs had long ago become numb.

She drew in her breath. "This is it," she murmured, her voice cracking from both dryness and emotion.

Her eyes turned to Sirion. She had never seen him so tired, so beat down. He'd worked for so long to remain strong and give her strength and hope, but the effort had taken its toll. The crushing weight of everything pressed down on her chest. Their time would soon run out, but she could not let that happen before she shared what filled her heart.

"Thank you," she told Sirion, breathing out the words with the deepest sincerity. "Thank you for protecting me and suffering so much on my behalf."

Sirion gazed at her, and though exhausted, he smiled. "I couldn't do anything less for you. And I'd do it again if I had to."

Though tears pricked at her eyes, an almost peaceful resignation settled inside Makilien, and she spoke with a smile coming to her lips. "I never imagined I would meet someone like you. When I thought you died, I didn't know how life would ever be normal again. I thought about you and longed for you every single day. I can't put into words the joy I felt when I realized you were alive." She let out a sad little laugh. "I just want you to know how thankful I am that Elohim allowed me to meet you."

Sirion breathed out, the light in his eyes showing her how much those words meant to him. "I've lived a long time and have had many opportunities for a relationship, but I always felt Elohim telling me to wait. I am glad I did because I know now I was waiting for you."

Makilien swallowed hard, coming almost undone at this. "I don't know what you see in me compared to others, but I'm glad you did too.

They shared a loving smile, and Makilien could see signs of tears in Sirion's eyes.

All was quiet for a long moment, but then Aedan sighed. Makilien looked down to him.

"I never told her," he said forlornly. "I never told Vonawyn how much she means to me . . . never told her I love her."

"She knows," Makilien said, trying to comfort him.

He nodded, but hung his head. "I still should have told her before I left. I should have known never to leave it unsaid."

They fell silent after these words. The light had increased around them, time drawing ever nearer to their perilous fates. Makilien knew at any time the fortress door would open. Despite her efforts to fight it, a growing panic gnawed at her, biting into her pounding heart. She wanted not to think of it, but she realized, when the dreaded time came, it wouldn't end quickly. It would be long and painful. Vayzar would see to that. Icy chills prickled along her skin, and she shivered hard. *Elohim, I am so afraid of what is coming,* she cried in her heart. *I don't think I can do this.*

Trust me.

The gentle words came to her mind. Words the same as when she'd had to come to terms with believing Sirion to be dead. She knew she must obey them . . . no matter what.

Sensing her struggle, Sirion made a request to take their minds from what was coming. "Tell me what has been happening in Elimar. The little, everyday things."

Makilien looked up at him, holding his gaze and gratefully seizing on this lifeline. "Everything is beautiful and green right now, and all the flowers are blooming. There must be hundreds of butterflies. Everyone says spring came early this year. We all spend most of our time outside."

"Where are you living?"

"In a lovely little house not far from Lord Elnauhir's. My father works at the stable. I help him sometimes. He loves it there." Smiling wistfully, she thought of her family and their quiet life. "Leiya has been raising frogs." She let herself laugh. "Elmorhirian helped her catch tadpoles a few weeks ago, which started a water fight. The three of us got soaked."

Sirion smiled widely as he imagined this, and Makilien went on, recounting everything she could think of from life in Elimar. Everyone listened intently, letting themselves be carried away by the peaceful images.

Then, the fortress door opened. Vayzar strode out. Makilien felt the dread that began as a sickening ache in her stomach spread throughout her entire body. She swallowed hard a few times, but couldn't bring any moisture to her throat. She tried to breathe deeply, but could only take shallow breaths. Uncontrollable trembling set in as fear wrapped around and smothered her.

In desperation, her gaze sought Sirion. She found strength in his eyes, strength and acceptance. Tears pooled up in hers as reality set in, hard and cruel.

When Vayzar reached them, he didn't waste his time in taunting. Voice devoid of even the smallest particle of pity, he ordered his men, "Take him."

Two strode toward Sirion and cut the ropes. He sucked in his breath and groaned quietly as searing pain ripped through his shoulders and across his back as his arms came down. The men shoved him forward.

Raw, consuming panic flared inside Makilien.

"No!" she cried, struggling against her restraints.

And Vayzar enjoyed every moment of it. He watched her in cruel delight, teeth showing in a vicious smile. He would milk this for all it was worth.

"Take me instead," Jered said suddenly.

"Oh, you'll get your turn shortly," Vayzar replied. "You all will, ending once and for all with Makilien."

He grabbed Sirion's arm and jerked him to face her. "Say goodbye," he said, delighting in how it ripped her heart to pieces.

Makilien's tears poured down her face as her eyes locked with Sirion's, and a sob of sheer agony broke free. Sorrow stole her breath away. Determination building, Sirion found a last remnant of strength and pulled away from Vayzar. He stepped toward Makilien, taking her face in his hands. Makilien's eyes closed for a moment, relishing their warmth and gentleness, the first time she'd felt his touch since the battle a year ago. Her eyes opened again and her tears flowed unchecked as she looked into Sirion's eyes so close to her own. From the deepest part of his heart, Sirion told her, "I love you."

He pressed a kiss to her forehead just before the guards grabbed him by the arms and yanked him away from her.

Voice trembling with the crushing grief, Makilien replied, "I love you, Sirion."

The guards pulled him farther away from her, but he fought against them just long enough to hold her gaze for a moment more. "I will see you again soon."

In his voice, she heard the hope and anticipation for their lives beyond this one. Choking and trying to fight the suffocating hold of despair, she nodded, and Sirion ceased resisting the guards, allowing himself to be taken away, into the fortress. His chest rose and fell heavily. He'd resigned himself to his fate, but trepidation pounded in his heart at the manner in which it would come. At that very moment, words flowed into his mind that he'd memorized as a child from the scrolls about Elohim that his uncle had taught him from.

Quietly, Sirion murmured, *"Through You we will push back our adversaries; Through Your name we will trample down those who rise up against us. For I will not trust my bow, Nor will my sword save me. But You have saved us from our adversaries, And You have put to shame those who hate us."*

Whether Elohim came to the rescue now or allowed this fate, Sirion knew with comforting certainty that He was the greatest force and power in this world, and, in the end, would throw down all evil.

Vayzar scowled at him. "Shut up. No amount of muttering is going to save you now."

Down into the reeking pit of the dungeon they descended. Sirion continued to recite verses in his mind. When they came around the corner and he beheld the sight of the torture chamber, prayers once more took over. Wormaw waited for them. The man's expression was like cold stone, yet an eerie anticipation glittered in his eyes.

"Bring him over here," he rasped.

They shoved Sirion toward a tall contraption and pulled off his torn shirt. Then they chained his arms up over his head and backed away. Wormaw stepped to a table where many of his torturous instruments lay. Vayzar watched eagerly as the alchemist picked up and swirled a vial filled with yellowish liquid.

Sirion tried to breathe normally and slow his heart, but fear clawed up around his throat. Yet, greater than the fear of pain was his fear for Makilien to have to endure such horror. He prayed with everything he had inside him that Elohim would somehow spare her at least.

In a last, frantic effort, Makilien yanked and twisted against her ropes until her wrists bled, but they would not give. At this final defeat, she released an anguished sob and hung her head. Large teardrops splashed to the ground as her cries echoed through the courtyard, tormented and crushed by the horror of losing Sirion again to such a grim fate.

"Elohim," she cried. "Help us. *Please*, help us!"

She wanted it to end, wanted desperately for it to be over, but Vayzar would make her stand there and wait until each of her friends was dead before coming for her.

"No," she sobbed again and again.

She couldn't bear it. She didn't have the strength.

Somewhere in the horrible, drowning pain, she heard the fortress door open again. For a moment, she knew the deepest despair she'd ever experienced, too terrified to look up. If Vayzar had returned, Sirion was dead. Truly dead.

"Makilien."

At Aedan's voice, she did look up to see someone running toward them. She blinked rapidly to clear her eyes.

"Derrin?" she gasped.

He skidded to a halt in front of her. In his hands, he held three swords. Looking her in the eyes, he said, "I've been a terrible fool. I am so sorry."

He dropped the swords and yanked out a dagger with which he sliced through Makilien's bonds. Speechless, she watched him do the same for Aedan and Jered before he turned back to her.

"We have to get to Sirion before it's too late."

Makilien needed no further prompting. She immediately grabbed up one of the swords from the ground, fighting mightily against the numbing weakness in her arms. Aedan and Jered rushed to take the others. With Derrin and Aedan in the lead, they raced into the fortress and down the halls.

Makilien pleaded with Elohim that they would make it in time. At the dungeon stairwell, they rushed down without hesitation. When the four of them burst into the chamber, Vayzar, Wormaw, and the guards spun to face them. Makilien's eyes went straight to Sirion. She nearly had to grab Aedan to steady herself against an onslaught of dizziness brought by the overwhelming rush of relief. He was still alive.

"Kill them!" Vayzar shouted.

Six guards yanked out their swords and rushed at them. Though exhausted, determination, adrenaline, and emotion propelled Makilien. She swung her sword upward to meet the advancing blow of one of the guards. The two of them slowly moved around one of the tables. The others fought close by, Aedan and Jered each taking on two of their foes.

It was a close match, but Makilien would not be defeated now. One wrong move from the guard left him open. Seeing this split-second chance, Makilien whipped her sword around, and it sliced into the guard's side. He moaned in pain, grabbing at the wound as he stumbled and crashed into one of the tables before falling to the floor.

Makilien took this moment to look across the chamber. Vayzar had disappeared, but Wormaw remained. A glint of metal caught the light, and Makilien's eyes locked on a long dagger in his hand as he stalked toward Sirion. Her heart leapt into her throat, choking her.

"Sirion!" she screamed, and, as time seemed to stand still for a moment, the devastating realization that she could not reach him in time almost killed her.

Hearing her cry, Derrin looked up from his fallen foe, eyes catching on Wormaw and the dagger. He lunged forward, throwing himself between the alchemist and Sirion. He raised his sword to defend, but it was too late. With a snarl, Wormaw drove the dagger into his chest. The breath rushed from Derrin's lungs. Pain seared through his chest, spreading to engulf his entire body. His sword slipped from his fingers, landing with a dull clatter. Makilien shouted his name, but her voice was hollow. His hands tingled and cold crept up his arms. He stared into Wormaw's face, meeting those disturbing, pitiless eyes. The man sneered and grasped the hilt of the dagger again, jerking it free of Derrin's body. Derrin gasped and sank to his knees as Wormaw fled.

Vision wavering, he fell to the floor.

"Help him," Sirion's voice came from above.

Makilien appeared, kneeling beside him, face pale. Her hand pressed down over the wound soaking his shirt. He tried to breathe, but felt like he was drowning.

"Makilien," he choked. Her gaze fell on his face, her desperate eyes filling with tears. "There's nothing you can do. It's over."

She shook her head in denial, the tears spilling over.

"You must listen to me," Derrin told her, the abnormally hard pounding of his heart striking him with urgency. "This is all my fault. These months you and Sirion have suffered is because of me."

"You don't have to talk about that now."

But he had to speak. He couldn't let all the turmoil that had built up over so long remain inside. "Yes, I do. If I wouldn't have tried to kill Sirion, Vayzar may never have found him and you two wouldn't be here." He grasped for her hand, and Makilien squeezed his tightly. "I hope by this I can give you both your lives back."

Behind Makilien, Jered released Sirion from his chains. Sirion dropped down beside them, and Derrin looked at him.

"You're a better man than I am. I don't know if I could have done what you did for Makilien." His eyes shifted back to her. "I've always loved you, but I should have accepted your choice. I cared more about my own desires than yours. I'm sorry."

Tears trailed down her cheeks. "It's all right, Derrin. I forgive you."

He smiled weakly, but his throat filled with liquid and he coughed. Blood coated the inside of his mouth, and he could hardly draw in a breath. The fear that had haunted him in the last couple of weeks descended with terrifying intensity.

He let out a panicked gasp. "Makilien."

She gripped his hand tighter. "What is it, Derrin? What can I do?"

"I need to know, is it too late for me? Would Elohim still take me after everything I've done?"

"Yes, Derrin," she assured him. "No one is too far gone. You just need to trust in Him, and He will save you."

Darkness closed in around the edges of Derrin's vision, and he could hardly feel Makilien's trembling hand anymore. As his strength bled away, he declared, "I do trust Him. I know I can't save myself."

Voice breaking, but carrying hope, Makilien said, "He loves you, Derrin, and you'll soon meet Him face-to-face."

Peace unlike anything he'd ever possessed before freed his heart and chased away the fear, replacing it with anticipation, and he knew this was exactly what Makilien and Aedan had always tried to tell him.

"Thank you. I only wish I had listened sooner."

Makilien managed a weak, wavering smile. "I look forward to meeting you again. I don't know how to thank you for saving Sirion."

"I know he will always take care of you, and that makes me glad."

Her face faded from his sight, and Derrin let his eyes close. Releasing one last painful breath, the world slipped away.

Makilien watched the life leave him, and mournful tears slid down her cheeks. She squeezed his limp hand once more and laid it on his chest. Sirion put his hand on her back, and Makilien met his eyes. Derrin's sacrifice had given them another chance.

:Chapter Twenty-three:

The Choice

Makilien sat in a daze, staring first at his face and then at his blood covering her hand. Derrin had been part of her life for as long as she could remember, whether for good or bad. After everything they'd been through, she couldn't quite seem to grasp the fact he was gone.

Aedan gently broke into her thoughts. "We have to try to get out of here before Vayzar sends more men."

Makilien looked up as if waking from a dream and realized he was right. Wiping her cheeks with the back of her hand, she nodded. She hated to leave Derrin here, but they had no choice. Rising to her feet, she looked down at Sirion. He was nearly spent and struggled to rise. She took his arm, and Jered grabbed the other.

Once standing, Sirion said, "Give me a sword."

"Will you be able to use it?" Jered asked incredulously.

"I might have no choice," Sirion replied.

Aedan handed him one of the fallen swords and picked up another, along with the key ring. Now, they left the torture chamber and hurried down the hall. At Jaeson's cell, they stopped, and Aedan hastily searched for the right key.

"What happened?" his father asked.

"Wormaw killed Derrin," Aedan answered, voice low and breaking a little. Finally, one of the keys fit and unlocked the door. He pulled it open. "We have to get out of here."

He gave his father the extra sword, and they went on. Up the stairs, Aedan led the way to the exit. Hearts pounded and prayers were made for a successful escape. But, halfway there, the group skidded to a halt. Standing in their way was Vayzar, Ryelan, and over a dozen guards.

"Going somewhere?" Vayzar sneered.

The guards unsheathed their swords.

"Is there another way out from here?" Makilien whispered, leaning close to Aedan.

He shook his head. Makilien's heart sunk painfully. They were outnumbered and trapped.

As they scrambled for a plan, Sirion suddenly stepped forward, eyes on Ryelan. "Is this truly what you want? To stay with him and see us all die?"

Ryelan swallowed, but said nothing.

Sirion's voice lowered, but it carried the full weight of the seriousness of this moment. "It's time to choose, Ryelan. Your family or Vayzar."

"Yes, Ryelan, it's time to choose," Vayzar said. He dropped his voice, his next words only for Ryelan. "And you better choose carefully."

Everyone watched him. For a brief moment, Ryelan stood unmoving. Then, very slowly, he withdrew his sword.

"Good, now kill him once and for all," Vayzar ordered.

His face setting in a hard, grim expression, Ryelan approached them. Sirion shook his head in deep regret and walked to meet him. Makilien gasped and took a step after him, but Aedan held her back. This struggle was between Sirion and Ryelan, and only they could end it.

They stopped a couple feet apart, and Sirion looked into his brother's face. Through the cold wall Ryelan held between them, he caught the deep pain in his twin's eyes.

"You don't have to do this," Sirion murmured, trying so desperately to break through the wall. "I can't fight you."

The conflict was there, in Ryelan's expression, but in the end, Vayzar and the past had too strong a hold on him. With an anguished cry, he swung his sword toward his brother's head. In a move more reflex than anything, Sirion threw his blade up to block just in time. The shriek of metal echoed against the stones. But excruciating pain tore through Sirion's back, and he nearly dropped his sword.

Groaning, he stumbled toward the wall to put more space between them, but Ryelan came after him with another blow. Sirion blocked again, but this attempt was weaker, and Ryelan's blade nicked him just under the chin. He fell back, blood trickling down his neck, and his back hit the wall. Blinding pain shot through him on impact, stealing his breath away and stunning him. Taking full advantage of this, Ryelan knocked his sword out of his hand. Sirion tried to move away, but Ryelan's blade pressed against his chest, pinning him against the wall.

"Ryelan!" Makilien's scream halted everything.

He looked where she stood wide-eyed with terror.

"Don't do this, please!" she begged, and Irynna's face flashed in Ryelan's mind, and her pleas for him to leave this all behind.

"Kill him now while you have the chance," Vayzar broke in.

"No, listen to me," Makilien said, voice rising in desperation. She took a step forward. "Think of your parents. They died at the hands of Shaikes who were on the same side as the men you are serving. Will you now be just like them and kill your own brother?"

"Remember your life was spared," Vayzar countered. "We raised you and elevated you to where you are now, to a place of power and respect. Don't throw it all away."

Chest heaving, Ryelan stared at his brother, caught directly in the middle of two warring sides.

"Ryelan," Sirion said, voice shuddering with pain, "remember back to when we were children. I know you trusted Elohim when I did. Turn back to Him."

But Ryelan shook his head. "It's too late for me. I'm sure He forgot me long ago."

"No," Sirion told him firmly. "He has *never* left you. You turned from Him, and He is just waiting for you to turn back."

"Fairytales," Vayzar spat. "A bunch of silly nonsense for the weak. You've already thrown your lot in with us. There's no escaping that."

"Derrin did," Makilien cut in. "He saw how wrong this is, and he gave his life to protect Sirion. Don't waste his sacrifice."

Ryelan grimaced, the struggle tearing apart his mind. His sword pressed into Sirion's chest, drawing blood.

Sirion lowered his voice. "Please, you can't do this. Think of how it would hurt Mother and Father if they were here. Remember what it was like as a family. Did you get any of that from these men? Was there any love? Do you really want to be heartless like them?"

Each breath Ryelan drew shook as Sirion watched the walls he'd erected against his emotions finally crumble.

"Elohim, help me," he gasped in a whisper.

Shaking, his sword fell away from Sirion's chest.

"Ryelan," Vayzar snapped, voice icy with warning.

He glanced at him and the guards, his mind racing. In a swift movement, he placed his sword back against Sirion's chest and stepped closer, speaking so only he could hear.

"If we fight them here, we'll all die. We don't have the numbers or the space. Back the way you came and to the left is a meeting room where we can barricade ourselves. There is no way out, but there is more room to make our stand, and it will give us time to prepare."

Sirion inclined his head in understanding. Holding his brother's trusting gaze, Ryelan stepped back, looking like he was about to kill him.

"Ready?" he murmured.

Sirion nodded.

Ryelan glanced once at Vayzar who watched with great anticipation.

"Now!"

He pulled his sword away, and Sirion lunged for his own.

"Go!" he told the others.

They raced back down the hall.

"After them!" Vayzar bellowed at his men. "I want them all dead!"

Sirion led the way and found the room. He flung open the door. "Everyone inside!"

They poured into the room. Ryelan was the last one to enter. He and Sirion slammed the door shut, engulfing the room in darkness. They dropped the barrier just as Vayzar's men reached the door. The guards slammed into it, but the heavy oak didn't budge.

Standing in darkness, they heard Vayzar's curses drift in as he joined his men. He shouted, "There is no way out of there. You're trapped! I will get in."

As Vayzar sent men to bring back something to break down the door, Ryelan made his way over to the wall and found a torch. In a moment, a flame flared to life. He lit a couple more and placed them in their holders before he turned back to the group.

"It's only a matter of time before they get in, but at least here we have room to fight."

Makilien looked at him, eyes tearing up with gratitude. "Thank you, Ryelan."

He nodded, but only met her eyes briefly.

Now, with so little time left, Makilien turned all her focus on Sirion. She hadn't even had a chance to check if he was all right after being handed over to Wormaw. Her searching eyes found a fresh acid burn on his side, but even more than that, a multitude of other scars. Her heart ached painfully over this.

"Are you all right?" she asked, voice quivering and her eyes smarting with tears.

Sirion didn't even say anything. He only nodded, dropping his sword, and stepping toward her. Makilien let hers fall as he pulled her into his arms. She curled her arms into her chest and burrowed into his, ever mindful of the wounds he bore for her. Overcome, she wept softly for a few moments as he stroked her hair.

"I've missed you so much," she cried.

"And I you," Sirion murmured in her ear, voice thick with emotion. "I thought about you every day of my captivity."

When they parted, he gently wiped the tears from her face, giving her an encouraging smile. "Everything will be all right. I don't think Elohim has brought us this far to die now. But if He has, it will still be all right."

Makilien nodded in complete agreement. At that moment, she felt more confident and stronger than she had in days. At least they had a chance to fight, and either live or die together.

Nearby, Aedan stood with his father. They said nothing for a long moment, but finally, Aedan turned to him.

"So you did consider what I said?"

"I did." Jaeson looked deep in his son's eyes. "It isn't too late for me, is it?"

"No, as long as you are alive, it is never too late."

Jaeson sighed with relief, but his face was still troubled. "I am sorry, Aedan, for what I've done to you. I wish I could undo all of it."

Aedan shook his head. "It's all in the past. As far as I'm concerned, it's forgotten."

"It will take longer for me to forget," Jaeson said, voice still tinged with guilt, "but I thank you for your forgiveness."

Commotion came once again from outside the door. Vayzar's voice bellowed in the hall. Then came an echoing crack as something sharp hacked into the door. Again, it came and the wood splintered.

Makilien looked up at Sirion. He took her hand and squeezed it, his eyes calm and reassuring. She drew in a deep breath, and they retrieved their swords.

The door shuddered and splinters fell to the floor. Standing in a line, the six of them raised their weapons to meet their foes. Makilien prayed, speaking to her Lord with a calm heart, thanking Him for this last bit of time she had with Sirion and for a less horrifying way to die. She prayed that, even now, they would be delivered, but accepted the fact they probably would not be. The door cracked more, and they could see through to the guards in the hall. Only one more strike, and they would get inside.

Someone shouted Vayzar's name, and the guards paused in the act of delivering the final blow. Conversation buzzed on the other side of the door.

"What!" Vayzar shrieked. After a moment, he ordered furiously, "Leave them for now and get to the gate!"

All the guards rushed away, and when the echo of their footsteps had disappeared, everything fell silent. Makilien and her companions looked at each other.

"What do you think is happening?" she asked. "Do you think it's a trick?"

Before anyone could answer, someone moved outside the room.

"Open the door. It's Jorin."

Ryelan and Jaeson frowned in confusion, but Makilien said, "He's with us."

She may have laughed at their surprise if not for wondering what was happening.

Removing the barricade, they let Jorin inside. Looking at them with the barest hint of a smile in his eyes, he announced, "Your friends are here. They are attacking the gate as we speak."

Makilien's eyes grew round. "But there are only seven of them. How can they take on Vayzar's force alone?"

That hint of a smile grew just a bit as Jorin replied, "I think you'll be surprised."

:Chapter Twenty-four:

Old Foes

T he ringing clash of battle echoed toward them when Jorin pulled open the fortress door. Makilien and the others stood stunned at the sight. Close to fifty Elves and Eldorian soldiers fought against Vayzar's men. A roar blasted the air. Makilien's eyes rose to the sky to see multiple dragons soaring overhead. Joy and relief flooded through her, bringing tears to her eyes, and she shared a smile with Sirion.

The fight filled the front portion of the courtyard. A handful of men noticed their presence and turned to engage them. Jaeson and Ryelan hurried to meet them, but Jorin turned to the four wounded and exhausted friends.

"Find somewhere safe and stay clear," he told them, leaving no room for argument. "No use having you die now."

With a nod, Sirion took Makilien's arm and guided her toward the far side of the fortress. Aedan and Jered followed behind, making certain no one attempted to follow them. From a safe distance, they watched the struggle. Vayzar's men outnumbered Eldor's force at least two to one, but the dragons, despite being unable to use their fire for fear of harming their friends, evened the odds.

As Beregon's opponent fell, incapacitated, he lifted his eyes. Taking in those around him, his gaze landed on one man in particular. Halen had made his way to the far side of the battle and was just entering the fortress. The memory of Sophine's battered body just after he'd rescued her came fresh to Beregon's mind. All the pain and emotions of that time rose up inside him, and he rushed after the man.

At the door, Beregon slowed and took a cautious step inside. He could see nothing ahead in the dark hall, but as he went on, he caught the faint echo of footsteps. He hurried after them, following the sound.

Deep inside the fortress, he paused at an open door. A rustling of movement and commotion came from within the room. He peered around the doorframe to find a massive storeroom. Halen was at one side, stuffing anything of value into a sack. Fingers flexing around the hilt of his sword, Beregon stepped into the doorway.

"You may think you can take your spoil and disappear, but I won't see that happen."

Halen spun around, grabbing his sword. Instant recognition jumped into his eyes, and he scowled. "If you want to live to see that wife of yours again, you'll pretend you never saw me."

Beregon shook his head, taking a step farther into the room. "I won't let you leave here to be free to hurt countless more people. Whether you come with me alive or dead is your choice, but I'm going to see that you receive justice for the atrocities you've committed."

Halen dropped the sack of valuables and took his sword in both hands, stalking toward Beregon. Sneering hatefully, he asked, "How is your wife these days? She used to be such a pretty thing. Now with those scars . . . I'm surprised you still wanted her."

Beregon's fingers squeezed tighter around his sword, and his blood heated. In a deathly calm voice, he said, "Don't give me further reason to kill you."

"You just try," Halen spat.

He drove into Beregon with the fury of a wild beast. But Beregon was ready, and they exchanged a flurry of crashing blows. He bided his time, giving ground and letting Halen's furious attack wear him out. They circled the perimeter of the room. Halen's sword flew wildly, knocking things off shelves and scattering them across the floor. Beregon thought this was done in a reckless fit of rage until he half stumbled on a bag of grain, and realized it was probably intentional. At last, he pressed forward with his own series of brutal attacks. Halen was larger than him, but Beregon matched his strength and stamina. Both slashed high and low, hoping for their opponent's defense to fail.

Halen growled, his expression cruel. "When I'm finished with you, I'm going for your wife. She may not get me much, but I'm sure I can find someone who'd pay something for a blind wretch."

Voice low and controlled, Beregon replied, "Even if it takes my last dying breath, I will never let you harm Sophine again."

He pressed on with his attack, but Halen was right there to counter.

The minutes drew out long, and the combatants panted with exertion, but neither one would concede defeat. Arms straining, Beregon attacked twice, and then fell back to defend.

Hacking at the other man's blade, Halen said, "Once Vayzar's men have control, you'll be a dead man. You can't fight all of us."

"I won't have to," Beregon replied with confidence. "Lord Darian's men will have this victory."

Halen gave a short, cruel bark of laughter. "They are out-numbered."

"That didn't stop them from defeating Zirtan."

Fresh anger and frustration flared in Halen's eyes, and with a sudden burst of manic energy, he redoubled his attack. Feeling his strength wearing down, Beregon struggled a moment to accurately block.

After a string of wild attacks, their swords locked. They stood for a moment in a battle of strength, but then, before Beregon could react, Halen released the grip of one hand to drive his fist into his opponent's ribs. Gasping, Beregon retreated to buy time to recover, but his foot caught against something on the floor and he fell back. Instead of hitting the floor, he crashed into a long table at the far side of the room. Halen was on top of him in an instant, the blade of his sword swinging down toward Beregon's throat. In that tiny space of time, Beregon let his own sword drop to the floor and reached out to grab Halen's arm just before the blade reached him. Holding Halen's wrist with both hands, he tried to force him away, but Halen was able to put his full weight behind his weapon.

The gleaming edge of the blade inched closer to Beregon's throat. He could see the bloodlust in Halen's eyes. His arms shook with effort, and he glanced desperately to his left and right. A glass bottle half full of a sickly, dark green liquid sat close by.

Returning his eyes to Halen, he watched the man's left hand drop toward the dagger on his belt. Having no other choice, Beregon shoved Halen's sword back with all his might and reached for the bottle. Halen's dagger slipped from the sheath as Beregon gripped the bottle around the neck and swung at Halen's head. The bottle shattered, sending glass shards and liquid spraying everywhere.

Biting pain stabbed into Beregon's side, but Halen's aim had been thrown off, falling low and barely finding flesh. Dazed, Halen staggered away from the table, his sword and dagger clattering to the floor. Blood ran down the side of his head, mixing with the dark, foul smelling liquid sprayed across his face. He brought his hands up to wipe it away, sputtering and cursing. All at once, the curses turned to a shriek, and he ground his fists against his eyes. In the same moment, Beregon became aware of a burning sensation creeping along the back of his hand where the dark liquid had sprayed him, as well as along his chin and neck.

Halen's shrieking and cursing rose in intensity as he clawed at his eyes. Beregon's gaze swung about the room, landing on a large barrel in the corner. He ran over to it and lifted the lid. Finding it was a water barrel, he hurried over to Halen and grabbed him by the jerkin. The man put up only a minimal struggle as Beregon dragged him to the barrel and dunked his head in it. Halen panicked at first, thinking Beregon was about to drown him, but when Beregon let him go, he plunged his hands into the water and brought great handfuls to his face.

Beregon stood transfixed for a moment before he winced, his entire hand feeling like it was on fire. His left sleeve had also been spattered and now leaked through to the skin. Tearing the sleeve off, his soaked it in the water and used it to wipe the acidic liquid from his hand, neck, and chin. Inspecting the back of his hand, he found it had turned a deep red, but now that the liquid was gone, he only felt the prickling sting of raw flesh.

By this time, Halen's moaning and gasping had quieted and he wasn't so frantically scooping up water for his face. Beregon backed away from him, retrieving his sword. The other man would be mad as a hornet once he gathered his wits, and Beregon wasn't about to give him the chance to strike at him while he was unarmed. Clutching his slowly bleeding side, he watched Halen push himself upright and turn to face him, water still streaming down his face, now a bright, mottled red.

Halen swayed momentarily, his eyes darting here and there as he blinked rapidly. His expression went blank before twisting into a horrible scowl as he spit out another string of curses. His hands once again covered his eyes, and he sank to his knees.

"What have you done?" he screamed. "I can't see!"

Beregon stood still for a moment, suspecting a trick to draw him close, but then Halen let out a dreadful wail.

"You've blinded me!"

And Beregon realized this was no trick. The bottle of green he had used in defense had indeed blinded the man. With the magnitude of what had just occurred still sinking in, he stepped closer and placed the tip of his sword at Halen's throat.

"Do it," Halen rasped. "End it! I won't live like this."

As much as he wanted to end the man's miserable life, he said, "No, I will not take my vengeance. I will let you live with the vengeance of Elohim. And every day for the rest of your life, you will remember my wife and the joy you stole from her. Thanks to you, she will never again see the blooming of a flower, the sunrise of a new day, or the faces of those she loves, and now neither shall you."

"No!"

On his hands and knees, Halen scrambled about for his weapons, but Beregon gathered them up. He turned from the man now, leaving him to grope along the wall. Walking back down the hall, Halen's screaming and cursing echoed behind him.

The battle was turning. The men and Elves of Eldor now had the numbers. Fear of defeat pulsed throughout the enemy. As Jorin's latest opponent dropped before him, he found Vayzar standing just on the other side. The man looked from the dead man to Jorin, his face wiped clean of expression.

"What are you doing?" he demanded.

Jorin smirked, taking great pleasure in saying, "I am fighting for Eldor."

Vayzar's eyes bugged. "You fight for me!"

"No." Jorin stepped over the fallen man's body, his sword rising as he approached Vayzar.

The other man backed up, hatred spewing from his eyes. "I gave you another chance. Don't blow it again."

At this, Jorin's smirk grew. "A chance I only sought in order to gain information."

"What?" Vayzar screamed. "You were supplying them with information?"

"Yes."

With this word, Jorin attacked, and Vayzar reacted savagely.

"How dare you give aid to our enemies! Your brother would be ashamed."

"My brother cared as little for me as you do," Jorin retorted.

He swung low, but despite Vayzar's smaller stature, the man held his own.

"Zirtan was right to discard you," Vayzar spat. "You're worthless. You always have been." He jabbed his sword at Jorin's legs, but Jorin jumped back. "What can you possibly see in these people?"

Feelings and emotions growing inside that he'd never fully experienced before, Jorin answered, "Forgiveness, honor, love—things you could never understand and I am only beginning to." Unleashing his full force, Jorin drove his opponent backward.

Though Vayzar was successful in blocking, he knew Jorin's strength would win this battle. He glanced over his shoulder, his cunning mind working in a flash. Maneuvering around near one of his men, Vayzar reached out to grab the man just as Jorin completed a powerful downswing. His blade found flesh, but not Vayzar's. As Vayzar's human shield crumpled, he made a hasty retreat, pleased to glance back and find Jorin now occupied by a new opponent.

Scurrying away from the fight, he spotted Wormaw. He called to him and together they entered the fortress.

"We must get out of here," Vayzar said in a rush. "We can still rebuild elsewhere, but the men are being overtaken. We can't be here when Eldor's force takes control."

They rushed to the storeroom and hastily gathered what supplies they needed to make their escape. Back out in the hall, they came upon Halen. On hands and knees, he crawled toward them.

"Help me."

"Help yourself," Vayzar sneered, and shoved him away with his foot.

Nearly apoplectic over this unexpected turn of events, Vayzar led the way to the back door. After making sure the coast was clear, they ran out into the courtyard.

"We'll get the horses and make our way to the forest before the dragons come after us. From there, we'll head to the coast. We'll be able to find friends there who can help us rebuild."

They turned toward the stable, but halfway there, they slid to a halt. A large group of men and women who had broken free of the grinding house stood in their way. At their head was Ren.

"There!" he shouted, pointing. "Get them!"

The men rushed forward. Vayzar and Wormaw yanked out their swords. Defenseless, several of the men fell wounded, but Vayzar and Wormaw found themselves overwhelmed by numbers. Vayzar fought like a madman, slashing recklessly, but someone grabbed his arm. Before he could break free, more hands latched onto him and ripped his sword away.

"Unhand me!"

A fist plowed into his ribs and then his chin. More men joined in. Still, he fought to pull away.

"Wait!" Ren ordered.

The men ceased beating their captives and looked to their leader. With revenge flickering in his eyes, he said, "Let's take them to the storehouse and then . . . we'll burn it."

"Yeah!" the men cried in hearty agreement.

"But what about the city?" someone asked. "What if the smoke kills everyone?"

"The wind is from the southwest," Ren replied. "It will miss the city."

For the first time, fear overtook Vayzar's anger. He struggled madly as he and Wormaw were dragged toward the shadelin powder's storehouse.

"You can't do this to me!" he shrieked.

Inside the storehouse, someone produced a torch and handed it to Ren. Standing before Vayzar and Wormaw, he declared, "This is for the lives you have taken and destroyed."

He turned toward the barrels. With help from the others, they broke open several and tipped them over. With a large amount of shadelin powder covering the floor, the men hurried back, and Ren dropped the torch. The powder ignited immediately. Those who held Vayzar and Wormaw shoved them forward and ran out, slamming the doors shut.

Vayzar rushed to the doors, ramming his shoulder against them, but they would not budge.

"Let me out!" he screamed, beating his fists against the wood. "You can't leave us here!"

Behind him, the fire blazed, and thick gray smoke billowed up, slowly rolling toward them.

"You!"

Vayzar turned to Wormaw, distracted by the blistering tone of his voice. His one good eye was trained on Vayzar, wild with fear as firelight danced in the other.

"You said this plan would never fail!"

"It wasn't supposed to," Vayzar shouted. "If Ryelan wouldn't have lost Makilien . . ." He stopped here, shaking with fury, thinking of how at every turn, every plan they'd ever conceived had been foiled. If Zirtan had not been defeated, if Jorin had never lost Makilien, if Makilien had never defeated Zendon . . .

The smoke overtook them. Vayzar tried to hold his breath, but it was not long before he needed oxygen. At last, he inhaled. Immediately, his lungs burned as if he'd breathed in the flames. Tears welled up, and his stinging his eyes watered. He took another breath, but with each one, he felt like his lungs were collapsing in on themselves even as his throat squeezed shut. He coughed and gagged, clawing frantically at the door.

In that moment, he knew with absolute certainty it wasn't Ryelan who was responsible for his defeat, not Makilien, nor Jorin. It was Elohim.

"Curse You!" he gasped. Sinking to his knees, he drew in one last breath. "Curse You!"

:Chapter Twenty-five:

The End

U nspeakable joy flowed through Makilien and filled her
eyes with tears. The surrender of Vayzar's men marked
the end to this struggle. At last, the nightmare was over.
"Thank You, Elohim!" she murmured.

Looking up at Sirion, the joy and relief in his eyes alone
was enough to make her cry. Smiling, they embraced carefully.

"It's all over," Makilien said.

Sirion said nothing, but let out a sigh, thinking of all they
had endured to get to this point.

Parting, Makilien took his hand. "Let's find the others."

Moving through the soldiers, they soon came upon familiar
faces. With smiles breaking across their faces, Halandor, Torick,
and Néthyn hurried toward them. Makilien hugged her father,
but stood back to watch the reunion between Sirion and their
friends. The intense emotion of that moment had her wiping
her cheeks.

As Sirion finished greeting these few, someone called out
his name. He turned as Elandir and Elmorhirian raced through
the crowd. When they reached him, they just barely restrained
themselves from hauling him into enthusiastic hugs. Eyes alight
and eager, they greeted him, and Elandir said, "You completely

had us believing you were dead. Please, don't *ever* do that again."

Sirion gave a small laugh, shaking his head. "I certainly don't plan to ..."

His eyes caught on another familiar face, and he felt emotion especially heavy. Leaving the two Elf brothers, he met his uncle. Glorlad grasped Sirion's shoulders, having to resist the incredible urge to embrace him as well. Tears collected in the noble Elf's eyes as he looked into Sirion's.

"Thank Elohim for so great a miracle," he breathed. "I've not known such great sorrow since your parents died, but He has restored the joy I have in you."

Sirion smiled, and tears clogged the back of his throat, thickening his voice. "It is good to see you, Uncle."

Gilhir joined them then, the joy in his eyes matching that of his lord's. Sirion greeted him warmly. This trusted captain and his uncle had always been his closest family, yet now he felt someone missing.

He looked over his shoulder for Ryelan but could not find him among the mingling group. He turned back to his uncle.

"You heard about Ryelan?"

"Yes," Glorlad answered, now searching the faces as well. "Is he ..."

"He is here, and he has realized the error in what he has done. He helped save our lives. I will find him."

As Sirion left his uncle to search for his brother, a short distance away, Makilien came upon another set of familiar faces.

"Darian! General!" she exclaimed. "I didn't expect to see you here."

The king and Nirgon smiled.

"With a threat like this to Eldor, we had to see that it was taken care of," Darian said. "And see all of you returned safely."

Makilien smiled, but then sobered. "How are you after . . . Ryelan's attack?"

"I am well," Darian assured her. "No adverse effects."

Makilien was relieved to hear so and quickly went on to tell them of Ryelan's change of heart.

"There you are."

Ryelan looked over his shoulder from where he stood alone at the corner of the fortress. Sirion approached him and stopped beside his twin.

"Our uncle is here," he said. "And Gilhir."

Emotions Ryelan hadn't felt in years stirred inside him. To see the faces of loved ones after so long . . . He swallowed. Fear strangled the emotion and the longing. He said nothing.

"I can take you to them," Sirion said, watching him.

Ryelan shifted and hung his head. Finally, he turned pained eyes to Sirion, voice breaking. "I can't . . . I can't face them after what I've done."

Reaching out, Sirion put his hand on his brother's shoulder. Ryelan looked away and flinched at the touch, despising himself.

"Ryelan," Sirion said with enough firmness to bring his brother's eyes back to him. His voice softened. "I understand the guilt of what you've done and how it must weigh on you, but we are your family. I've already forgiven you, and Glorlad has as well. I saw in his eyes how much he desires to see you."

Ryelan drew a heavy breath, his fear heightening, but his longing grew with it as memories of his uncle and Gilhir, though hazy, appeared in his mind. Slowly, he nodded and turned toward his twin.

Sirion led the way to where their uncle waited. With pounding heartbeats, Ryelan followed, uncertainty pulsing in his mind. Did his uncle truly wish to see him? Before he was completely prepared, he looked up, his eyes meeting those of his uncle. He froze, his heart pausing for a moment, and could go no farther. But he did not need to. Glorlad closed the distance between them.

"Ryelan," he breathed, and before Ryelan could speak, his uncle drew him into his arms.

Ryelan was slow to return the embrace, but when he did, his nose stung with tears that rose up to his eyes. He held them back with effort, but he was overwhelmed by the true love and forgiveness displayed by his uncle and brother, something he'd grown up without.

When they parted, Glorlad beckoned Sirion closer and laid a hand on both their shoulders, looking at them together.

"What a joyous day this is," he said. "To see a sight I never dreamed possible—both of my brother's sons."

With the excitement and adrenaline wearing off, Makilien could see Sirion was fading, and she wasn't far behind him. But she made it her mission not to find any rest or comfort for herself until his more urgent needs were met. She couldn't have been happier to see Lintar among the Elves. He was the most skilled healer she knew besides Vonawyn and Lorelyn. Leaving Sirion's side for just a moment, she hurried over to the Elf.

"Lintar!"

The dark haired Elf faced her and smiled. "Makilien." His keen eyes took in her signs of weariness as well as the blood drying around her wrists. "What can I do for you?"

"It's Sirion. He really needs to be looked after," she told him.

"Of course." Lintar searched the crowd, finding Sirion. "The soldiers have begun setting up camp outside the fortress. We'll take him out there. I only need to get my supplies from Ruby," he said, speaking of one of the dragons.

He followed Makilien back to Sirion. After taking a preliminary look at Sirion's wounds, he led them out of the fortress. In the lush grass along the river, the soldiers were unloading supplies from their dragon companions and beginning to pitch small tents. In a shady spot under a small tree, Lintar told Sirion to sit while he gathered his medical supplies.

With Makilien still holding his arm to help support him, Sirion gratefully sank down into the cool grass and released a long sigh. Makilien dropped to her knees in front of him, expression troubled at how pale he was. Catching her eyes and the concern in them, he said, "I'll be fine."

She gave a little nod and took his hand. "I just hate seeing you in pain."

"It won't last forever," Sirion murmured.

When Lintar returned, he set to work, carefully and meticulously cleaning the torn flesh of Sirion's back. It was a long and painful process. Now that Makilien had seen the wounds herself, she knew she could become physically sick if she allowed herself to dwell on it. She wished with everything inside her that she could take at least some of his pain, but she could only hold his hand while Lintar worked. Even when he unknowingly squeezed it so hard it hurt, she refused to let go. When he grew weaker and swayed a little, she grabbed his shoulder and held him steady. His eyes stayed closed in an effort to block the pain, and he didn't see the two tears that escaped and tracked down her cheeks.

When at last Lintar finished, Makilien helped him lightly wrap bandages around Sirion's wounds.

"What you need now is plenty of water and rest," the Elf told him. "And food, but I think rest is more important right now."

Sirion nodded. Food was the last thing on his mind.

"I'll see if there is a tent ready for you," Lintar said.

While he went to check with the soldiers, Makilien just stared at Sirion, thinking of his wounds and all the many scars that were so noticeable now out in the sunlight. It took several moments before the constricting of her throat eased enough for her to speak.

Looking at him through teary eyes pained with regret and sadness, she asked in low voice, "What happened to you?"

Sirion stared down at their hands, and for a long moment, would not speak. Finally, he met her eyes. "I don't know if I want you to know." He shook his head, wishing he could bury all the memories of the past months. "You shouldn't have to know about such things."

Makilien swallowed hard, struggling to bear the thought of what he must have endured. She squeezed his hand, and her voice trembled a little. "I won't make you tell me. But if you need to talk about it, I am here, always. I will listen to anything. I don't want you to carry it alone."

Sirion hesitated. He wanted to shelter her from the horror, but she was strong, and if she would one day soon be his wife, he couldn't keep it from her.

"I will tell you . . ." He looked around, eyes focusing on the fortress for a moment before coming back to her. "But not here. When we are all safe back in Elimar, then I'll tell you."

Makilien nodded, swallowing again.

A moment later, Lintar returned. He and Makilien helped Sirion up and led him to one of the tents near the river.

"I'll help you get situated," Lintar told him, and Makilien remained outside as the Elf helped Sirion in.

Once he was settled in comfortably and would be able to rest, Lintar came out, and Makilien followed at his side.

"Now let's see to you," the Elf said.

Makilien shook her head. "There are others far more in need of care than me, like Aedan and Jered. Anyone can help me with my wrists." She looked up at him, eyes large and still rimmed with moisture. "Sirion will be all right, won't he?"

Lintar paused and faced her. "He is badly injured, I won't try to tell you otherwise, but it isn't anything that won't heal." A comforting smile came to his face. "It will take time, but with proper care, he will be all right."

Makilien breathed out a sigh, heart beating deeply in relief. "Thank you."

The Elf nodded. "Are you sure you don't need me?"

"Yes, go see to the others."

"Just make sure you get some rest too," Lintar told her. "You need it just as much as Sirion."

"I will."

They parted, and Makilien's eyes scanned the growing camp. The soldiers tended injuries and offered food to the freed men and women from the fortress. She noticed the people of Carel watched the odd gathering from the city gate, but few dared to venture closer, not with twenty dragons standing guard or circling above. Once again, it hit her that they were safe, bringing a soothing comfort to her wearied heart.

A little smile lifted her lips, and her eyes landed on her father walking toward her with Halandor who carried a supply pack. Her smile grew as they drew near.

"Let's get your wrists taken care of so you can get some rest," Halandor said. "Do you have any more injuries?"

Makilien shook her head. Thanks to Sirion, she could answer, "No."

She sat down in the grass, and Halandor cleaned and bandaged her raw skin while her father offered her water and a little food from the pack. She accepted it gratefully, but like Sirion, she was too tired to have much of an appetite.

Just as they finished, her eyes caught on two men carrying a stretcher out of the gate. On it lay Derrin's body. Her throat squeezed tight. Eyes watery, her gaze met her father's as he watched her.

"He saved Sirion's life," she murmured. She swallowed hard against the lump in her throat. "He should be buried in Elimar. It shouldn't be here."

Her father nodded, and Halandor said, "We'll see to it."

Eyes fluttering open, Makilien took in the bright canvas of her little tent. The material billowed lightly in the breeze, and in the warmth of the late afternoon sun, she felt a particular peace and joy that she had not experienced in a very long time. Life was normal again. Not the normal she'd tried to accustom herself to in the last year, but the normal she'd known before—before Sirion's disappearance. She could think of no words to adequately thank Elohim for bringing them through this, and let the joy in her heart rise up in thanks for her.

Feeling much more rested, she sat up and crawled out of the tent. Soldiers milled about, some talking to groups of freed captives. She looked at their faces, witnessing the joy in their eyes, a joy she could well understand.

Spotting her across camp, Makilien's father came to meet her. He put his arm around her shoulders and pulled her close to kiss her temple.

"Sleep well?"

"I did," Makilien answered. "Better than I probably have in a year."

"It's been quite a year."

"Mmm," Makilien agreed. "I can hardly believe . . ."

Her voice trailed off as her gaze found Sirion just leaving his tent. They'd only been separated for a few hours, but the upwelling of love he caused in her heart made her realize just how much she wanted there to be a day they would never have to be separated again.

"Go on," her father said with a smile in his voice. "I won't keep you."

Makilien broke from her thoughts and smiled lovingly up at him before crossing the distance between her and Sirion. His face was serene and rested, and his eyes held a joyful contentment that added to feelings in Makilien's heart. She studied him as she drew near, never wanting to forget a single detail. His dark hair just brushed his shoulders as a breeze rippled through camp. He saw her immediately, and his smile, one that always made her feel so loved and safe, drew her close.

Sirion studied her as well. In a plain, pale blue linen dress and her hair slightly tangled from sleep, he didn't think she'd ever been more lovely.

"You are beautiful," he murmured when she reached him.

Makilien blushed and laughed a little. "I'm not so sure, but I'm glad you think so." Eyes more serious, she asked, "How do you feel?"

"Like everything is perfect."

That brought a smile of contentment back to Makilien's face. Sirion took her hand, rubbing his thumb over her fingers. "I was thinking, now that I've had a chance to rest, I would like to talk to your father."

Her eyes sparkled, and she motioned over her shoulder. "He's right over there."

Sirion glanced at him, and then back to her. "Excuse me for a few minutes?"

"Of course." She watched him walk toward her father, anticipation fluttering in her chest. Was this really happening?

It all seemed like a dream. A very good dream that she hoped never came to an end.

As Sirion approached, Néthyn smiled kindly.

"Do you have a moment to talk?" Sirion asked.

"As many as you need," Néthyn answered, and the two of them walked together toward the edge of camp to allow for privacy.

"I think I already know what this is about," Néthyn said, glancing at Sirion with a smile.

Sirion felt his own smile spreading and turned to face Makilien's father. At first, he found himself hesitating. Even after the multitude of enemies he'd faced, he realized he was anxious about asking for Makilien's hand. He imagined how difficult it was for a father to entrust his daughter's wellbeing to another man, any man, and Makilien was particularly special. Drawing a deep breath, he plunged in.

"While we were captive, I asked Makilien if she would marry me, and she said yes. But I won't consider it done until I have your permission and blessing."

Néthyn stood silent for a moment, his face calm, yet with a wistful expression in his eyes, reminiscing over how the years had flown by. It seemed like such a short time ago that they'd lived in Reylaun and he'd tucked Makilien in bed at night. Part of him missed those days and his little girl, but he didn't wish for them back. They enjoyed lives filled with purpose now, and Makilien had a whole new and exciting aspect of her life yet to live.

With this in mind, he nodded. "You're a good man, Sirion. I appreciate the honor and integrity I've seen in you. You've certainly proved beyond any doubt that you love and will care for my daughter. I love seeing how happy she is with you. Though it is hard to let her go, I gladly give you my permission and blessing. This is something I have always wanted for her."

"Thank you, sir," Sirion said, breathing out contentedly. "I don't think I can say how blessed I am to be the one who has won her heart, and I will never treat it lightly."

"I'm glad to hear it. Makilien is a precious gift to me and her mother, and I know she will be to you too."

With a few final, heartfelt words, they parted, and Sirion returned to Makilien who waited not far away. At her hopeful look, he grinned causing a smile to break out on her face. Once he stood before her, he took her hands in his and said, "Your father has given his permission and blessing." He paused, looking her in the eyes. "Is this still what you want?"

"Yes," Makilien replied with all the surety in her heart. She shrugged, shyness creeping into her smile as she admitted, "Actually, I wanted it even before I knew you were still alive. I was devastated to think it would never be."

Sirion smiled tenderly and looked down at her hands. "I wish I had a ring for you."

She just shook her head. "I need no ring. Only your love."

"And you have that always." He drew her closer and kissed her forehead. Still holding her close, he said, "Now, shall we announce the news?"

Eyes sparkling in pure joy, Makilien nodded. "Yes, let's."

Still holding hands, they walked over to where their friends were gathered. Makilien and Sirion stood before them, Makilien's arm looped around Sirion's. Smiling at the group of expectant faces, Sirion announced, "Yesterday, while Vayzar had us tied up in the courtyard . . . I asked Makilien to marry me if Elohim delivered us, and she said yes."

Though most already had subtle smiles on their faces, they now broke into full grins. Cheers and congratulations rose up, adding to Makilien and Sirion's joy. At one point, Elmorhirian elbowed Elandir hard in the ribs.

"What did I tell you? I said give them a day or two of being reunited and they'll be engaged. I told you."

Makilien and Sirion chuckled, and Makilien shook her head, thinking of what delightful people she had in her life. She went on to accept a big hug from Halandor and from a couple of the others. Everyone was overjoyed for the two of them.

Once the commotion had died some, Makilien had a private moment with her father.

They embraced for a long moment. As they parted, Néthyn clasped his hands around her shoulders and said, "I am so very pleased for you."

Makilien breathed deep. "Are you?"

"Yes. I know how much you love him . . . and he loves you."

"He's done so much for me." Just thinking of the day before made Makilien have to wipe the corners of her eyes.

Néthyn hugged her again. "When did my little girl so quickly grow into a woman?"

"Trials have a way of maturing us."

"Yes," her father agreed, "but I am not at all disappointed in who you have become and in the choices you've made."

Tears welled in Makilien's eyes again. "Thank you. I never want to do anything to displease you."

:Chapter Twenty-six:

New Life

akilien stood at Sirion's side, watching the last of the fortress walls crumble as six dragons pulled against the chains attached to the stones. All that remained after the dust settled was a heap of rubble. The end to Vayzar's brutal reign. And with it, they could return home. Soldiers were already packing up camp and loading supplies onto the dragons.

Satisfied, Makilien and Sirion turned and walked back toward the breaking camp and joined a small group of their friends.

"I just spoke with Nirgon," Halandor told them. "He said any of the soldiers are willing to give up their places on the dragons. Makilien, I was thinking you, Sirion, and Aedan should take that offer so you can get back to Elimar to recover."

Makilien glanced at Sirion. She hated to force any of the soldiers to return to Eldor on horseback, but she was terribly anxious to return home. "I guess if they truly don't mind."

"Not at all."

Overhearing the conversation as he and his father joined them, Aedan said, "I won't be heading back to Elimar right away. I would like to, but as long as I'm this far north, I want to visit Reylaun and check on Mother and Rommia."

Makilien was a little disappointed that he wouldn't yet be returning home, but she understood his need to check on his family.

"Besides that," he continued, "I saw Laena last time I was in Andin. Her store burnt down, and she would like to come to Eldor. She doesn't have anyone to travel with so I promised, after I was finished here, I'd come for her."

This caught Halandor's full attention. "Is she all right?"

"Yes," Aedan assured him. "She's been staying with friends, but since the store is gone, there is nothing to keep her in Andin."

Halandor was silent for only a moment before he said, "I will go for her and bring her back to Eldor."

"I'll go with you," Loron told him.

"So will I," Torick was quick to offer. "Who knows how many men still lurk through Eldinorieth who won't learn of Vayzar's defeat for some time. We don't want any mishaps along the way."

Halandor smiled in gratitude.

An unmistakable glint in his eyes, Elandir stepped closer and nudged him. "So is this the woman you've always avoided telling us about?"

Halandor side-glanced at Elandir and Elmorhirian's grinning faces. "Perhaps."

"Come now, you can't hide anything from us, and you know it," Elandir pressed.

"Especially not a romantic relationship," Elmorhirian added.

"I never said there was a relationship."

Elandir's grin only widened. "*Yet.*"

"Besides, this 'not relationship' seems pretty serious," Elmorhirian insisted. "Look how quick you were to offer to get her."

Halandor shook his head. "You two are impossible."

Makilien had to chuckle to herself. She had never seen the Elf brothers able to fluster Halandor before, but she detected just a hint of it in his voice. Though Elandir and Elmorhirian were loath to let it go, Halandor said nothing more, and instead followed Aedan, Torick, and Loron to retrieve and saddle their horses.

Aedan's father followed them.

"Would you object to me joining you?" he asked his son. He hesitated, reaching up to rub the back of his neck. "You see, I would like to apologize to your mother and meet . . . your sister?"

"Yes, you have a daughter. Rommia." Aedan smiled at him, putting him at ease. "I'd be glad to have you with me." He paused. "There is something you should know though."

"What is that?"

"Mother remarried a couple years ago."

Jaeson glanced at his son. "Is he a good man?"

"Yes. Maybe you remember him. Simon? He's a farmer."

"I think so." Jaeson nodded slowly, thinking this over. Finally, he decided, "Good."

After the men had their horses saddled and supplied, they returned to their friends for farewells. Makilien hugged and said goodbye to Halandor first. She was distinctly pleased for him, remembering the look she'd caught between him and Laena. There had always been something keeping the two of them apart, whether war or Laena's store, but things had changed now, and it excited Makilien to think of their future.

When she came to Aedan, she hugged him carefully. "Come home soon, all right? We miss you in Elimar."

"I will," Aedan promised with a smile, but his face grew more serious. "If something were to ever happen and I don't make it back, will you tell Vonawyn how I feel?"

"You will come back," Makilien said with confidence. "But yes, I would tell her."

"Thank you."

As the men were mounting up, Tanzim appeared leading his big roan horse.

"Are you joining us, Tan?" Aedan asked.

"I am," the Shaike answered with a jerk of his head. "I followed you this far. Gotta see you make it safely home."

Aedan smiled, and final goodbyes were exchanged. Riding away from camp, Jaeson looked curiously at his son.

"So who is this girl waiting for you in Elimar?"

Aedan looked at him and then to the horizon, a smile in his voice. "Vonawyn, Lord Elnauhir's daughter."

Jaeson's brows rose a little. "You love her?"

"From the moment I first saw her."

This brought a little smile to Jaeson's lips. "I look forward to meeting her. I hope she will receive me well."

"She will," Aedan assured him. "I've never met anyone with a kinder heart."

Makilien was a little sad to see so many of her friends go. It had been so good for them to be together again. But a short time after they left, Beregon and Sophine joined those who remained, filling some of the gap and bringing their own special joy.

"Good news," Beregon announced with a broad smile. "I believe Jorin now has his trust in Elohim."

Makilien gasped. "Really?"

The blacksmith nodded. "I just spoke to him. He wants to go to Eldor. He is speaking to Lord Darian now to ask his permission."

"That is incredible," Makilien breathed. She shook her head, still taking in the wonderment. "If you would have asked me a year ago if I believed this could happen, my answer would have been a definite no. I am so pleased."

"So am I," Beregon said.

After the others expressed their surprise and happiness at this, Makilien asked, "So Beregon, are you and Sophine staying here?"

Beregon looked down at his wife. "I'm not sure. The house and shed are gone. We'd have to rebuild."

"In that case, let me invite you to come with us to Eldor," Elandir said. "I'm sure we could use your services in Elimar. Either that or Minarald. There is plenty of work there."

"Or in Elindor," Elmorhirian chimed in eagerly. "We're soon going to rebuild the city and there will be more than enough metalwork to be done."

Beregon's gaze shifted again to his wife. "What do you think?"

Sophine's face glowed. "I think it sounds wonderful. A fresh start, away from the memories of this place."

With a smile, Beregon squeezed her hand. "I do too." To the others, he said, "It looks like we'll be joining you. After all, with so many appealing offers, how could we refuse?"

Makilien was elated. She'd become so fond of the two of them, and loved the idea of seeing them often. She shared a hug with Sophine, and everyone talked with excitement about the future. Elandir and Elmorhirian spoke animatedly of numerous housing arrangements, and Makilien started to worry they would overwhelm Beregon and Sophine, but the couple just looked to be drinking in all the prospects of a new life.

The Elf brothers' chatter finally halted when Nirgon joined them. Once everyone had greeted him, the general looked at Sirion.

"If you are not busy, Lord Darian would like to speak to you. You and Sophine."

Sirion nodded, and he, Sophine, and Beregon followed Nirgon to where Darian stood with a few of his men. Nearby, the men who had surrendered after the fight sat in a tight group, closely guarded by the soldiers. Sirion glanced at them, but fixed his eyes on the king as they came to stand in front of him.

"I hope I haven't taken you away from anything," Darian said.

"No," Sirion told him, still chuckling inside over the Elf brothers' teasing, but his mirth faded at the seriousness in Darian's expression.

Looking between Sirion and Sophine, he said, "The reason I wished to speak to you is in regard to Halen." The king glanced over his shoulder at the men behind him. "I have decisions to make about our prisoners, and I know Halen has caused the two of you, in particular, so much pain. I can have him hanged for the atrocities he's committed. He certainly deserves no less. Or, I can have him brought to Minarald with the others where he will be imprisoned for the rest of his life . . . the decision is up to you."

As the weight of this decision sank in, Sirion's gaze turned from the king to Halen. The man sat miserably among the captives, dull eyes unseeing. If he could hear the conversation, he made no show of it. Painful, vivid memories flashed into Sirion's mind. The countless beatings. The cruel, twisted satisfaction in Halen's eyes as he'd loomed over Sirion while he lay battered, bleeding, and semi-conscious after each one. He let out a shuddering breath, not realizing he'd been holding it, and squeezed his eyes shut for a moment.

Then he glanced at Sophine who stood silent beside him. The scars Halen had left her were even deeper and more painful than any he would live with. A muscle twitched in his clenched jaw as he contemplated his answer. The man didn't deserve to live. Didn't deserve mercy. But to be put to death would seal his fate for eternity.

Drawing in a deep breath, Sirion looked into the eyes of the king. The words were hard for him, and he did not know how Sophine would feel, but he said, "I won't ask for his hanging."

He swallowed down the tightness that had locked around his throat. "In prison he will still have a chance to know the truth. If he doesn't . . ." Sirion gave a small shrug. "He will have been given every opportunity."

Perhaps, had the man been able to see, Sirion's decision would have been different due to fear he would escape, but there was no chance of that.

Darian's eyes slid to Sophine and Beregon. "What do you say, Sophine?"

She said nothing for a moment, reaching up to clasp Beregon's hand on her shoulder. Slowly, she nodded. "I agree with Sirion."

With the sun at its peak, those remaining at the fortress were just about ready to leave. Sirion moved through the men, searching. He'd barely seen Ryelan all morning. At last, he found him attaching his belongings to his horse. Ryelan glanced up at his brother's approach.

"Would you like to take one of the dragons instead of riding?" Sirion asked.

Ryelan sighed, staring at his saddle, and did not answer for a long moment. Finally, he met his brother's eyes. "I'm not going to Elimar with you."

Sirion came closer. He hadn't considered the possibility of leaving Ryelan behind. "Where are you going?"

Ryelan shrugged. "Wherever I end up, I guess."

"Why won't you come with us?" Sirion asked, his eyes searching the depths of his twin's.

Ryelan shook his head, still burdened by guilt. "I can't just leave behind what I've known most of my life and slip right into your life. I wish I could, but it's impossible with the memories I carry."

Sirion held his gaze steadily. "Your actions are forgiven, Ryelan, by all of us and by Elohim. He can help you adjust to a new life."

Head hanging, Ryelan murmured, "I know . . . but I have to learn how to forgive myself before I can accept His forgiveness."

He returned to his work, and Sirion let out a long sigh. He wanted so much for his brother to come back with them, to be a family again, but he knew he could not force him. He prayed for him to change his mind, but Ryelan seemed set on his plans.

As Ryelan was finishing, someone led a saddled horse up beside his, and Irynna appeared.

Ryelan eyed her and the horse. "What are you doing?"

"You sent me away once," Irynna said, voice even, yet not harsh. "I won't let you do it again."

Ryelan's shoulders sagged. "Irynna, please, go with them to Eldor. Life will be much better for you there."

But she shook her head steadfastly. "The life I want is with you, whether it's here, Eldor, or anywhere, whether easy or difficult. You're all I have now for family."

Ryelan breathed out heavily. "I don't want this for you, but . . . I don't have it in me to force you away."

A smile spread across Irynna's face, and she mounted her horse. Just before Ryelan mounted up, Sirion embraced him tightly, fighting the emotions of letting go. But, at least this time they could say goodbye.

Parting, Ryelan looked into his eyes. "I will visit . . . someday."

Sirion took hope from this and watched his brother swing up into the saddle. Taking up the reins, Ryelan looked down at him once more. "Goodbye."

Sirion cleared his throat, but his voice still came out rough. "Goodbye, Ryelan."

Nudging his horse forward, Ryelan rode away.

Before she followed, Irynna looked at Sirion, her expression sad and regretful. "I'm sorry I deceived you. Thank you so much for all you did to try to help me. You were so kind."

Sirion nodded in acceptance of her apology, and Irynna rode on after Ryelan.

A short distance away, the two of them came upon Makilien. Ryelan halted his horse for just a moment as she looked up and met his gaze. He hesitated, fighting with his conscience.

"I apologize for what happened in Elimar. I hurt you deeply by my deception, and I am sorry."

"It's the past now," Makilien told him. "Think no more of it."

Ryelan said nothing, but she caught the gratitude in his eyes. As he and Irynna rode on, Makilien walked to Sirion, saddened by his expression. She wrapped her hand around his arm and leaned her head against his shoulder.

"He'll come," she said quietly. "I really believe he will."

Sirion stared after his brother for a long moment, but then looked down at her, a grateful smile on his face.

Now that the time was nearing to depart, Sirion had one more person to find. When he came to Jered, the young man stood near the soldiers, his arms crossed comfortably, reminding Sirion of the day they'd first met.

Jered smiled, blue eyes content. "About to leave?"

"Yes." Sirion looked over the area before his gaze settled back on his friend. "Are you coming with us?"

"I'd like to," Jered said wishfully. "I've never been south of Eldinorieth, but . . . I think it's time I went home to my family."

Sirion nodded, understanding.

Jered looked down at the ground and shook his head. "This whole thing definitely made me look at things differently. Actually, there's this girl back home . . . if she's still waiting for me. I didn't think I was the settling down type, but I've had a lot of time to think that over."

Sirion smiled. "When you see how quickly and easily your life could come to an end, things you thought were important turn out not to be and you see more clearly what is."

"Exactly."

"I hope things go well for you," Sirion told him.

"You too, my friend," Jered replied. "I'll be coming down to Eldor sometime after things are taken care of at home, so be looking out for a visit."

"I will," Sirion said with anticipation. He offered his hand. "Thanks for everything, Jered."

Gripping Sirion's hand tight, Jered nodded. "And thank you."

At last, it was time leave. As everyone gathered around the horses and dragons, Makilien spotted Jorin nearby with his horse.

"I'll be right back," she told Sirion and walked toward Jorin. Coming up behind him, she said, "I'm glad you're coming to Eldor with us."

He looked up and turned, a hint of disbelief in his eyes. "I still don't understand how you can feel that way, but . . . I'm glad."

She gave him a warm smile. "The more you come to know Elohim, the more you will understand."

For the very first time, Makilien watched a smile take hold of Jorin's face, and it filled her with a joy she would carry for a long time. With this, she hurried back to Sirion.

"Ready to go?" he asked.

"Yes, I'm ready."

The two of them climbed onto Carmine's back. Once all the riders around them had mounted, Carmine spread his wings. In moments, his mighty flaps took them into the air. Makilien looked down as the ground shrank beneath them. This gave her an entirely new view of the fortress rubble. The other dragons and their passengers rose around them. From the ground, Jered waved, and Makilien and Sirion lifted their arms to wave back.

Curving gradually, Carmine flew toward Eldinorieth. As the fortress and Carel disappeared behind them, they left behind all the pain and struggle. New lives lay ahead of many of them. As Makilien looked over her shoulder, her eyes caught and held Sirion's. The look they shared held a joyful anticipation of what was to come, and she couldn't wait to start their life together.

:Epilogue:

Little tingles skittered along Makilien arms and fluttered like butterfly wings in her chest. Her mother and Vonawyn had helped her prepare for this day for two months, and she could hardly believe it had come at last. The excitement of it made it difficult to breathe.

Though she faced away from the mirror, she could feel Vonawyn's light fingers expertly arranging her hair.

"Just about done," the Elf said, her voice musical with joy.

Makilien's heart beat a little faster. She glanced at her mother through the thin, glittery veil falling in front of her face. Hanna hadn't ceased smiling all morning, though she looked to be on the brink of tears.

"There, finished," Vonawyn announced with pleasure. "Come look in the mirror."

Makilien rose and stood before her reflection. Her breath stayed locked in her lungs at first, overcome with the moment. The wedding gown Vonawyn had created was radiant—pure white satin, embroidered and beaded tastefully, with thin lace sleeves open at the elbow, but falling almost half way down the skirt. Her dark hair fell long over her shoulders, curled beautifully. Now tears welled in her own eyes.

"What do you think?" Vonawyn asked.

"It is more beautiful than I imagined," Makilien breathed, voice trembling. "How will I ever thank you?"

She gave her friend a tight hug. Then she turned to her mother who looked her up and down.

"You are beautiful, Makilien," she murmured.

Makilien smiled and stepped closer to hug her. Hanna held her for a long moment, and when they parted, she had tears glistening on her cheeks.

"I am so happy for you."

"Thank you," Makilien replied, a little choked up.

A moment later, Vonawyn touched her on the shoulder. "I think it's just about time," she said with a grin.

The butterflies multiplied, and Makilien's heart beat yet faster. Vonawyn opened the door and the three of them left the room. Downstairs, they came to the hall just outside the ballroom in Lord Elnauhir's house. The doors were closed, but Makilien could hear the murmur of excited conversation from inside.

Standing at the door waiting was Makilien's father. When his eyes landed on his daughter, he held his composure, but tears glittered in his eyes. A wide smile stretched across his face, and he seemed at a loss for words.

They stopped, and Hanna turned to face Makilien.

"I love you, sweetheart. This is such a wonderful day for us."

They hugged again, and Hanna lifted Makilien's veil just enough to give her daughter a kiss on the cheek. She then smoothed it out, struggling not to cry.

Vonawyn touched Makilien's arm, elated for her friend, and gave Makilien her bouquet of pale blue roses and white lilies. She and Hanna then left quietly to take their places.

Makilien was alone now with her father. Smiling, she came to his side and curled her arm around his. He covered her hand with his other.

"You are so beautiful," he murmured, his voice thick.

She squeezed his arm.

In a few moments, the commotion inside the ballroom quieted.

"Are you ready?" Néthyn asked.

Makilien drew in a deep breath and nodded. She then looked up at her father with a grin.

"Are you?"

He chuckled. "As ready as I'll ever be."

Just another moment later, the ballroom doors slowly opened, revealing the many rows of seating and the lovely blue and white decorations. But Makilien's eyes were drawn to the end of the long aisle between the chairs. On the left side of the raised altar where Lord Elnauhir waited stood Vonawyn, Leiya, Lorelyn, Sophine, and Laena. To the right stood Aedan, Halandor, Glorlad, Gilhir, and Darian.

But none of these people held Makilien's attention. As she and her father walked down the aisle, her eyes were only on Sirion. Dressed in a crisp white shirt and black suede jerkin, his hair trimmed back to chin length, she thought him the most handsome man she'd ever met, and she loved him more today than she ever had before. One look in his warm brown eyes and all her nerves quieted.

Sirion watched her approach, and didn't know if he even breathed in that time. His heart pounded against his ribs, and he felt amazingly blessed.

At last, after what seemed the longest walk she had ever taken, Makilien and her father reached the end and now the ceremony truly began.

"Who gives this woman to wed?" Lord Elnauhir asked.

"I do," Néthyn answered, his voice surprisingly clear and strong.

Makilien turned to give him a hug, and he led her up to the altar. He squeezed her hand before letting it go. She smiled into his eyes and then turned to face Sirion.

Makilien heard most of Elnauhir's words, but she felt almost in a dream state as she looked up through her veil into Sirion's face. He held her gaze, his eyes overflowing with tenderness and love.

Elnauhir spoke of the paths Elohim had led them on both to and from their meeting and on through the growth of their relationship. Makilien reflected on these things and the incredible events that had led to this day.

At last came time for their vows. Though Makilien had worried beforehand that she would forget them, they were now perfectly clear in her mind, spoken straight from her heart.

"I, Makilien, take you, Sirion, to be my husband, to love, honor, and obey. To be your helper, and to follow you through sickness and health, through good times and bad. To remain faithful always and to walk together on this path Elohim has set before us until death do us part."

Eyes shining, Sirion echoed her words with his own heartfelt vow, "I, Sirion, take you, Makilien, to be my wife, to love, honor, and cherish. To be your protector and provider, and to lead you through sickness and health, through good times and bad. To remain faithful always and walk together on this path Elohim has set before us until death do us part."

Tears brimmed in Makilien's eyes and her smile gleamed through her veil as Elnauhir concluded, "By these vows given before those gathered here and before Elohim, our Lord, I pronounce you man and wife."

Makilien's heart leapt in her chest.

Sirion took the edges of her veil and lifted it back. Drawing her into his arms, he kissed her tenderly. Makilien closed her eyes, lost in the joy of their shared love.

When they parted, Sirion took her arm in the crook of his, and they faced their friends who were cheering and wiping their eyes. Makilien didn't think her smile would ever leave her face. To think of where she'd come from and to know that Sirion had chosen her made her heart swell with love for him, and she thanked Elohim with all the words she could find. His guiding of her life was something she would forever behold in awe.

In the midst of her thankfulness, Sirion leaned close and whispered, "I love you, Makilien. I will love you and take care of you until there is no life left in my body."

And Makilien knew without any doubt that it was true. Her heart and her trust were safe with him. Overflowing with her own love, she rose up on her tiptoes to kiss him again as their friends looked on with great joy to witness the start of this new life and adventure.

Map & Guides

Northern Wilds
(Goblin Territory)

Aldûlir

Reylaun
Andín

Carel

Eldinorieth

:N:

W   E

S

Pronunciation

NAME	PRONUNCIATION
Aedan	Ay - dan
Aldûlir	Al - doo - leer
Antiro	An - teer - oh
Arphen	Ahr - fen
Baltar	Bal - tahr
Beregon	Bayr - e - gon
Carmine	Cahr - mine
Darand	Dahr - and
Darian	Dahr - ee - an
Demera	De - mayr - a
Derrin	Dayr - in
Dolennar	Doh - len - nahr
Elandir	E - lan - deer
Eldinorieth	El - di - nohr - ee - eth
Elimar	E - li - mahr
Elmorhirian	El - mohr - heer - ee - an
Elnauhir	El - nah - heer
Elohim	Ee - loh - heem
Emaril	E - mah - ril
Falene	Fa - leen
Gébrale	Gay - brayl
Gilhir	Gil - heer
Halandor	Ha - lan - dohr
Halen	Hay - len
Indiya	In - dee - yuh
Irynna	Ī - rin - uh
Jaeson	Jay - son

Jered	Jayr - ed
Jorin	Johr - in
Laena	Lay - nuh
Leiya	Lee - yuh
Lokye	Loh - kī
Lorelyn	Lohr - e - lin
Loron	Lohr - on
Makilien	Ma - kil - ee - en
Meniah	Me - nī - uh
Minarald	Mi - nahr - ald
Néthyn	Nay - thin
Nirgon	Neer - gon
Reylaun	Ray - lahn
Rhûnland	Roon - land
Rommia	Ro - mee - ah
Ryelan	Rī - lan
Shaike	Shayk
Sirion	Seer - ee - on
Sophine	Soh - feen
Torick	Tohr - ick
Tôr	Tohr
Vayzar	Vay - zahr
Vonawyn	Vah - nah - win
Wormaw	Wohr - mah
Zirtan	Zeer - tan

Character Guide

Aedan - Makilien's best friend from Reylaun.

Antiro - Makilien's black horse who can understand Human language.

Arphen - Former leader of the griffons who died helping Aedan defeat Zirtan.

Baltar - The founder of Eldor.

Beregon - A kind blacksmith in Carel.

Carmine - A red male dragon.

Darand - Former king of Eldor.

Darian - Son of Darand and king of Eldor.

Demera - Younger sister of Gébrale and daughter of the former king of Rhûnland.

Derrin - A young man from Reylaun who was in love with Makilien and joined Zirtan's forces.

Elandir - The oldest son of the Elf lord Elnauhir.

Elmorhirian - The youngest son of the Elf lord Elnauhir.

Elnauhir - The Elf lord of Elimar.

Emaril - A green male dragon. Mate of Indiya.

Gébrale - King of Rhûnland. Demera's older brother.

Gilhir - A high ranking Elf captain from Althilion.

Glorlad - The Elf lord of Althilion and uncle of Sirion.

Halandor - A Half-Elf man of Eldor. Close friend and mentor of Makilien.

Halen - A cruel slaver who takes delight in other's pain.

Hanna - Mother of Makilien.

Indiya - A blue female dragon. Mate of Emaril.

Irynna - A former slave girl who was rescued by Ryelan.

Jaeson - Father of Aedan.

Jade - A young green dragon. Daughter of Emaril and Indiya.

Jered - Slave of Vayzar who becomes close friends and allies with Sirion.

Jorin - Younger brother of Zendon.

Laena - Kind shopkeeper in Andin.

Leiya - Makilien's younger sister.

Lorelyn - Wife of the Elf lord Elnauhir.

Loron - An Elf of Elimar and close friend of Makilien and Halandor.

Makilien - A young woman of Reylaun who killed Zendon.

Meniah - Son of Elohim who gave his life for the people.

Néthyn - Father of Makilien.

Nirgon - General of Eldor's army.

Rommia - Aedan's younger sister.

Ryelan - Sirion's twin brother who was thought to be dead for many years.

Sirion - Half-Elf from Althilion. Nephew of the Elf lord Glorlad.

Sophine - A former slave to Halen. Wife of Beregon.

Tanzim - A Shaike formerly in service to Zirtan.

Tôr - A male griffon serving Eldor.

Torick - A man of Eldor and close friend of Makilien and Halandor.

Vayzar - Zirtan's once appointed governor of Reylaun and bitter enemy of Makilien.

Vonawyn - Daughter of the Elf lord Elnauhir.

Wormaw - A cruel and twisted alchemist working with Vayzar.

Zendon - Zirtan's general who Makilien killed in battle. Older brother of Jorin.

Zirtan - Evil ruler who tried to gain control of Dolennar, but was defeated by Aedan.

BOOKS BY MOLLY EVANGELINE

Makilien Trilogy
Truth
Courage
Trust

Pirates & Faith
The Pirate Daughter's Promise
Every Tear
A Captain's Heart
Finding Faith

FOLLOW ALONG ON THE JOURNEY AS MOLLY
EVANGELINE WEAVES AN EPIC NEW TALE OF FAITH,
FANTASY, AND ADVENTURE IN

ILYON CHRONICLES

www.ilyonchronicles.com

Made in the USA
Lexington, KY
03 December 2015